D0272488

MORLAIS

MORLAIS

Afterword by John Pikoulis

SEREN

Seren is the book imprint of
Poetry Wales Press Ltd, Nolton Street, Bridgend, Wales
www.serenbooks.com
facebook.com/SerenBooks
Twitter: @SerenBooks

ISBN: 978-1-78172-280-0
ISBN Ebook: 978-1-78172-295-4
ISBN Kindle: 978-1-78172-294-7

A CIP record for this title is available from
the British Library

The publisher works with the financial assistance
of the Welsh Books Council

Cover illustration:
Pigeon House by George Chapman © The Estate of George
Chapman

Printed by The CPI Group (UK) Ltd, Croydon

MORLAIS

A butterfly came over the red-painted iron railings of the school playground and fluttered in a bewildered scatter-brained flight across the yard. The macadamised surface threw the sun's flash upward; the wet uneven floor breathed out wisps of steam and cast a dazzling glare from its slowly evaporating puddles. The butterfly tacked and staggered, looping upwards from the burning sterility of this unexpected vast absence of green and growth. Its wings beat hysterically, striving to keep its tiny body afloat against the downward thrust of the metallic blue sky; and the burning white ground stretched illimitably beneath. An old man leaned on the railings of the allotment from which the butterfly had thoughtlessly ventured. He wiped the sweat from his wizened face with thin, blue-pocked hands. Between watching the butterfly and waiting for his grandchild to come out to play he lost himself in a doze; the chant of voices dimmed by glass gave a dreamy rhythm to his breathing.

Two twos are four, four twos are eight,
Eight twos are sixteen, ten twos are – TWENTY.

He tried to single his grandson's voice out of the incantation and, nodding his head and keeping time with his hand, he saw the kid sitting on the back steps outside the coal cwtch and reciting his homework sulkily for a halfpenny off dadcu. He did not see the butterfly crash into the railings on the farside of the playground and tumble helplessly into the river whose cool purl had excited it to abandon. He did not see the dry silent yard. His eyes were closed against the harsh glitter of a showery June.

Sixteen pence are one and fourpence,
Twenty pence are one and eightpence.....

The bell rang down the green-tiled corridor. Ting-a-ling-a-ling, ting-a-ting-a-ting. The old man started convulsively – every day the bell roused him from his heavy leaning against the railings, – and fumbled in his deep pocket for Bobbie's 'lunch'. It was something he could do just nicely; dress himself in his Welsh flannel shirt, and old working trousers and torn old Sunday coat; knot his red muffler round his neck; sit impatiently in the back kitchen while his daughter Lizzie – Condon since her marriage, that is, – cut a hunk of bread and jammed it and wrapped it up in a bit of news-paper; then take it easy going down Glannant Street on his bent stick of briar – his best leg, he called it – to give the boy his grub at playtime.

But dang it if the blamed thing wasn't all tangled in his lining, and the kids pouring out into the playground like boiling water over an ant-heap, and the row they were creat-ing, screaming and hallooing enough to make your old knuckles jump and twitch, lost in the torn lining of pocket, in the darkness, pulling at the paper and ripping it, and ripping the lining, and Bobby shouting up from under the railings for his grub.

"A'right now, Bobby, a'right," he bleated, "it's got itself caught in my pocket. Lizzie should 'a stitched that 'ole up before, a'right."

"Come on, mun, I got to play, come on" Bobby yelled ruthlessly, his scornful impatience spurring the old man to renewed frenzies of doddering.

"Here it is, here it is," he said, his head swimming as he felt his fingers clutch the bread. He pulled it out in pieces, the crust first like a scalp, then the squashed and begrimed soft part, soaked to a jammy pulp.

"Here it is, here it is, boy."

"Chuck it down, then, quick. Come on, mun."

Bobby hopped up and down on his hobnailed, well-polished boots.

"Here you are, then."

Like feeding goldfish, great swirling goldfish that leaped up at you with gaping mouths from the swirling water. The old man dropped the bread and jam into his grandson's hands.

"Solong," Bobby yelled, turning round and racing across the yard to the red-bricked lavatories, stuffing the crust into his mouth and wrenching a piece off as he ran.

The old man departed as un-noticed and as broken as the butterfly. And the playground rejoiced over its double victory, screaming and leaping and violently exuberant with children.

Bob Linton rushed out from the lavatories as impetuously as he had rushed in. His fly buttons unfastened, his blue serge trousers, much too long for him, coming down over his knees, his thin eager face tense and scowling, his hair clipped like a convict's except for the uncut fringe that covered his forehead. His hands were wet. He rubbed them in his jersey, then, cupping them about his jam-stained mouth, let out his Tarzan gang call.

"Yuhoieehoieeooee," he yelled, his feet planted firmly astride, his head thrown back. That done, he put his hands on his hips and looked stern; but his tongue, uninterested in the great design, crept up his bottom lip in an attempt to lick the snuffles that bulged in two bubbles under each nostril of his pug nose.

"Here, chief. Here, chief. Here, chief. Here, chief."

His four lieutenants saluted smartly and clicked their heels.

They lined up in front of the lavatory and mysteriously put their fingers in their right ears. Bob replied by tugging three times at his fringe of hair,

"Morlais Jenkins," he snapped.

"Morlais Jenkins," they muttered, clenching their fists.

"No cowards' fists now," Bob warned. "Keep your thumbs inside your four fingers. Otherwise you might split 'is eye, and then there'll be a row off Master. Understand?"

"Yes, o chief," came the reply, four times.

"Right. Get 'im in the corner by the girls' railings, see? They can't see us from the classrooms there, and it'll do 'im good for the girls to see 'im 'ave a licking," Bob snapped.

"Where is the varlet now, chief?" Dicky Owen asked, wiping his nose with the sleeve of his jersey with the grand flourish of a buccaneer drawing his cutlass across his tongue.

"Still within doors, Cap'n Dick. The cur is doing his composition to get good marks off teacher. Till 'e comes out, disperse. Surround 'im when I give the signal. O.K.?"

"O.K., chief." Again four obediences.

"Better 'ave a pee first," Teddy Barnes said. "Get the decks cleared for action right off."

Bob, like a true leader, being already cleared for action, did handstands against the lavatory wall while the others slipped stealthily inside.

Morlais Jenkins was sitting in the front desk in Standard Five class-room, Miss Meredith standing behind him, her hand on his shoulder as she leaned forward to look over his shoulder at his exercise book.

"Have you nearly finished now, Morlais?" she asked, a suspicion of impatience in her light, gentle voice.

Morlais turned his head to one side, looking up at her like a chicken.

"I'm on the conclusion, now, Miss," he said, and dropped his eyes as he felt himself flush.

She was so very close to him, bending over him like that with nobody else in the class-room at all. There was such warmth in her, such an enchanting elusive scent that seemed to blow from her, from an incredibly beautiful other-world where she was, such fullness in her white smooth throat and deep blue eyes and her hands pink like fruit drops. His little body swayed in his awareness of her mystery like a slender weed in the river bed. He tucked his leg more acutely under his bottom so that he was almost lying on his exercise book, and dipping his pen in the inkwell continued his painstaking and fervent scrawl. He had written three sides already, during the last lesson; for forty minutes his tongue had licked slowly back and fore along his lips, the pendulum to his thoughts, and his ink-stained fingers gripped the scratching pen so hard that they had become cold and cramped. Looking down at him she sensed the effort and the absorbing concentration which possessed the child, holding him to his pen and book and subject without respite or remorse. But she did not sense the confusion her own presence had created in him, stalling his ideas, diffusing and breaking the tide of his work, holding his pen poised and useless a little to the right of the last full stop.

"You'll never finish at this rate, Morlais," she said.

She looked at her watch, and then out through the window where the children were flashing like dragonflies in the playground.

Annie Burroughs, the tea monitor, poked her head inside the classroom,

"Miss Brown says to come to the staff-room for your tea, Miss, as it's getting cold, Miss," she shouted officiously.

"Tell Miss Brown I'll be along as soon as possible," said Miss Meredith. "Ask her to put the saucer over my cup, Annie, will you?"

"Yes, Miss," Annie said. And as Miss Meredith turned again to the window Annie gave Morlais's elbow a sharp jab that sent it off the desk. He fell onto his exercise book, and a great gout of ink sullied the marvellous clean page of his thoughts. His involuntary shout made Miss Meredith swing round in time to see Annie leap away from Morlais's desk.

"Annie," she shouted, her voice sharp and dangerous.

Annie disappeared in a scurry of black stockings and green print.

"I'll settle with her again," Miss Meredith said.

She looked down at the close-cropped head bowed over the spoilt page.

"Never mind," she said. "It won't look so bad when it's dry."

When he still sat silent, unmoving except for the right hand which brushed a heavy tear off his cheek, she pulled a desk up beside him and took his pen from his hand.

"Let's see," she said enthusiastically. "Where are we now?"

She turned the page back and skimmed the content of his essay,

"There, it's nearly finished," she said happily. "The shepherd has followed his barking dog Fan through the snow drifts to the thicket where the orphan girl is trapped, and he's wrapped her in his sheep skin coat and carried her to his cottage in the shelter of the pine trees. After she has had some hot milk he puts a rug round her and sets her on the settle by the fire. Now how shall we finish it?"

Morlais didn't move, neither his body nor his lips. His eyelashes were brilliant with brimming tears.

"Suppose we end it like this," she said, dipping the pen in the ink-well, 'And so, nodding drowsily in the friendly blaze, the little girl fell contentedly to sleep.' Is that all right, Morlais?"

He still stared at the blot, moodily, stonily.

"Do you like the word friendly for describing a fire? "she asked. "Can you see why I call it friendly?"

He seemed to shrink away from her, from his composition, from any intellectual idea at all.

"Oh well, I see it's no good us going on like this," she said with vexation. "You'd better go out to play and let's hope you're more sociable when you come back."

He slipped out from under her arm and left the classroom, dragging his feet. She considered his peaky shoulders and bony knees and curiously oval head. Then, shrugging her shoulders, she put his pen down and went down the corridor to her cup of tea, rubbing the ink off her fingers with her transparent scented handkerchief.

In the corridor Morlais rubbed his eyes fiercely with his fists. Nobody must see that he'd been blubbing. He hated himself for blubbing like that, for trembling like a jelly inside himself; if only he wasn't like that inside. He wanted to be like Bobby Linton, having a gang of his own, and stealing from Granny Thomson's sweet shop and from the coal trucks in the siding, and knocking people's doors and running away, and shouting at old Forrest the farmer. Not desolate, soft – oh hell. He heard Miss Meredith's footsteps behind him, light and curt, and he hurried out of his daydream and along the corridor to the playground entrance. But as he hurried through the lobby a hand plucked at his sleeve, and David Reames popped out from behind a coat.

"Hallo, Morlais," he said, smiling.

"Hallo," Morlais said. "You gave me a fright then."

He was trembling.

He was very glad David had waited for him, in a way.

"Haven't you got anything better to do than wait in here?" he said gruffly.

"Well," David ruffled at the rebuke, "I wasn't waiting, really. At least I just waited, that's all. I thought you'd be coming all the time."

"What d'you want, then?" Morlais said rudely. "Any of those standard three kids in your class been hitting you?"

"No, nobody today," David said. "They've been very good today."

"Well, you just tell me if any of them try to be funny,"

Morlais said, "and I'll pick a scrap with them on the way home and give them a bloody licking, too. Coming out the yard?"

"Yes, please," David said, skipping involuntarily at the unexpected invitation. He was two standards below Morlais.

"Don't say, please," Morlais said sharply. His skin was pink again. "P'r'aps your mother've learnt you to say please for everything in your house, but that's not the same as school, see?"

"Yes," David replied blindly, accepting as a strange fact, hard and uncompromising as all facts, the axiom that what is right in one place is wrong in another. His mother had made him constantly sensitive in his behaviour to other people, to old people and visitors mostly, but in this school he seemed to be contravening every convention. He found the children of colliers disturbingly offensive and proper. And there were so many of them, and all so strange and noisy and vivid; all the faces bewilderingly new; all the names strange, too, as strange as the accent of their speech; and it was so tiring having to learn the names and fix the right name on the right face and presence, especially when they were never still, and always teased or ignored or sniggered at him and stopped talking in groups and tossed apart when he approached them. The first time he came to school he had worn a yellow silk blouse and velvet trousers with yellow buttons, and his mother had driven him down in the car because she wanted to talk to the Master. All the children had gathered gaping round the car and eyed him and his mother, his beautiful tall mother, as they went through the playground.

"That's the new manager's kid at the top pit," he'd heard their awed whispers.

From the first playtime they'd treated him with a mixture of scorn and reserve, timid reserve. Bob Linton had made a set against him right at the start, fingering his velvet trousers derisively and saying "Puss, Puss, Puss," and imitating his lisp and making sarcastic remarks about his own chauffeur being ill. And the girls were all silly towards him, simpering and stressing their aspirates. The first few weeks he cried his eyes out as soon as he reached home, mostly with relief at getting indoor, in sanctuary, away from the playground and the shouting and the indecision, away from the broken pavements and stony roads and grey rows of houses from whose doorsteps fat women regarded him critically and gossiped as he hurried on out of earshot. And although things had stopped whirring round and had settled down in his mind and outside him, he was still nervous and cautious and ill at ease. Whenever he saw Morlais he felt a warmness break into fire inside him, as it did when he saw his mother waiting at the garden gate for him on his way home from school. For the Master had put Morlais in charge of him on the first day.

"Yes," he said, "I won't say please, then. Where shall we go?"

"Out," said Morlais, putting his hands into his pockets and trying to roll a little as he walked.

As they went down the corridor David coughed nervously.

"Morlais," he said.

"What?"

"Mother wants to know please would you like to come and have tea with me today – with us today, would you?"

David swallowed hard after daring his great request. His eyes were big and apprehensive,

"Will you?" he repeated, in his trepidation taking Morlais by the sleeve,

Morlais shook his sleeve loose,

"Don't do that," he said. "Only girls touch each other. It's soft."

"Sorry," David said, utterly crest-fallen.

They passed out through the door into the glare and dazzling movement of the playground.

"I'm going to pee," Morlais said, dashing off to the lavatories and leaving David alone. Terribly alone.

Well, Morlais thought savagely, he shouldn't have asked. It's his own fault for asking. Why won't he leave me alone, not be after me all the time, the blessed nuisance? I'd like to wring his neck. What does he want? He's got a farm hasn't he? And a big house? And his father's the manager of the pit, and rich. What does he want, pestering me all the time? And now this. And I've left him there, and Bob Linton will be after him, and –

He saw Bob Linton standing forbiddingly in the entrance to the lavatory. His nonchalance it was that was so sinister. Morlais turned back and returned slowly towards David, his head bent and his feet slouching slovenly along. David was still in the same place, standing stiffly like a nervous old woman surrounded by the tide,

"Coming down this way?" Morlais said roughly.

"Yes, er –" David choked the please back just in time. "Thank you," he said.

"Oh," – Morlais felt properly sick of him – "What's the use of telling you anything? Isn't please the same as thank you?"

"Is it?" David said, trying to remember when he said please at home and when thank you." They must be different or there wouldn't be two words for them, would there?"

"Oh hell," Morlais said, his eyes harsh with vexation.

"Now then, Morly, none of them swear words when you're in good company," Teddy Barnes said, attaching himself to them. "You know little Davy's mammy said 'e's not to talk with boys wot use bad language. For shame on you."

"She didn't say so," David said, bravely, standing timidly by Morlais.

Teddy burst into laughter.

"Whassup now?" Dicky Owen said, poking his head round David's shoulder – there was one on each side of them now.

"Davy's mother says 'e can swear as much as he likes," Teddy Barnes roared. "I wish my old woman would say the same to me. Strap across the bum it is in our 'ouse if she catches you cursing,"

"My mother never said such a thing," David said, stamping his impotent feet and trembling on the verge of tears.

"Well, you just said she did, you dirty little fibber," Dicky Owen shouted. "Get away from, here with your old lies."

He gave David a cuff that sent him reeling.

"Bully," hissed Morlais, white as a sheet.

"'Ere, did you 'ear that, Dicky?" Teddy Barnes said grimly, closing his fists and squaring up,

"Called me a name, didn't he?" Dicky said, "What did you call me, Morly Jenkins, you dirty little scum?"

Morlais edged away from them, shaking with fear of the physical pain he felt in their clenched and waiting fists.

"Well, say it, mun. Where's your tongue?"

Morlais was shaking feverishly.

"What's wrong, boys?" Bob Linton said, coming up behind Morlais.

"This dirty skunk of a teacher's pet is calling me out of names," Teddy said, moving his fists up and down like pistons.

"Didn't think 'e 'ad the guts," Bob sneered. "Better be sure what 'e said, though, Teddy. 'E'll cleck to Miss Meredith for certain."

"Never mind about that," Teddy said grimly, "I know I'm in the right."

"Give 'im a sock, then," Bob said, pulling once at his fringe of hair.

David screamed at the top of his voice.

"Bullies –" Morlais's mouth was open on the word as Teddy Barnes' fist crashed into it. Bob Linton had put his foot out behind him and spragged him as he reeled back. He fell flat on his back on the hard surface of the yard; the others piled on top of him. A loud scream of delighted hysterical excitement ran across the girls' yard, and the railings swarmed with shouting bobs and pigtails. A whistle blew urgently and peremptorily.

"Look out," hissed one of the squirming pile of boys. "Master's coming."

"Get up, you fools," Bob said, leaning against the railings as though he had nothing to do with the scrap.

"Ooh, let go, leggo my leg," Dicky Owen bellowed, kicking out with pain and flinging David back. He peeled himself off the pile and rubbed his bleeding ankle.

"You dirty little biter," he snarled, looking at the teeth-marks in his white skinny leg. He started to his feet to go for David, and crashed into the headmaster.

"What's all this?" said the Master, puffing his purplish cheeks outwith indignation. "What are you up to now, Teddy Barnes, Dicky Owen? Get off that boy at once. Who is it?"

He bent down with a wheeze like a deflating balloon.

"Won't let go, sir," Teddy Barnes said, sweating and red.

"Come off at once, at once," said the Master, pulling Morlais by the collar of his jersey. "Who is it? Morlais Jenkins, is it?"

Morlais clung like a leech, his head buried in Teddy Barnes' belly.

"Come on, boy," the Master shouted, shaking Morlais as hard as he could.

Morlais saw who it was. For a moment he stared white and uncomprehending. Then everything in him caved in. He let go, slumped limply on the yard, and the breath went out of him with a grunt as the weight of Teddy Barnes' body crushed into his relaxed stomach.

"Come on," said the Master, "no silly tricks here. Get up boy. Stop shamming."

He yanked Morlais to his feet.

"Well, have any of you anything to say?" he asked.

No reply.

"Well, in that case we'll leave the matter where it is," he said. "I'll keep you all under observation, and if I have the slightest trouble from one of you," – he wagged his podgy little finger under Dicky Owen's nose – "I'll expel that boy from this school instantly." His words fell on them like the blows of a flattened hand.

"Go to your places," he said.

As they filed into school from lines David came up to Morlais, who was bathing a torn lip in the lobby, and said, "Will you come to tea with us, Morlais?"

"Yes," said Morlais quietly. "If my mother's a-willing."

And as David was leaving for Standard Three room Morlais caught him by the sleeve.

"Dicky Owen's got a lovely cut on his leg," he said. "Seen it?"

David smiled, the most tremulous difficult smile; it seemed to come out of the heart of him.

"Go on, scoot," Morlais said, "see you after school."

"See me too, you swab," Bob Linton shot from the corner of his mouth as he filed past.

Morlais felt sick at that, sick and oppressed.

"Are they all in now?" Miss Meredith called – she was playing the piano in the hall for the march in – girls on one side, boys on the other.

"All in, miss," Morlais replied.

She sighed with relief, clamped the piano lid down and taking her music score and her keys in her arm came out through the lobby.

"You know what I said just before you went out, Morlais?" she bent over him as she passed, light as a shadow. "Never mind. It'll be alright when it dries."

Her hand touched his tousled hair, and she was gone.

Only then did he cry. Only then. When there was no need to cry. Curse himself, oh curse, curse, curse.

The remaining two lessons – sums and nature study – were a slow agony for Morlais. He sat through them with pain and difficulty, and the reluctant struggle of his bruised mind with the area of a rectangular garden and the parts of a bluebell was as laborious and painful as the struggle of a snail whose shell has been crushed to reach the grass and thistles on the margin of the flinty road. Whenever Miss Meredith asked him a question he froze up, black and vacant. His mind was dead.

"You'd better go to bed early tonight, Morlais, and have a good rest," she said. "For if you're as dull as this during the scholarship exam tomorrow you'll never pass through to the County School."

He didn't care, didn't understand, even. Nothing had any meaning or attraction. When the bell went, he was going to run, *RUN*. Bob Linton mustn't catch him. If Bob Linton were to hit him with his fists at dinner time he'd lie on the ground and die. Die. Die.

To flee the anguish of death was all his desire. To run when the bell rang. Home.

"Now if the outer sides of the garden are ten yards by five, and I mark off a gravel path all round it, two feet wide, what will the area of the garden inside the path be? How would you tackle that, Morlais, if it happens to be on the scholarship paper tomorrow?"

Miss Meredith stood close to him, looking at him expectantly, appealing to him with all her secret power, the power so much deeper than words. Silently she was wanting him to answer her, willing it. He felt her unspoken wish pervade him, stir the bitter mud up in the troubled waters of his being. And he shut her out. As if his soul was a deep-sea squid excreting a pall of inky fluid he blotted out her question and her presence inside him. The sunlight coming through the window, through the jamjars of wild flowers ranged along the window sill, the dust swirling in the shaft of light, burning his sullen sight like a hostile sword drawn against him – *him* – against, him the whole universe had directed its malignance, against *him*.

"You won't answer, then?" she said, taking offence at his refusal.

"Well, you tell him, Hetty," she said sharply, turning from him to the eagerly lifted arms behind and around him.

"Please, Miss," Hetty began, beaming with excitement at knowing something that Morlais Jenkins didn't know, "please, Miss..."

And then she stopped, faltered, and slowly drew down her hand and covered her mouth. She didn't know it after all.

The bell rang.

Morlais was in the yard, in the open air, almost escaped and away from the menace whose terror so oppressed him.

He raced across the yard as blindly as the butterfly had done, earlier in the day. Flash. And out through the school gates into the road.

Free.

He had turned the corner into the street the buses used before the school spewed out its brawling brood. The road was quiet and safe. The houses reassured him, the parlour windows with frayed curtains, the clean doorsteps and scrubbed pavements in front of the tidy houses, fat Mrs Morris suckling her baby in the sunlight and shouting across the street to Mrs Jones Top – he knew he was safe among these safe things. He stopped running and walked slowly down the street, and his body began to tingle with reassuring warmth.

Free.

He felt in his trousers pocket, hoping he had brought his Saturday halfpenny to school with him. He hadn't spent it on Saturday – Saturday had been cold and drizzly and he'd decided to wait until a sunny day when a packet of sherbet would taste so deliciously cool and sharp, poured into a glass of water and fizzing against his lips in the sun's glare.

He felt thoroughly. Hanky, dickstones, twigs, penknife, lump of chalk his father used underground for marking his dram of coal, string – but no halfpenny. Well, he'd have to hurry home and get the halfpenny out of his Sunday trousers, and come back to the shop to spend. He began running, and involuntarily he skipped and threw his hands up into the lovely sunlight as though he were scattering flowers.

Half way down the grimy street he turned off the pavement and went across the ash-covered space where the buses waited for people to go shopping to town. There was a red bus waiting, a huge red bus throbbing away impatiently, its fixtures rattling rhythmically, brr-rr, brr-rr, brr-rr, the driver in his fine uniform, peaked cap and braided coat, talking to the conductor and drinking cold tea from a bottle.

It was a fine thing, that huge bus, throbbing away, and the driver was fine and strong, being able to drive the bus to town, round corners and down hills. Three times he'd been on that bus to town. Oh boy. Some day he'd go again, perhaps, when his mother wanted to buy him a new trousers or something. In the bus, to town.

Remembering the halfpenny and the sherbet he tore himself away from the bus and went towards the house. At the corner of his own back lane he looked back at the bus. It was still there, red and throbbing, like the winding engine at the colliery, great, great.

He wandered up the back lane, slowly. He never hurried in the back lane unless he was playing fox and hounds with the other boys. Usually he just moved slowly, peeping through the back doors at the men sitting in their shirtsleeves on the kitchen steps and the women hanging clothes on the line and the little boys feeding the chickens and white rabbits that browsed in the wilderness of ragwort and dock leaves.

In the afternoons the back lane was full of colliers, sitting on their heels against the wall, black faces, black hands, having a Woodbine and a bit of a chat before going into the house and bathing. Morlais liked sitting there with them, half-hearing their talk, smelling the cold mousy smell of pit-dirt that was always about their clothes, and wondering at them going down the shaft, down down in darkness, and cutting at the face the hard coal, bruising their hands and their arms that knotted and tensed with the strength of the bus and the winding engine. Some of them were good footballers, and would have a kick about in the back lane in their working clothes. You should see the welt they gave the ball, their heavy hob-nailed boots with iron toe caps. And when their wives and mothers called out that the bucket of water for their bath was boiling on the fire, and they went indoors, he still stayed on in the back lane, still possessed by their movement and rude vitality and loud laughter, till hunger called him home.

Today the lane was empty. Empty ash boxes and buckets worn too thin with use in the kitchen to serve any other purpose than holding refuse, the outside leaves of cabbages thrown over the back walls of the narrow strips of vegetable garden at the back of each house, a few empty salmon tins which the cats of the street nosed and pawed about, miraculously never cutting themselves on the sharp scalloped edge the tin opener had made. The lane that was as familiar and characteristic a part of him as his skin, hands, clothes. Empty.

His own house was the end one in the street, and therefore had a side door opening into the rough square at the end of the lane and at right angles to it. The door was painted red; years ago his father had painted it red; now it was a worn pink, faded and bubbled and flaked; it wouldn't shut properly and his mother was always on about getting it mended, and his father always saying alright, one day when he had a bit of time he'd do it up for her; you could see into the back, into the kitchen too, if the kitchen door was open; his mother didn't like everybody seeing into the kitchen; it was so *common*; she said, everybody listening every time there was a row in the kitchen about something; and it was against that door that Morlais' sister Doris was leaning when he came out of the back lane. He didn't see her for a moment because there was a boy leaning against the wall right up against her, concealing her from him. But when he saw her, and the boy leaning close up to her, he stopped dead. The spasm of revulsion that seized him at seeing them made his legs stop dead. He frowned and his face settled into a sulk and self-consciously he made himself walk on towards her.

He knew the boy alright. He took milk round for the Co-op and lived in Fochriw Row and played centre half for Fochriw Corinthians. And Morlais had seen him playing billiards in the Lucania once when the door swung open to let a man and his greyhound out. He had seen the green cloth flooded with lamplight, the swirl of blue tobacco smoke, and this boy standing over the table in his shirtsleeves chalking his cue. His legs were a bit bandy and his eyes were narrow and he had hair on the back of his hands.

Morlais felt sick, seeing him leaning against the wall talking to Doris. She had her hair in curlers, her neck bare except for a few rat tails, and she was leaning with her back to the wall so that her belly was puffed out against the cord of her washing apron. She had a sweeping brush in her hand and the buttons of her blouse were undone in the middle, exposing a glimpse of smooth fat flesh.

The milkman said something to her and she gave him a push, laughing at him silkily.

"Let's pass, Dor," Morlais said, pushing her to one side and trying to brush past her without lifting his head.

"Oh, you again, is it ?" she said. "Mam's waiting for you; she wants you to run down James the grocer's for some corned beef for dinner."

Morlais squeezed under her arm and through the back door.

"What would Maggie Jane Rees say if she knew you wanted to meet somebody else up the mountain?" his sister said as he pushed the door to behind her. Her voice sounded slimy to him, rich dark slime like the drain pipe Dad cleaned out last week, repulsive slime that was like velvet, like a frog's back, like a pup drowned in the river.

His mind was wandering through its dark tunnels.

"Watch that tub there, boy," his mother said.

He woke up with a start as he barked his shin on the edge of the wooden wash tub on the kitchen floor. He rubbed his shin hard, dancing on his other leg.

"Serve your faults," she said, wiping the suds off her fat red arms and pushing her sweaty wet hair back from her perspiring forehead. The table was piled with clothes already washed and wrung half-dry. A clothes-horse covered with washed underwear steamed in front of the fire. The steam and the sun's heat and the drone of bluebottles made his skin itch with discomfort. There was no room to move in the little back kitchen and the window was filmed over with condensing steam. He picked up the tattered copy of Rob Roy which he was reading and opened it at the dog-eared page where he had left off at breakfast.

"Don't start reading in here," she said sharply. "Nor out the back, neither," she snapped as he turned to the door. "Put that old book away now and go down James's for some corned beef. The order 'aven't come up and there's nothing in the 'ouse for dinner."

"Oh pot." he said, passionately.

He shut the book and dropped it carelessly onto the settle.

"Go on now, like a good boy," she said, immersing her arms once more into the tub. "I been working since seven this morning. Go on now out the way."

He watched her scrubbing the soiled linen, her stubby fat hands swollen and red.

"Well, go on," she said. "You'll be late for school if you don't watch."

Still he watched her, expending his curiosity upon her movements. She rubbed the things against the corrugated board, back and fore, soaping them, rubbing them, rubbing them hard. A wonder the skin didn't come off her fingers the way she rubbed. Sweat running down the crows' feet of her eyes and the sharp vertical groove in her forehead just over her nose. Her mouth sagged as she bent over the tub and rubbed so hard that the suds rose up in great snowy heaps and broke into web patches on her old green blouse. She never wore her teeth when she washed.

She was washing his father's working pants. They never came quite clean, and she didn't rub them too hard because they were all darns and frayed thin patches that would go through if she weren't careful with them. When she had scrubbed them to her satisfaction she wrung them dry and put them on the floor beside the tub. Then she looked up at Morlais, "Teacher tell you anything today?" she asked, smiling at him.

He evaded her eyes as though he had been caught doing some shameful act. Looking at her washing, on her knees by the tub, examining her – "No," he said.

"Didn't she say nothing about the scholarship tomorrow?" she said. She sounded thirsty to hear something, something from his own world, something entirely apart from her perpetual scrubbing and washing.

"No," he said, stubbornly, refusing her what she asked of him.

"Well, I expect she knows you'll do alright tomorrow, don't she?"she said, still appealing to him.

He enclosed himself in a sulk and shrugged his bony high shoulders.

"Oh well," she said, sighing as she bent down to the tub once more. Then, with exasperation, she looked up again and snapped at him "I told you to go down James's, didn't I? Go on now, when you're told, will you?"

He turned away from her towards the door, halted and pondered, then slipped through the passage and upstairs. He remembered about the halfpenny and the glass of sherbet. His hands trembled with new joy as he opened the tin box in the bare little room in which he and his brother Dilwyn slept.

26

He pulled out his Sunday best trousers.

The halfpenny wasn't there.

He pulled the lining of the pockets out. Nothing. He pulled his Sunday coat out, searched the pockets in vain, flung it on the floor, and feverishly began to yank everything out of the box, all the neatly folded clothes, coats, jerseys, shirts, stockings, all the old books and toys, the bag of marbles placed there in readiness for next season, and nowhere, nowhere among all his possessions was the halfpenny to be found. He searched long after he knew it was gone, long after his eyes had blurred with tears and he couldn't see anything but a hot swirl of clothes, and in his impotence he clawed his nails into the floor. A long splinter jabbed under his thumbnail, and he jumped with the sudden pain of it. He caught his thumb round the joint to check the jumping pain, and as the blood surged under the nail he began to sob.

"Morlais, Morlais," his mother called from the foot of the stairs. Her voice made him jump as if she were shaking him by the neck of his jersey. There was a tone in it he knew better than to disobey. So he stopped sobbing, suddenly, not as a baby stops when it is given the toy it's screaming for, but as two lovers might stop if a pimp peeped over the hedge and encouraged them to consummate their ecstasy.

"What 'ave you been doing up there all the time?" his mother said angrily.

"I've lost my Saturday 'a'penny," he said.

"You can look for it after school tonight, then," she said. "There's no time now. Get you off to James' or there'll be no dinner for you today."

He went straight out through the kitchen into the yard. Doris was pulling the rabbit hutch out to clean the dust away from the corner of the yard.

"Do us a favour, Mor," she said carelessly,

"What d'you want?" he asked sulkily.

"Tell Ben James I can't meet him tonight as we arranged.

Tell him – well, say I've got to go to Chapel, will you? Say I'll see him tomorrow night. See?"

"Go and tell him yourself," he said.

"Come on, be a sport," she said. "Only tell him, that's all."

He kicked the weeds between the flagstones, head bent all the time.

"I'll give you a halfpenny if you do," she said, silkily now.

He raised his head and looked at her straight.

"I won't," he said.

She laughed, loud and derisive.

"Don't then," she said, pushing him out through the back door. "I tell you what's wrong with you. You've got a dirty little mind and you know more than you should. See? Well, don't expect me to do you a favour next time, that's all."

She took him by the scruff of his neck and pushed him into the lane, shutting the door after him.

"He's gone now, anyway, Mam," she shouted into the kitchen. And she went on cleaning and singing Lily of Laguna loud enough for anyone to hear.

Morlais kept to the back lanes all the way down to the shopping street at the bottom of the village. He tried to go as fast as he could; that is, he hurried every time he remembered he had to fetch corned beef for dinner. But most of the way down he was preoccupied with the things that had happened to him that day, and the things that were still to happen. Bob Linton and his gang would be still after him, and he would have to go to the manager's big house for tea, and somebody at home might notice his lacerated lip and he'd have to tell them some story about falling down – hateful questions demanding a lie in reply and all the torment of lying – oh, how dangerous and monstrous and endless the day was.

Peeping through an open door in the back lane of Fair Prospect Road he saw a fox. His heart leapt like a salmon in him. A fox. A real live fox, its sharp nose pressed against the wire netting of a ramshackle cage. Long black hairs growing on the lovely smoothy slope of fawn fur below its eyes, its bright questing eyes. Its chain rattled as it ran belly-to-straw up and down the cage. He looked at it with hound's eyes, his pulse quickening with the primitive excitement of standing face to face with an unexpected wild creature. A fox. He breathed slowly between his closed teeth, unconsciously baring his lips. Then, unaccountably, he ran. Ran away from it, and from himself facing it.

At the bottom of the lane he bumped into two little girls from his own class.

"Where are you going?" Winnie Morse asked him.

He looked levelly at her, her squint and her clubfoot and her torn frock.

"Down James's," he said curtly.

"We're playing house," Rhoda James explained.

She was chubby, red-cheeked and yellow-haired, and her eyes were blue. He liked her alright and played with her often. But not since she had started going with Winnie Morse, from whom he shrank instinctively.

"Yes, we've built the 'ouse, see?" Winnie said, pointing proudly at the rectangle of stones within which were placed broken pieces of china and real doll's tea things and some whelk and limpet shells that Rhoda had brought back from last year's Sunday School outing to Barry.

"Like to step inside for a bit of dinner?" Rhoda asked. "It's all ready now."

He grinned.

"I'm too big," he said, "and my boots are dirty, too."

"No, don't you worry about that," Winnie said, "you just come in. We was just saying we've got everything we want 'ere except a man to sleep with."

Rhoda giggled nervously.

"Wouldn't you like a bit with Rhoda?" Winnie sneered.

He looked at her with fear, seeing her club foot and sharp squinting eyes as something witchlike and horrible. He was at the mercy of her tongue and her spite and her wickedness.

"Come on in, mun," she said, warming to her mockery. "There's nothing wrong with it. Even your father and mother do it."

"They don't," he said, visibly wincing.

"Alright, no need to shout," Winnie said, shrugging her painfully skinny body and waving her bony arms as though she were a marionette being jerked by the devil. "But you wouldn't be alive if they didn't. Would he, Rhoda?"

"I don' know," Rhoda said, giggling hysterically.

"'Course you wouldn't," Winnie said.

"I was born because my mother and father got married," he said, retreating behind the earthwork of another argument.

She broke it down at once with a final thrust and appeared before him again in all her malice.

"That's got nothing to do with it," she said with scorn, snobs running down her nose in her excitement. "My sister's got a baby, and *she* isn't married. So there."

"I don't care," he said, reeling from her cruel logic, "I can't help that. Your sister isn't everything."

And once again he ran away, stumbling and demoralised and ashamed beyond words this time. And Winnie's laughter followed him, her jibes completing his rout.

He turned now out of the back lane and down the steep hill into the shopping street, past the police station and the iron monger's where he had bought his penknife last birthday and over the railway crossing into the Square. The hot noon and the dry wind covered his boots with a thin white coating of dust and irritated his throat. He walked along the pavement, keeping to the shelter of the window shades which the shop keepers pulled down with long hooked poles. The shop windows were full of flies; flypapers black with them, butter and fruit and cheese crawled over by them. He watched a bluebottle crouch in a bubble of fat in a rich side of bacon, and when it flew away he pressed his face against the hot pane of glass to see whether he could discover the pile of tiny white eggs it had secreted in the meat. His father had found a knot of flies' eggs in the meat last week, and cut them out with a knife and put them on the fire, Morlais had imagined those foul eggs maturing in his stomach; in bed that night he had lain with his mouth open to let the flies crawl up his throat and escape. In his imagination he identified himself with the lion on the treacle tin, bees swarming in its stomach. For a week since that day he had been coughing all the time, his throat morbidly irritated by the apprehension of the bluebottles hatching out in the lining of his stomach.

The Square was fairly busy. Boys like himself sent on errands dawdled outside the Italian shop where the young colliers played nap and listened to the gramophone. The baker loading his van with bread and dainties had an inquisitive audience. Others, their shopping done and brown paper parcels tucked under their arms, walked homewards alongside the ice cream cart, rubbing their hands against its white paint as though they could thereby capture the essence of the ice cream they could not afford to buy. And every time Luigi shouted his wares they took up the cry, hallooing like huntsmen, "Oice cree-um, oi; oice cree-um, oi." Morlais watched them till they were round the corner at the top of the hill. Then he wandered down the Square, regretting bitterly his lost halfpenny, and hurrying past the row of old men who always occupied the red bench outside the Workmen's Hall, went into James the Grocer's to fulfil his mission.

The shop was full as usual. He hated the shop for many reasons, not the least of them the fact that he always had to stand waiting among a crowd of women who, even if they came in after him, pestered the white aproned assistants for immediate attention and leaned over his head to place their baskets on the counter and see that the scales tipped in their favour. Their voices were harsh and self-assertive, their clothes stained and soapy, their laughter unrestrained and unlovely. And his legs ached with the long wait, jostled about on the sawdust-strewn floor by the impatient nagging women who were so much bigger and self-confident than he. But he hated the shop for a deeper reason than that. He hated it because of Benjamin James, the son of the bald pursy proprietor. Benjamin James was courting his sister Doris.

There was no chair to sit on, so he moved across to the corner where he could watch the girl cutting ham on the gleaming steel cutter. The operation fascinated him, the steel teeth that held the ham in position, the whirring circular blade that cut the meat in such wonderfully thin strips – it was fused in his mind with the breathless tales of the Scarlet Pimpernel over whose brilliance the guillotine was always suspended, like this cutter, relentless, baleful, inhumanly cruel.

"'Owbe, Morlais," Benjamin James shouted, leaning over a pyramid of raisins, his blue, clean-shaven chin shining like his smooth glassy eyes and the sharp bridge of his nose. "What d'you want, boy?"

Morlais jumped awake from his reverie by the ham cutter and grinned nervously in reply to Benjamin's loud greeting.

"Tin of corned beef," he said.

"Right you are," Benjamin said pleasantly, taking a tin of Fray Bentos off the shelf and tossing it into the air before handing it over the counter. "Put it on the book, is it?"

Morlais shrivelled up at the effusiveness of the man. He wasn't kind; his actions were too cocksure, too demonstrative, too smooth to be kind. He leaned over the counter and ruffled Morlais' hair with his huge hand – he wasn't very tall but his hands were huge. Morlais moved away.

"Any message from Doris?" Benjamin asked, still with his buttery smile.

"No," Morlais said.

"Oh well, no news is good news, I suppose," Benjamin said, brushing his greasy hair back from his narrow forehead and beaming, beaming.

"Well, solong boy."

Morlais turned and went out of the shop without a word.

He was passing the Italian's shop when he bumped into his brother Dilwyn, who was coming out of the doorway.

"My sister wouldn't go with you if you paid 'er a fortune," Dilwyn was shouting to one of the boys in the shop, "She's particular, boy." And he crashed backwards into Morlais.

"Oh, it's you, is it?" Morlais said impatiently. He and Dilwyn were always fighting. They fought in bed and in the back garden and at meals. They quarrelled when they were playing Cowboys and Indians or anything else, quarrelled and pummeled each other until one or the other went home crying. Dilwyn was nine years old and had been kept back for a second year in standard two. He never tried to work in school, and he was out all hours of the night, messing about the billiard hall and the railway sidings and the Italian's shop and the football field. He took a row from his mother or a strapping from his father without flinching; they couldn't do anything to chasten him. He mitched when he should be in school, staying away to pick whinberries on the mountain in summer or watch the engines taking the loaded trucks away; Morlais hated him. And he in return did all he could to upset Morlais. He played up to Bob Linton's gang, persecuted David Reames, hammered on the floor when Morlais was reading in the kitchen; he was a proper swine. And when Morlais saw a halfpenny packet of sherbet in his hand he knew at once where his lost halfpenny had gone to.

"You stole my halfpenny," he said.

"No I didn't," Dilwyn rejoined, his face going stony and stubborn.

"Where d'you get the money to buy that sherbet, then?" Morlais said viciously.

Dilwyn hid his hand behind his back.

"What sherbet?" he asked viciously. He was ready for a fight.

"You little thief," Morlais said. "I'll tell our Mam you been stealing again."

"Tell 'er, then," Dilwyn sneered, "That's just what you would do, mammy's pet."

Morlais clenched and unclenched his hands and trembled and flushed. "I'll hit you sick," he said. His voice quivered.

"Try it on," Dilwyn mocked, his eyes narrowing.

Morlais hit him as hard as he could. His fist seemed to crash into Dilwyn's watchful eyes, close, swimming close to his own. But he hit nothing. Dilwyn's head swayed to one side and as Morlais overbalanced Dilwyn's fist hit him sharply in his stomach.

"Here, what's the game, you kids?"

A towering blue-uniformed policeman lifted them both off the ground and shook them like dirty carpets. "Stop squabbling and get off home while you're safe. See?"

Frightened and quiet they hurried away. At the top of the hill Dilwyn said "You can 'ave a drink of the sherbet if you want to, Mor."

"I don't want any," Morlais said, clenching his teeth and turning his head away and covertly wiping his eyes with the sleeve of his jersey.

"I suppose you'd rather tell our Mam about it, wouldn't you?" Dilwyn said bitterly.

Morlais didn't reply.

"If you tell 'er I stole your 'a'penny I won't tell you where Bob Linton's gang is going to wait for you after school 's'fternoon," Dilwyn persisted.

"I don't care where they're waiting," Morlais said.

"They'll knock you sick," Dilwyn said threateningly.

"I don't care, I don't care," Morlais said, the hot day burning out his whole being with its ruthless pitiless glare. He ran a few yards ahead of Dilwyn and then slowed down. He wanted to be by himself. That, was the only thing he wanted.

He didn't say anything about the halfpenny when they

reached home. His mother was angry at his long absence and her vexation froze him up. So until dinner was laid he went down the garden to pluck leaves for the rabbits and when he "kneeled before the wire netting of their cage he forgot everything except the vision of their dull little eyes and their furry white heads and sensitive nostrils snuffing eagerly at the green stuff he pushed through the netting.

"Tweek, tweek, tweek," he whispered, laying his cheek on the stone flag and peering up at them.

"Can you see their teeth, Mor?" his sister Hetty called, coming in through the side door.

Hetty wasn't dark like the rest of them. Her hair was straight and flaxen, her face thin and sharp with a light wax-smooth glow like a Japanese lantern. When she laughed her cheeks and eyes seemed to become transparent, reflecting the clear flame of her merriment.

And she was always snuggling up to people, putting her arms round her mother or Doris, putting her head against their sopping wet aprons and hugging their thighs, or pulling her father's yellow-stained moustache and lighting a match for his pipe, or putting her forehead against Morlais's and counting how many eyes he had. Her hair was tied in a pigtail by a white rag bow and when they were playing engines she used it as both whistle and communication cord. She was the youngest of the family, seven years old, and as she had been home ill a lot with her perpetual cough she was still in the Infants' school. She was always taking things for her cough, and if the medicine tasted nasty Morlais would drink half of it with her; but the cough never went from her for long. It kept her awake at nights and she could only relieve it by curling up against Doris' warm body and pressing her face into the heat of her breasts.

She came skipping down the yard and knelt beside Morlais.

"Isn't Mrs Rabbit getting fat?" she said wonderingly.

"She's 'aving babies, Dad said," Morlais informed her.

"Well, she won't be able to run after them if she gets much fatter," Hetty said. "Let me give her a bit of dinner, Mor, is it?"

They were both lying on their tummies watching the two rabbits nibbling the green lettuce leaves when their mother came to the kitchen door and called them.

"Get off that cold stone at once, Hetty," she shouted. "And come on in to dinner now straight. It's time for school."

Reluctantly they separated themselves from the rabbits and from the all-absorbing pleasure of watching them eat the green leaves and went indoors to eat the cold dinner that always accompanied the steam and heat and sharp temper of washing day.

Dinner was a quick and silent meal. They pulled a chair each up to the linoleum-covered table by the small window and took a plate and knife and fork from the enamel bowl in which the crockery was always placed after washing up. It was nondescript crockery, chipped and cracked and diversely patterned; they used it always for week day meals; when they had a visitor to tea and on Sundays they put the bowl in the pantry and used the set of blue china made in Swansea which Mrs Jenkins had received as a wedding present from her parents. Doris cut bread, holding the loaf against her stomach and handing them a round each. Mrs Jenkins went on with her washing, for she wanted to get the boiler empty of clothes in order to put water on the fire for her husband's bath. Dilwyn ate most but finished first; he was apprehensive throughout the meal, glancing up at Morlais to see whether he looked like clecking about the halfpenny. But Morlais had no sort of look on his face at all; he ate expressionlessly, scarcely lifting his eyes from the plate, never speaking except to ask for the tomato sauce.

"I'll 'ave a bit, too," Dilwyn said, growing optimistic and feeling hungry in consequence. "Cut us a hanch of bread, Dor."

Doris cut a thick round which he dipped into the pool of sauce on his plate and stuffed into his mouth.

"Take your time, mun," Doris said, "scoffing it like if you didn't 'ave no manners at all."

She supped daintily at her cup of tea, her little finger held away from the rest, sticking straight out in a way that was held nice in all the tea drinking functions with which mining village life abounds. Her free hand was busy scratching an itch between her breasts.

"You ought to see the way they do eat in the pictures," she said severely, "you'd learn a bit of manners then, p'r'aps."

"Never mind about manners now," Mrs Jenkins said, poking at the boiler full of clothes, "let them finish their grub and get to school."

"I'm off," Dilwyn said, jumping up from his seat and drawing his jersey sleeve across his mouth to wipe away the crumbs and sauce. "Solong."

The door slammed behind him as he ran out, whooping like a redskin.

"How long is it before Guy Fawkes?" Hetty asked.

"There's the bell," said Mrs Jenkins. "You'll 'ave to leave your dinner and run, Morlais."

Morlais stopped eating, laid his knife and fork aside, and pushing his chair back half stood up.

"Don't stand like that," Doris said, "your bum sticking out and your face in the butter. Look at 'im, Mam, 'e's a proper yell."

She laughed loudly like most people with no sense of humour who think they have seen something funny. Morlais' lips were quivering.

"Shut your row," Mrs Jenkins said angrily to Doris, and putting her stirring rod down crossed over to Morlais. "What's the matter now?" she said.

The unusual gentleness of her voice broke down his last resistance. Heavy tears laboured down his cheeks and fell onto the table, while he stood there bent forward and holding the chair behind him, his shoulders shaking and his throat gasping for breath.

"Are you feeling bad, bach?" she asked, taking his head and pulling it into her stomach. "Are you feeling bad?" her voice troubled and quiet.

Hetty put her knife and fork down and slipped nervously out of her chair. She stood watching her mother and Morlais weeping against her wet washing clothes; Hetty's eyes distended and she walked backwards from them. When Morlais suddenly choked with sobbing she turned and ran out of the room.

"There then, there then," Mrs Jenkins said, her voice rhythmic with the soothing rise and fall of old lullabies.

Doris yawned and smiled to herself.

Morlais clung to his mother's clothes, to the pitch darkness into which his tears flowed, black rivers of pain; and the warmth of her body against his wet cheeks and the calmness of her hand smoothing his head soothed the immense trouble upheaving in him.

"God spare my boy," she said softly, her breast heaving as his own blind agony communicated itself to her.

"What's up with him?" Doris said, sipping her tea. "Leave the kid be, Mam, I would. You pet 'im too much, that's what's wrong."

"Shut your mouth," her mother snapped back, her face suddenly raw with jealousy and defiance. "What do you know about 'im, eh?"

She bowed her head over Morlais and kissed his close-cropped high head.

"What is it, Morlais cariad, what is it?" she said, almost singing the words. "Try and tell us what is it."

Morlais stilled himself, steeled his body to be calm, and after a deep pause tried to tell her of his terror.

"Bob Linton is –" the tears welled up again in a great flood engulfing his pitiable effort at articulation and his wet face sought oblivion again for its tormented weeping. He stamped his feet on the floor and tore at her apron.

"Oh, Morlais, don't, don't," she said, herself shaking with the anguish that consumed him. She looked wildly round and seeing Doris she spoke to her as if she were a sudden deliverer.

"Tell 'im not to," she said, gasping. She didn't seem to recognise Doris. "Tell 'im," she said.

"It isn't anything," Doris said, "only some scrape 'e's got into in school. That boy Bobby Linton 'ave quarrelled with 'im and is going to give 'im a lamping, by the look of it. It isn't nothing to weep about."

"Is it?" Mrs Jenkins said, like a child. "Is it?"

She seemed unable to isolate Morlais' immediate trouble from the amorphous subsoil of potential trouble into which all human roots reach, the black earth of the past and present and future whose sap wells up silently in dreams and intuitive fears, budding into writhing flowers in the hidden gardens.

"Is it?" she said again. "Is it?" the words a passive incantation and then, fiercely, she wrapped her fingers in his hair and pulled his raw face out of the darkness and looked down on it, "Is it Bobby Linton is after you, Morlais?" she said, passionately brooding over him.

His lips opened to say 'yes' but renewed weeping thrust them gibbering apart.

"You wouldn't think there was all these tears in 'im," she said softly.

"Let 'im wash 'is face and get to school," Doris said, "They won't touch 'im now. And if you're not a-willing to let 'im fight 'is own battles you'd best go up and see the Master and tell 'im what it's all about."

Tired of the scene she poured herself another cup of tea.

"Yes," Mrs Jenkins said. "Yes, I'll go up. Come on, Morlais, go out the back, there's a good boy, go and wash your face a bit and 'ave a spell. I'll tidy myself up and come to school with you, see?"

Her arm round his shoulder she led him to the bosh in the back yard, took the carbolic soap out of the rack and pulled a dry tea cloth off the line.

"There now," she said, and went indoors, rubbing her eyes with a trembling and suddenly weary hand.

"Hetty gone yet?" she asked.

"No," Doris answered. "We'll be getting a bad name in the school and that's a fact. She's in the parlour hiding."

"Hiding?" her mother repeated, too exhausted to comprehend. She flopped shamelessly into a chair.

"Send 'er off, Doris, there's a good girl," she said.

Doris pulled herself out of her chair with a lazy sigh and shambled into the passage. After a minute she called out "She've gone, Mam. Must 'ave gone out the front way. I'm going upstairs to change."

"Alright," Mrs Jenkins said, to herself apparently, for her voice was too quiet for any other to hear.

After the cold water and the rough contact of the gritty soap block Morlais's face burned palely, the air like ice against his cheeks and smarting eyes. He hung the wet tea cloth on the wall and poured the water away and somehow, as he bent his head back and tried to touch the wall by curving his back and reaching beyond his head with outstretched arms, he felt different. He straightened himself, saw that no one was there to hurry him to school, and slipped quickly on his knees by the rabbit hutch. The rabbits were in the dark inner compartment, but their smell was there. His nostrils communicated their strangeness to him. Mrs Rabbit going to have babies, blind squirming little babies. Funny, about babies, baby rabbits, blind, Mrs Rabbit, fat old Mrs Rabbit having them. Somehow.

The house was listless, droning with flies, and his mother, when he peeped through the kitchen door to tell her he was going, was fast asleep. Her head hanging loosely, nodding

foolishly as she snored, her face exhausted and expression-
less, around her the heap of washed underwear and the
unwashed dishes on the table, a wasp fretting round the dirty
meat plates. He wanted to wake her, to tell her he was going,
in the hope that she would come with him perhaps, his talis-
man, protecting him. And yet, if she came, how sneakish he
would feel, mammy's pet, everybody calling him a baby, a
cleckerbox, and Bob Linton waiting till his chance came. He
stood indecisively in front of her, wanting her to wake but not
able to put his hand out and touch her. Not touch her.

And the front door knocker made the house jump out of its
silence.

She started up with a seared bewildered look.

"Who is it?" she said, "Quick, go and see."

She took the long comb from the sill and pulled, her grey
hair back hurriedly while Morlais went to the door. Her hands
trembled with haste and sleep and uncertainty. Her husband
it might be, hurted underground.

It wasn't.

"Are you Morlais Jenkins?" the tall and beautiful lady said,
standing deferentially a yard back from the door-step.

Morlais lowered his head in utter confusion.

"Could I have a few words with your mother, Morlais?"
she said.

Her voice moved him like music, charming his confusion
into obedience.

"I'll fetch her," he said, looking once at her, her fawn coat
and exalted eyes melting his single look. He stumbled along
the passage, bumping into Doris who had come downstairs,
to see who was there. She went stooping into the kitchen and
snatched a towel from the fireguard to cover her soiled vest
and knickers, her silly red knickers.

"Get out the back," her mother hissed, pulling her apron
off with nervous fingers. "Show her into the parlour, Morlais
quick."

Doris ran out the back and Morlais returned to the front door.

"She's coming now if you'll come in," he said.

She waited in the darkened parlour, enclosed by the formality of rarely used furniture and half-drawn blinds, feeling herself cut off from the spirit of life in the house, held at a distance by the ornamental fire irons, the green table cloth, the antimacassars on the polished stiff arm chairs and the cold portraits of dead people.

"Mrs Reames?"

She turned with a slight bow an a serious sensitive smile to the woman whose stockinged feet had taken her by surprise.

"Yes," she said, "how did you know me?"

Mrs Jenkins, fidgeting at the door, smiled weakly and with a lift of her hand conveyed the statement she could not put into words. A miner's wife, all the miners' wives, naturally they'd know the manager's wife. They'd talked about her... but not *to* her... they couldn't talk *to* her; when she was there they were frigid, naturally, not with unkindness. It was no good.

"I've come to see you about the trouble Morlais and David – my son, you know. Morlais has been so kind to him –"

"Yes," Mrs Jenkins said thinly, "Morlais do talk about him."

"Does he?" she said, so gently, and with a sudden joy. But Mrs Jenkins retreated from her unintentional intimacy.

"Yes," she said deferentially.

"There's some trouble in school, I believe," Mrs Reames said. "Some of the boys have been bullying David, I suspect, and Morlais taking David's side has let himself in for trouble, too."

Morlais in trouble. Yes, she knew that. That was somehow natural now. She knew about it, she'd let him weep his trouble into her. And she would heal it for him. But now it was all tangled up with this tall other woman, and her world of cut

glass and perfection which she could not enter, or understand, and which dismayed her.

"I didn't know your David was in it, too," she said
tonelessly.

"Yes, he is," she insisted, "it's all his fault that Morlais is
involved." Mrs Jenkins clung to her own world, afraid to share
with this other woman something she could only understand
as long as it remained her own. But the voice was so gentle,
asking her to help.

"I thought perhaps if we two mothers went up to school
and had a few words with the headmaster, we'd be able to
settle it," Mrs Reames said.

"Yes," Mrs Jenkins said, feeling herself, her son, their
common trouble, taken up into this starry beautiful woman's
trouble and watered down in it; like a root pulled out of the
earth and dipped in pellucid river water, the earth encrusting
it all washed away.

"D'you think we might go up to school together?" Mrs
Reames asked.

Well, her son's trouble was enfolded in her own now, like
before he was born. To protect him she must walk with this
other woman up Glannant Street, everybody seeing the two
of them incongruously together; worse than walking naked
up Glannant Street; to protect her son.

"It seems the best," she said, staring woodenly at Mrs
Reames's grateful smile.

She put her Sunday best on quickly; it made her feel worse,
wearing her black stockings and best shoes and shiny black
hat and the six year old coat with black fur round the collar.
On a hot day, and a week day. Mrs Reames dressed so
perfectly, and coolly, waiting for her in the parlour.

"Come on, Morlais," she said, gripping his small hand
tightly.

Mrs Reames took Morlais' other hand when they left the
house, and miraculously he felt at ease, her hand softly

enfolding his, and her gentle voice about him, asking about the scholarship, and books he was reading. He flowed along, a river in sunlight.

Doris in her soiled undies watched them go down the street, smiling as she scratched the red spot between her breasts.

"Mam looks a fool," she said aloud, and wandered downstairs to sit by the fire and look for blackheads with the hand mirror, in comfort.

"Well, I don't think Master Linton will trouble either of them again, do you? Mrs Reames said, standing at the school gates and extending her gloved slim hand to the quiet perspiring woman in Sunday primness.

"No," said Mrs Jenkins, not seeing the gloved hand, not seeing anything. A blur of people it had been; faces of people at doorways all up the street, sardonic amused blurs of faces, cold neighbours; faces fading courteously before the gentle voice end the scent of this woman; the Master's purple face, steaming with indignation before the pale unformed frightened faces of small boys, whose trembling voices apologised meaninglessly, whose heads hung; faces of people troubled and smiling, smoothly effaced by the gentle voice of this woman who commanded such respect, this woman who effaced her, whom herself she deeply hated.

"And Morlais can come straight up to tea with David?"

The smiling interrogation so gently confident of her reply.

"Yes," she said.

"There's no need for him to change," she said, "I like him just as he is, in his jersey and inkstains. I'll send him home before dark. Well, thank you very much for your help, Mrs Jenkins, and for all that Morlais has done for David. I hope we see more of each other soon."

She went like a wind among flowers, so gracefully.

And Mrs Jenkins, feeling herself free, turned savagely

home, to Glannant Street, and the back lanes, and the loaf of bread she needed for her husband's broth, and the unwashed dishes; turned to her deep and narrow self with savage relief. Back to her washing, to forget the loveliness of this other woman as she had already forgotten Morlais, whom this other woman had taken away.

"This is our house," David said, turning the handle of the green and white garden gate. "Mummy's usually waiting at the gate. I expect she's reading on the lawn today."

He held the gate open, waiting for Morlais to enter. Morlais hesitated. Standing in Glannant Street, his feet on miner's land, standing in all the places he knew and the houses in whose kitchens he had played, in whose sheds he had made boats and bows on wet afternoons, where he was at home. David's face tried to ask him to step in. The neat gravelled walk invited him to merge himself among the untrodden lawns. He hesitated. Then David lapsed into the language of the street.

"Come on, mun," he said, swinging on the gate.

Morlais crossed the threshold.

Well, it was like fairyland, now the green and white gate excluded the street; Fairyland discovering itself softly as they walked up the winding path. And oh! The big house, with a trellised porch covered with roses, and the white bench in front of the great French window which opened right onto the green grass. And the red earthenware dogs on each side of the porch. And a real dog, too, a puppy, black and white with rough curly fleece bounding out of the French window and barking effusively to see David coming home.

"Oi, Jockie," David shouted, dropping his bag and pushing the dog away. "Take your dirty paws off my clean things, will you?"

Morlais looked at David, then at the dog. It was so lovely, so new and strange, all of it swimming round him like sea water, green and exciting like the great bottles of sweets on the counter of Granny Thomson's shop.

"Can I smooth him?" he asked David, timidly.

"We'll have tea on the lawn today," she said. "It's a shame to eat indoors on such a fine afternoon, isn't it, Morlais?"

She was wearing a dress of purple silk with tiny flowers stitched on it. It burned coolly against his cheek as she pulled his head against her slim hips and tousled his hair with her fine hand.

"Slip in and tell Margaret to bring tea out here, David dear," she said.

It was so much a part of her, the closely cropped lawn and the roses and the peacock bushes and the sunlight. And the thrush flitting across them and renewing his song from the cloudy ramparts of the hydrangeas.

"Do you like it here, Morlais?" she asked.

"Yes," he answered, looking up with a burning in eyes and throat.

"You must come here more often, then," she said. "David is a bit lonely here, all by himself. He finds the place *big*."

No one had talked to him like this before; like an equal. He flushed with an exquisite discomfort, abasing himself at the too great honour of a shared confidence. She was talking to him, only him, and he wanted to die almost at her gentle intimacy.

"David tells me you're sitting the entrance exam to the County School tomorrow, Morlais?" she went on, sitting on the grass beside him. Now he had to look into her eyes every time he answered her. They were sort of violet.

"Yes," he said.

"And he said you're the best scholar in the class," she went on.

He flushed with delight and shame.

"Do you want to go to the County School?" she asked.

Till then he hadn't thought about it; he'd never envisaged

the County School, or going there, or anything. But her words and her presence and the kind excitement in her voice suddenly made it clear to him.

"Yes," he said, starting up with the physical shock of seeing in his imagination another place, harder to achieve, stranger, fuller of unknown forward-reaching achievements than anything yet... sort of violet, and glowing, and encouraging him to try, try, try, the new place was, which he saw when he looked up into her eyes.

"I'm sure you'll do well tomorrow," she said, patting his head. "And always – in the County School, and College, and life."

But it was too heady, this wine of new things, this sudden revelation of a vast trembling world where before there had been nothing except today and this person and this thing. The vision went; and he was on the lawn, by Mrs Reames, David's mother, who was speaking to him in her gentle voice.

"I'm sure your mother will be proud of you," she was saying.

And he frowned inside himself at that, feeling something dark and resentful seize him, the cold recollection of home, outside the green and white gate.

"Can Morlais see the thrush's nest, Mummy?" David asked.

"After tea, darling, if you like."

"No, now, Mummy, please," David said, putting his arms petulantly round her neck and squeezing his tummy into her breast and face, Morlais went hot at the closeness of the contact, the boy pressing against her, demanding a kindness of her.

"Alright," she laughed, unlocking his hands behind her neck and rolling him over on the lawn like a puppy. And both of them laughing, and happy. Their happiness caught Morlais up into its swirl of light and taking hands they ran three together across the lawn.

"Here it is," David said, under a speckled laurel bush.

"Quietly, David," she said, stooping over the bush and breathlessly parting the leaves. "She's on the nest now," she whispered. "Look, Morlais."

She held the leaves apart while Morlais stood on tip toe close against her and – and *saw* the bird, bright eye facing them unwinking and full breast and sharp beak and long flattened tail, in the nest fashioned carefully in the secret heart of the bush.

"Ooh," he said, marvelling.

She released the leaves softly, restoring the bird to itself.

"Don't disturb it," she said, smiling.

Morlais would have flushed the bird, shaken the branch and made it go. But she said no, don't disturb it, and it was still there, a bird, brooding in the bush, unseen now, protected by her words and by the enfolding leaves. He gazed back at the silent bush, and shyly at her, too, two inviolable things.

"And now how about some tea?" she said.

"Let's have a race back, shall we, Mummy?" David asked, tugging at her frock.

She started running at once. Morlais and David streamed after her, caught her, almost, and they sprawled in a laughing heap by the tea wagon, at the demure feet of the uniformed maid. And the maid was Maggie Thomas, Doris's pal, and she looked at Morlais as if she didn't know him. His laughter stopped with a shudder inside him.

"That'll be all, Margaret, thank you," Mrs Reames said.

Maggie went with a little bow and Morlais took the serviette Mrs Reames held out to him with fingers that felt big and unsteady.

But she and David were unchecked; the stream of happiness flowed on.

"And lemon cake," David shouted, taking off the shiny plate covers from dish after dish. "And chocolate éclairs, and mince pies. Oom! It's like a birthday, Mummy."

Morlais felt perilously exalted and embarrassed at discovering the feast laid in his honour. He was too self-conscious to look up, too proud, in a strange frightened way.

"Yes," she said. "This is to celebrate all the correct answers Morlais is going to get for his sums in the scholarship tomorrow."

"Yes," said David, "can I have the biggest sum first?"

Morlais was thinking again of the exam, the County School, the high path along those strange upland pastures whose blue ranges had disclosed themselves to him in her voice and eyes. And the exam he had resented, for the nagging of teachers and the drudgery of homework which were its only associations, the exam his father was always reminding him about when he wanted to go out to play, had become wonderfully transmuted into something inexpressibly delicate and changeable, like an ice crystal or a tiny blind sparrow cupped in his excited hands.

They didn't have to eat bread and butter today. Just think of that. Only cakes if they wanted to.

Morlais started with bread and butter.

"I've got heaps of toys and things, a meccano and a train and rails and a tunnel," David prattled, "you can see them after tea. And a painting book that Mummy and I paint sometimes, haven't I, Mummy?"

"You can show him everything after tea, dear," she said. "Perhaps Morlais doesn't like trains, though."

"I do," said Morlais, "I like them sometimes,.'
She laughed.

"Just for a day or two at Christmas, is it, Morlais?" She asked, laughing gently at his qualified approval.

"Yes," he replied, surprised. For that *was* how he liked them, just for a bit, watching Dilwyn playing with his clockwork car or sometimes in the back lanes watching the children showing their birthday presents off. Only he hadn't realised that before, either.

"But books last longer, Morlais, eh?" she said softly.

"Yes," he said again, looking up at her and seeing her violet eyes watching him and seeing in them all the hours of lying in bed with a candle, when Dilwyn was still out playing, and a book.....

"David's a proper little dunce," she said mockingly. "He much prefers wasting his time with his toys. I'm going to grow his hair and tie it with red ribbon if he doesn't become more a man in his tastes."

She saw David's bottom lip quiver and his eyes cloud. She laughed quickly and bent over and kissed him.

"Silly," she teased, "thinking I mean every word I say."

He laughed instead of crying, changing in the last second, when his face was twitching with tears. It was a delicate difficult laugh, and two un-necessary tears came out of his eyes and like a sunshower glistened in his nervous little laugh.

A crunch of heavy boots on the gravel; a tall man in a black waterproof and old slouch coming past the rhododendrons.

"Oh, Daddy's coming," David said with petulant anger.

"David," she said sharply. "For shame."

"Well, I didn't want him to come yet," David said, looking at her desperately, as if she were being stolen from him.

Morlais sat rigid with discomfort, feeling the change in everybody and the brusque new presence of the manager. A cloud crossing the sun, and halting coldly over the day's warmth.

"Hallo, everybody," he said, tossing his coat and hat on the grass and rubbing his dirty hands together vigorously. He had a thick moustache and sharp eyes that looked at you. The manager. Morlais shrunk into his shell as he would before the Master in School or the minister in Sunday School, or a policeman. A big, square-shouldered man with a crisp broad voice, effacing the lawn and the sun and the intimacy that had woven its web round the three of them. Like his father coming home all black in his working clothes, and everybody having to move to let him strip and kneel in the tub before the fire while his mother soaped his great black back.

"Hallo dear," she said, turning to him, he bending over her with his red lips and brushing her white forehead with his heavy moustache.

"And who's the visitor?" he asked, turning the full force of his presence on Morlais; like a cold searchlight, a great, eye.

"This is a little friend of David's," she said.

He laughed a trifle harshly.

"Glad to see you're making friends at last, Dave," he said.

David went red, face and neck burning with the smart.

"Yes," she said with forced haste. "This is Morlais Jenkins, dear. I wonder whether you know his father. He works in the pit, doesn't he, Morlais?"

Morlais nodded inarticulately.

"Jenkins?" Mr Reames mused, scratching his head slowly. "What's his Christian name?"

For a moment Morlais couldn't remember. Dad, Dad, what did Mam call him sometimes? How idiotic, not knowing. Then it came with a flash and he blurted it out with a squeak.

"William," he said. And before relapsing into silence he added, "He's a master haulier."

"Oh, *that* Jenkins," Mr Reames said. "Oh, I know *him* alright."

He spoke with the same cold sneering undertone that stung David. Morlais floundered painfully in the implications of the steely voice, troubled at the cold inrush of men's affairs, another transcendent over-reaching world of great metal objects and fists, foreign to him in its cold unyielding power; yet terribly interwoven in his own being; men in the back lanes talking with great curses and spitting coal dust, his father heavy-booted and slow and hard-handed when he had done something wrong, the buses, and the shunting engines, but more than all these the pit, the pit, the inscrutable skeleton of power whose whirring wheels attracted him as completely as a nightmare.

"Can we go, Mummy?" David said, slipping from his chair and leaning passionately close to his mother.

"Don't slobber over your mother, boy," Mr Reames said sharply.

"Yes, alright," she said, putting David gently to one side. "Take Morlais up to your room and show him your things." Her voice was chill, as though her thoughts were no longer in her words. "Shall I get some more bread and butter for you, Denis?" she said, turning in to her husband.

As David led Morlais away Mr Reames said curtly, "No thanks. You don't seem to have eaten anything but cakes. You're spoiling that kid, making a namby pamby of him.

"Come on," David said passionately, tugging Morlais fiercely away, "let's go somewhere where he isn't."

They went through the French window into a great sunlit room of silver and glass and polished walnut and cool green chair covers.

Instinctively Morlais trod softly, like a beggar boy trespassing in a palace. The hall clean and solemn with ticking grandfather clock and brown dusk filtering through the fanlight. The thick green pile of the stair carpet taking the sound out of his steps, the winking brass stair rods; David running upstairs on all fours like an eager dog.

A corridor of muted green light with white bedroom doors and light green wall-paper. Then David's room. He had a room of his very own; his rocking horse by the window, a Hornby engine and a network of siding and station rails all laid out in the corner; oh, and heaps of things. He shut the door carefully behind Morlais, and then, with a proud little gesture, said "This is my *own*."

Morlais stood and looked, his mind glowing with the wealth of it. *All* these things, *all* these, just his, David's... What would he do if he had such riches? His fingers itched with the intoxication of it....

David rode the rocking horse, and then let Morlais have a ride. There was nobody in the room, only the two of them; Morlais became a jockey, digging the wooden flanks with excited heel. Then the engine, David manipulating the points officiously, Morlais sitting tensely beside him, too enthralled to speak. David let him work the green flag in the toy guard's lead hand.

Then David tired.

"Let's go into the garden," he said with a pettish sigh, no longer satisfied by the toys. "Let's look for Mummy."

They slid down the bannister.

When he saw his mother he flung his arms and heels up with a whoop and scuttled across the lawn to her; she held her arms out and swept him up.

He hugged her and kissed her, and she put him gently down, a little embarrassed.

"Go on, puppy dog," she admonished, gentle and severe, "take Morlais to the river."

"Yes, come on, Morlais," David shouted, his face rosy with delight. He ran through the bushes, stooping like a pheasant, Morlais running behind him. The river sounded close, David halted and put his finger to his lip.

"There may be some man-hunters in their canoes," he whispered, and with extreme caution parted the bushes and stepped softly onto the sloping bank of the brook.

"None," he said, and lapsed again into his sudden ennui, as though his energy had suddenly dried up.

"Let's go back now, shall we?" he said.

"Is there any trout in the river? Morlais asked.

David shrugged his shoulders.

"I 'xpect there is," Morlais said.

He knew the river well. It came down the gash in the hills and flowed through farm land into the Reames's garden. Thence it went through the colliery and for the remainder of its way seaward it was polluted and black. But above the garden, in the rocky hill pools and long shallow reaches in the farm meadows, Morlais and the other boys of the village knew where the trout were. Jersey sleeves rolled up, knees numb and wet with kneeling on the half-submerged boulders, fingers icy with groping under the stones, in the dark holes where the soft feel of slippery flesh betrayed the coveted trout...

"Let's 'ave a try, is it?" he said.

He rolled up his sleeves end began groping at the edge of the pool, his face almost touching the water, serious as a craftsman or an artist. David squatted on the pebbled verge, both excited and bored.

"You try the next pool," Morlais said.

But David was afraid of plunging his arm out of sight, in cold green water, under dark boulders.

"Got one," Morlais hissed, his arm suddenly stiffening as he thrust it further into a cranny.

"What *are* you doing?" her gentle voice said, over his head. "Your shoulder's in the water, Morlais. You'll be *soaked*."

"It's alright," he said, thrilling to see her standing tall and beautiful on the bank. "It's a trout." And he fought to get his fingers in its gills and his palm underneath its belly with savage determination to excel before her. She and David watched in suspense.

"Got it?" David shouted, dancing with excitement as Morlais slowly drew his arm out of the water.

He didn't reply. Carefully now. Carefully, drawing his hand out, the trout crushed between his cupped palm and the smooth underside of the stone. Tail first he pulled it carefully out of the hole, and then, ecstatically, his hand closed over it completely and up it came from the troubled pool, a beauty, stippled with red and blue spots, its tail impotently twitching in his relentless grip.

"Ooh," they gasped, bending over his hand in wonder.

And, "what are you going to do to it now?" she asked, like a little girl.

For reply he jabbed its mouth open with his finger and bent its head back. Its eyes bulged. Crack. It spine snapped, and it twitched convulsively in his white wet palm.

She said "Oh, poor little thing."

But David was silent with the fierce frightened delight that children find in torture – in flies placed in the spider's web and sucked to death by the longlegged murderer, straddling his victim under their enthralled eyes, in tearing off a fly's wings, ssp, ssp, the soft parting of gauzy wing from the body's sticky slot...

And Morlais felt all the strong manhood of the arch priest performing the sacrifice before a great devout audience.

With the deftness of long practice he plucked a bulrush and threaded it through the pink saw-edged gills and offered the glazing trout to Mrs Reames.

"Thank you very much, Morlais." she said. "But you must take it home with you. They'll want to see it, and you'll enjoy it for your own breakfast tomorrow."

"No," he said with insistent entreaty, flushed with determination to give it to her only, "*you* take it, please."

"Alright," she smiled, accepting his gift, "I'll eat it all by myself tomorrow morning, and think of you getting all your sums right at the same time."

Oh yes, he thought, flushed and happy. The scholarship exam. He rubbed his hands, glowing like red fruit drops, in his trousers.

"Let's play across the river," David said sulkily, feeling outplayed.

"Alright, you two play about for a little," she said, "while I finish my chapter. But don't be more than half an hour. It's time for Morlais to go. Remember, he's got to have a good night's rest before this exam he's going to do so well in."

"We won't be long." David said curtly.

"Well, look after him, Morlais, won't you?" she smiled. "See he doesn't get his feet wet – he's not as strong as you. And don't go through the hedge into the colliery, whatever you do."

"Oh alright," David sulked. "Come on, Morlais."

Morlais watched her go through the bushes, carrying the trout on its bulrush string, a soft scented swirl of blue silk fading into the green laurels. Then he smiled. Another half hour of this enchantment, half an hour's delight in the paradise of this garden.

"Come on," he said, "let's cross over,"

And he gave David his hand, telling him where to put his feet, careful not to wet his feet, observing religiously her last commandment.

First they looked for nests in the bushes and hazel trees. But they drew a blank and again David fell into his fatigued discontent.

"Let's go through the hedge into the colliery," he said. "Come on."

"But your mother said we wasn't to," Morlais objected, stubborn and dismayed,

"Oh, it's alright," David said with quick glibness. "She's always fussing if I go anywhere. Come on. We'll just climb through and have a little look at the engines. Nobody'll know."

There was malice in his determination to trespass on her will.

"Come on," he said, stamping his foot like a frustrated child.

"Only for a minute then," Morlais conceded. He also wanted to go and watch the engines.

Once through the hedge they forgot her admonition. It just vanished from their minds, which were now engrossed in the new scene, the great other world of the pit, as fascinating as a spider coming out for the sacrificial fly.

There were several acres of siding round the pit head, long black spines of slag like buried whales, derelict buildings cemented with the blown dust whipped from the trams at the pithead and the loaded wagons under the conveyor, winding rails wriggling like shining eels down the valleys of slag and tipped small coal; black all, and uncharted and fascinating, because trespassers were forbidden.

"Let's go over to watch that journey, is it?" Morlais said, pointing to a journey of trams which was scaling the steep incline of dirty rubble. "We can keep behind the trucks, and hide under the tumps; they won't see us."

"If they do it doesn't matter," David said proudly, "they all know my Daddy."

Morlais had forgotten that he wasn't with a gang of boys. Trespassing on the tips was one of their favourite pastimes; anyone caught got a kick from an iron toe-cap and perhaps a row next day from the Master, whose bamboo cane came whip across their trembling palms. But in David's company his habitual slyness was outmoded.

"Alright," he said, putting his hands in his pockets and strolling forward. The place had become desolate and ordinary.

They walked forward together to the bottom of the incline and watched the journey climbing up to the tip at the top, the collier riding on the first tram growing black and sharp in the setting sun as he topped the crest.

A stone whizzed past his head and thudded into the bank of shale beyond him. Another, and another – whizz… phut, whizz… phut. David screamed with sudden pain; Morlais turned and saw him wrap his hands round the calf of his right leg, doubled up with pain; blood trickled between his fingers. And behind him, between them and the house, standing on the top of a small tip black in the sun – Bob Linton and Dicky Owen and Teddy Barnes, hands raised to throw.

"Run," Morlais shouted, grabbing David's hand.

They ran blindly in the quick terror of this surprise attack. David kept Morlais back, dragging on his hand. Their assailants didn't shout, fearing to attract attention from the journeyman. So there was just a black nightmare silence through which the two boys ran, their lungs tearing, their eyes blurring with effort. A stone caught Morlais in the pit of his back. Jab, like a bayonet, a fierce stab of pain. He gasped and stumbled, letting David's hand go. Another stone went phut in the slag by his head. He pulled himself convulsively to his feet and ran on, leaping over the points of the rails and over the boulders of slag, running frantically past David, who was whimpering with breathlessness and terror.

It all happened in a flash; as if his head was a black bladder that suddenly burst – with a man's startled "Look out," and a high-pitched scream from David that broke off sharply as a hideous crash of steel overwhelmed it. Then silence, dark and terrified and trembling, paralysing his limbs.

He turned round slowly, slowly, sick right through himself.

The last three trams of the journey were piled on top of each other, askew across the track. The journeyman was running down the incline with gigantic tearing strides. Morlais saw a leg sticking out from under the wrecked trams, a leg with grey stocking and a small well-polished shoe.

"David," he said.

Then he screamed, "David. David," and putting his hand to his eyes ran mad, away from the wreckage, from the leg across which the disturbed bank poured a thin stream of slag, like sands running down in an hour glass.

He ran till he tripped up over a discarded pit prop. A man running from the pithead towards the shouting journeyman picked him up and shook him.

"What's up?" the man shouted, his apprehension suiting Morlais's hysteria. It was all intense, everything intensified and chaotic, nerves like highly charged wires pulled across each other, pulled to the limit of endurance and ringing terrible alarms in the anarchic wilderness of his mind. His body shivered dreadfully. The man let him go and ran.

A bit later another man took hold of him, and dimly he heard a blurred voice booming at him and was conscious somewhere outside himself of a face looming against him gibbering and huge as though seen in the concave reflexion of a teaspoon. A hand on his shoulder shook him, shook him, everything whirled around him and something erupted in his guts. When the hand closed over his mouth he knew he was screaming. Then the hand slapped him across the face, hard, with flat palm. And he was himself, still, clear, himself, standing against the man's knees, knowing that he was just going to puke.

The man held his head while he was sick, and encouraged him to get it up... tea, éclairs, mince pies, a lumpy pink stew. Then the man said "Are you O.K. now?" and he nodded yes. So the man said "Wait here then till I come back." But at that the black crags swirling with cruel blood surged round him, inside him, again, and as he felt himself being sucked under he grabbed the man's hand and screamed. So the man kept hold on his hand and the crags sank into watchful darkness, foiled for the moment. And to keep them buried in the blood he held on passionately to the man's strong black hand.

Then there were other men about him, their great boots and working trousers tied under the knees, talking over his head, snatches of their talk reaching him, terrifying him, "This kid was with 'im... Aye, Reames' boy, it was... William Jenkins's kid, this one is... Aye, there's Reames running over from the offices now.... Poor sod..." Then the man's hand led him across the network of rails and they, went up the stony lane to the pithead and past the smithy where the boys went to cadge dick-stones, into the ambulance room.

It was on a stretcher, on the table, under a grey blanket, the men standing around with bared heads, not talking.

Then a policeman, taking his name, from the man... No,

from his father, who was bending over him, asking him questions he couldn't make out. When he heard her voice outside he knew that that was what he'd been waiting for with such terror. Her voice streamed through and through him and he pressed his head, into the man's trousers, hiding himself. "I must see him," she said – he heard her distinctly; in the silence there was only her voice – "I'm alright, Denis. Let me go in, I *must* see him."

And then she was standing in the bare room crowded with men who turned away in silence as she stooped over the table and lifted the grey rug. Morlais heard her catch her breath, and then something seized his limbs and twisted up his heart. He let the man's hand go and as the black rocks swirled up at him he leaped over them, over the four feet of floor between himself and her and plunged his head into the soft folds of her coat, clinging to her with twitching fists, and for the first time sobbing.

Mr Reames took him roughly by the neck of his jersey, pulled him with violent rage. But her hand stopped him, and she turned to Morlais and took his head in her hands and rocked him against her, preternaturally calm.

There was a crowd of people at the pit gates, and a thin line all along the pavement of Glannant Street, falling silent as the ambulance came bumping down the stony road and up the street to the green and white gate, then talking again in pitiful undertones as soon as it had passed.

Mr Reames and the policemen and more men were asking Morlais how it had happened, what they were doing running across the tramroad... And she had been taken away from him and there were only these men all round him with their questions which he couldn't grasp, insistently demanding information which he couldn't shape into words. They gave him a glass of water which spilled down his chin and still he couldn't tell them. His father wrapped a rug round him and took him home, through a blur of silent people and a soft murmur of muted voices; and he was vaguely aware of his name being spoken sometimes as they went down the road and through the back lane and into the kitchen where his mother took him, putting him in the wicker chair by the fire.

She was asking him all the time if he felt better, and putting cushions behind his head and once she put a glass of hot milk and treacle to his mouth, which he pushed away. When he was lying in bed in the dusk his father came up and wrapped the eiderdown about him and carried him downstairs to see the policemen who were sitting in the kitchen. But he couldn't speak to them because it was all a turbulence of falling boulders in his aching skull. and he fell asleep.

He woke up in the middle of the night, pitch darkness on his eyes pressing like thumbs against his pupils, and he wanted to excrete.

He called out, "Dad. Dad."

Dilwyn stirred beside him, then lay still.

He called louder, "Dad, Dad."

Movement in the next room, the bed creaking, a match striking, an uncertain flicker of yellow light under the door. He sat up and climbed over Dilwyn and slid his feet down to the bare floorboards.

"What d'you want?" his father whispered, opening the door and peering sleepily through the candle flame.

"I want to go out the back," Morlais said.

"Alright, let's put my trousers on," his father replied, his bare hairy legs like white props to the Welsh flannel shirt in which he always slept.

They went together down the stairs and through the silent kitchen, the candle lighting up the dead fire and his father's working clothes laid out on the fender in readiness for the morrow, and then the wind whipped the candle out as they went through the back door into the yard. His father swore, in the darkness, and struck a second match. Morlais shivered, and everything became clear and orderly to him.

They went down the path, the wet grass swishing the dew against his bare legs. He wanted to get there badly.

"There you are then," his father said, pushing the W.C. door open. "Hurry up now. It's cold waiting out here." Then laughingly he said, "One thing about going at night, there isn't somebody from next door sitting on it." In their street there was only one lavatory between every two houses.

Morlais felt utterly at ease physically when it was out, and when his father asked him suddenly, as if by afterthought, "What was you two running across them tips for?" he made his mind up quite logically. He thought to himself, "Bob Linton and the others will have a row, worse than a row, if I say the real reason. And it's no good saying it, because there'll only be a lot more questions, and the cops coming to school, and it's no good because David's dead now and it can't make any difference." And he said quietly as he wiped himself with newspaper, "We was having a race, and I didn't see nothing in the way only the journey and that was going away."

His father said with a sharp voice. "You was trespassing."

Morlais said nothing, but waited in the dark little shed, although he ready to come out.

"And there's always a danger of the last drams breaking loose," his father said.

The candle flickered about the gaunt man, digging black caves under his eyebrows, from which his eyes glowed like wolves starving, and menacing pits of darkness under his raised arm. The night pressed down on his candle, which leaped up with a sudden desperate illumination and went out. The immediate darkness had the image of his father's lined face engraved in red flame upon it. And terribly out of the utter night his father's voice came in cold irrefutable judgment.

"You was responsible for that kid. You should never 'a taken 'im over the tips."

Then a match struck comfort out of the night. The candle

kept it at bay. But it had found its way into Morlais's head, wrapping itself, about the words it had engendered. And as they went back up the path the black rocks swirled up out of the sea of congealing blood and said "You did it. You were the one who –" but he fought against them, forcing them down before they could say the final words that would raze his brain.

"Well, get to sleep now, and don't worry about it," his father said, holding the candle up for him to climb into bed. "Remember, you got the scholarship to sit tomorrow."

The door closed, and the darkness inside him swirled into the darkness without, and he fell asleep at once.

The morning came grey and shaky, his bare legs quivering as he slid them onto the floor. His mother stood by him while he washed himself, bending his head over the cracked china bowl on the makeshift orange-box wash stand.

"Wash yourself proper now," she admonished. "You got to be at your best today, mind." She wiped the soap away from the back of his ears and then put her hand across his hot forehead.

"You make sure you got a clear head for them sums, now," she said severely.

She had cooked a bit of bacon for him this morning as a special treat; it was sizzling on the stove between two hunks of fried bread when he entered the kitchen. His father had long ago gone to work; the kitchen was quiet, waiting to fall back to sleep.

"Eat this bacon now," she said, taking it from the frying pan with a fork and putting it on his plate. "It'll do you good."

He breathed through his mouth to hide the sickening smell of fat and tried grimly to eat the plateful of repulsive food. He didn't want her to notice him; he shrank from being addressed at all; the day ahead of him boiled with accusing and insinuating inquiries, a scum of questions forming on the surface of the dark potion of the day.

Seizing his chance he threw the bacon onto the fire while she was washing the frying pan in the back yard.

"Now what about some Liver salts?" she asked.

He took the refreshing drink thankfully, but he smiled no thanks to her. She looked worriedly at his drawn white face, and her silence stung him like nettles. If she'd said something about it it would be better. Not this awful silence, and every sound in the lane made him start and look towards the door; when the milkman clicked the latch something inside him bolted in terror like a rat into a sewer.

He stood up unsteadily and wiped the crumbs off his mouth.

"Well, off you go, bach," she said, combing his hair back with her big tortoiseshell comb full of grey hairs. "And do your very best now, won't you?"

"Yes," he whispered, and went out through the back door. The bright day hung over him like a trembling knife.

He was too feverish with fear to foresee anything exactly. He was in the back lane, and turned out of it to cross the square where the buses stopped, and there was a bus waiting there, full of shop assistants going to their morning's work. But he saw none of these things objectively any more than he saw in his mind the quiet school room where he would sit the scholarship papers or the Master calling him to his room after the arithmetic paper and asking him to tell the gentlemen there what exactly had happened last night. Nor did he remember anything exactly of yesterday's happenings. But it was all inside him.

A dissolved fluid terror. He went on and on up the endless street, neither thinking nor seeing, but frightened, frightened, and as alert as a burglar.

He went through the school gates and slowly crossed the playground. Then somebody tapped one of the windows facing the playground. He didn't look round. He didn't even think. He ran. Ran to the corner where one of the railings was bent, slipped through and jumped knee-deep into the stream. He waded across, climbed the bank, crossed the gravel path and raced up the meadow. Somebody was calling his name; his lungs were throbbing, his eyes smarting and useless. It was like running in nightmare, or under the sea. He ripped his trousers as he scrambled through the barbed wire fence that separated the grazing land from the mountain and as he jerked himself   up and ran on he saw a red stain lengthen along his thigh. But he was on the mountain, with ferns and gorse and hidden cwtches in the rocks to hide in. He was safe....

A man's voice woke him in the middle of a dream in which Winnie Morse was thrusting her naked deformed body into his face and making foul accusations about his parents and foul demands on himself. She was kneeling to him grinning, and he started up and the man was blocking the entrance to the stone hut with his huge black body.

"There you are, you little devil," the man said with relief, his Davy lamp illuminating the dark dripping rock and the little body huddled in the corner.

Morlais let the man come over and lift him up, feeling with passive relief the strong arms flex under his shoulders and knees. Dully, he felt glad. A human presence was like warm water on a body starved and frozen into apathy.

The man carried him out, then set him down in the ferns on the quarry floor while he blew three times piercingly on a whistle.

"That'll let them know to stop searching," he said, grinning with his anticipated triumph. "I've found you," he said.

They took a long time to descend the mountain, following winding sheep tracks along the crest; Morlais watched fitfully the stars. Sheep were bleating in the darkness.

"You're heavy," the man said, wiping sweat from his eyes. "Damned heavy for nipper."

Again there were people grouped in the dusk, an excited tremor of talk making them move towards him as the man carried him down the last yard of the mountain path into the village. The dim groups eddied and broke and his mother was taking him from the man and crying over him.

Then he was in the kitchen, the door shut behind him, sitting like a bird that has been brought in out of the ice, feeling the warmth of the fire on his body and waiting, waiting, knowing something would be happening.

Then his father came in behind him, wiping his boots on the mat by the door. He came into Morlais's field of vision, stood between him and the fire, without speaking unbuckled his heavy leather belt. Morlais saw his face, like worn white stone. And then he knew what going to happen. His mother's cry and passionate entreaty were swept aside by his father and by himself, passively waiting in a paralysis of terror.

His father beat him with the belt, the steel buckle cutting into the flesh of his naked bottom. His legs squirmed under his father's arm and he cried too terribly to make any sound. Only his mother made any sound.

Then his father carried him to bed.

An hour later somebody touched him softly on the cheek and he woke full of the blessed knowledge that she was touching him on the cheek with her gentle hand.

"Morlais," she said, stroking his hair softly, bending over him with warmth and sweet scent.

He smiled, and she smiled back.

His father came to the edge of the bed, holding a candle over her raven's hair. He spoke slowly, a cold edge to his voice.

"This lady wants to know if you'd like to go live with her from now on," he said. "Do you want to?"

The rosiness of sleep drained from his face. It whiteness made his eyes glow.

"Will you come and live with me Morlais?" she said breathlessly, "Now that David's gone –"

"Alright," came his father's cold voice, "I've asked 'im once."

Morlais nodded his head, smiling.

Then he managed to speak, a thin whisper, "Yes."

She stood up, rigid like a woman in desire.

"You can go straight away then," his father said, setting the candle on the wash stand. And turning to Mrs Reames he said "You can wait downstairs."

"Don't make him get out of bed," she said quickly. "Let him wait till the morning, please."

"You take what's yours now," his father said, leading the way down to the kitchen.

His mother dressed him, kneeling before him with bent head and working his old boots over his stockinged feet. She knotted the laces twice each.

"Wait on the bed till I pack your clothes," she said.

He watched her back bowed in candlelight over the tin trunk. She looked at each garment before she put it into the bag. A pair of socks in which the darned heels had given way she laid aside.

"There you are, then," she said, standing up slowly as though her body ached all over with bending over the tin trunk. "Come on."

She took his hand and led him down to the kitchen.

Its light dazzled his blinking eyes. But soon they were out in the dark night, and she was holding his hand and talking to him gently.

The 'county bus' bringing the boys home from the secondary school stopped nonchalantly at the bottom of Glannant Street in the square of rough waste between the railings that fenced off the railway and the low wall along the river bank. A woman shaking a mop through a bedroom window watched the boys jump down from the bus. A benchful of old men smoking clay pipes watched them too. Three ragged children waiting at the station entrance for the train bringing the bale of evening newspapers also waited and watched. But nobody really noticed the bus or the boys. The arrival of the bus at five p.m. sharp every evening was unremarkable. The driver's yawn acknowledged the boring quality which invests regularity with the veil of invisibility. And the boys split up without bothering to say goodnight. Morlais himself walked sleepily, dragging his legs and letting his shoulders bow under the pressure of his satchel, and as he avoided the main street and turned into the back lane he too yawned.

He never went down Glannant Street unless he was with Mums. He didn't like going down the street by himself. Four years in the County School hadn't inured him to that. But in the deserted lane there was nothing to remind him of himself. He strolled homewards thinking of tea and homework and school, but not of himself.

Then something unforeseen happened. A boy – tall and lanky but obviously a boy from the gaunt immaturity of his body and slovenly gait – slid down the bank of rubble that separated the lane from the colliery. He was in working clothes – heavy boots, baggy oily trousers, leather belt inside which he had pushed his hands as though it were a pouch, tea-jack bulging his coat pocket, red muffler, cloth cap – and he was coming home from work. Morlais and he saw each other simultaneously. For an imperceptible second they stopped. Their bodies swayed ever so slightly, like young colts that shie. In the same second they continued walking towards each other. Morlais took a wad of cigarette cards out of his pocket; Bob Linton spat fluently, a long stream of juice; he was chewing tobacco the way the colliers do underground. Keeps the dust out of your mouth...

"Hallo, Morlais," Bob Linton said, stopping squarely in the lane and digging his black hands further into his belt. He looked like a young kangaroo proud of its virginal pouch.

Morlais looked up swiftly from his cigarette cards and flushed at the clumsiness of his pretended surprise.

"Hallo," he stammered, "I didn't think it was you. You're –"

"Aye," Bob spat again, then crossed his legs and leaned against the wall of the lane. "Working underground now. With my uncle. We cleared more drams than anybody else working on the hard face this week. We'll draw good wages this week, boy."

Morlais saw that he had blue eyes. Light blue, like laughing glass floating in the pale dirty uncertainty of his changing features.

"Yes," he said. And then, looking at the ground between Bob's feet, he said "Got any doublers?"

"Don't save cards now," Bob said. "Given that up. I could save a lot for you though, off the men. I'll ask them to save them for me, if you like. Is it?"

In his casualness there was an intense desire to please.

Morlais flushed.

"It's alright," he said. "I don't see you. And it's more fun saving them yourself, isn't it?"

"Alright," Bob said, kicking his steel-capped toe against the wall to make a white mark under the grimy surface of the stone. And then he said eagerly, "Lend us a card and let's 'ave a flip for the furthest, is it?"

"O.K.," Morlais responded swiftly, unhooking his satchel from his shoulder and dropping it to the ground. He gave Bob half his cards. Bob meanwhile marked a line with his toe across the lane.

"Throw from here, is it?"

"Right. You go first."

Holding the cards between the first two fingers of their right hands they flicked them into the air. The cards fell to the ground three four five yards away.

"I won you then."

"Mine that time."

"Goh, there's a beaut."

"Oi, keep your foot behind the line. That one don't count."
They were excited.

When they had thrown all the cards they picked them up
and started a second round.

"What's it like in the county school?" Bob asked casually.

"Alright," Morlais said. "There's a lot of big boys, and they
– it's alright, though. The masters are alright. There's one of
them collects bird's eggs, and we go on rambles –"

"They do say the masters do wear black gowns," Bob said.

"They do, too," Morlais said hotly.

"Do they?" Bob was incredulous. He whistled. "I'd like to
see them anyway."

"*You're* inching now," Morlais said. "Look, your foot's
right over the line."

"Alright, won't count that one, then," Bob conceded. "'S
the furthest I thrown, too."

He waited while Morlais flipped his card.

"How did you pass the scholarship when you didn't go to
school for the year before it?" he asked suddenly, as though
he had often puzzled the problem in his mind.

Morlais stopped, his hand poised to throw, and turned his
head round so that he looked Bob in the eyes.

"Mrs Reames taught me in the house," he said. His voice
had a sharp defiance in it and his shy brown eyes hardened.

Bob pushed his cap back, exposing a line of black sweat on
his dirty forehead.

"But she isn't a teacher?" he remonstrated.

"No, but she *knows*," Morlais said, raising his voice. "She
knows more than any of them."

Bob pulled his cap back and spat.

"They do all say different things about her," Bob said
slowly. Then he became aware of something strained,
something like a strand of hair pulled tight between the

fingers, and he didn't ask Morlais anything.

"I'm working in the same district as your father," Bob said.

Morlais, taken by surprise, looked nervously away.

"Are you?" he said, almost inaudible.

"He do bring the horse for our journey," Bob said. He flipped his card carefully. "That's a good one. Beat that." He watched Morlais throw. "I'm going to be a haulier when I grow up," he said.

Morlais threw his card listlessly. He seemed weak; his shoulders drooped.

"What are you going in for?" Bob said.

Morlais shrugged his shoulders.

"Don't know yet," he said. And then, with a flash, opening his whole eyes, he said "Ornithologist, I want to be."

"What the crikey's that?" said Bob, flabbergasted.

"Oh, in a museum, and watching where birds migrate from, and island sanctuaries," Morlais said.

"Coo," said Bob, visions floating in his head. Then he spat.

"My old woman will be after me for keeping the water boiling all the time," he said. "She'll be wanting to put the kettle on."

He handed Morlais his cards back.

"Your Doris was in our kitchen last night," he said. "She's going to get engaged to Ben James the grocer, she said. Said we'd see it in the paper."

Morlais was picking up his satchel and didn't say anything.

"I s'ppose you knew before," Bob said curiously.

"No, I didn't know that," Morlais said. "Well, solong."

"Solong," Bob said.

He stuck his hands into his belt and went off with a swagger. Morlais walked slowly home, dragging his shoes....

"You keep them feet off my floor, will you?" Maggie said with annoyance and alarm. "Look at them – covered with dust, they are. Take them out with you, you old thing you. Here, wipe them in this."

"Oh, alright," Morlais said, taking the duster from Maggie and dropping his satchel onto the rocking chair in which Maggie spent her winter evenings. Then, instead of going out, he picked a bun from the cake dish on the tea table and bit it slowly.

"Spoiling your tea again you are," Maggie said. She tidied his hair with careful indifference. "You're always starting at the wrong end you are. Wait till you begin smoking, my boy. You'll burn your lips, I'll bet." She laughed – her short loud laugh that only let itself go when the Reameses were out. "And when you get courting, my – I wouldn't like to answer for you then."

"Oh stuff," Morlais said, flushed and embarrassed. But he laughed nonetheless, reluctantly but completely, when she picked up her sheeny black skirt and kicked her leg up as though she were doing a Highland fling.

"You're daft," he said, looking at her starched cap fallen askew from her carefully combed and scented curls.

"And you are," she said merrily. "You ought to come to dancing class in the pally-de-dance Thursday nights," she said. "You'd be able to do that then. It's Old English."

"Dance," he said as scornfully as he could. And then, with ill-feigned inquisitiveness, "Are there boys there?"

Maggie laughed. "What d'you think?" she said.

She twisted a loose curl back into position, sneaking a glance at herself in the glass.

"Your Doris is there every Thursday," she said.

He turned away at once and unstrapped his satchel.

"She's engaged, isn't she?" he said, hiding his face from her.

"I don't know what she is," Maggie said. "None of my business, is it? She's a good sport anyway."

Morlais took out his books and pen case.

"Come on now, leave them things till you've 'ad a square

meal," Maggie said. "You're always at them old books. I don't know what you see in them. And *she's* always reading too, and books all over the place." She sighed. "If she 'ad to clean them – Well, one thing I can say, there's not a single book in our 'ouse, thank goodness."

" What's for tea?" Morlais said, easy again.

"Sardines on toast," she said, "take it or leave it."

She took a plate of buttered toast from the fender and putting it on the table proceeded to turn sardines out of a small tin, making them slide on the melted butter.

"Now sit down and eat that," she said. "And you can eat the tails as well, being as *she* isn't here."

Morlais started into the sardines while she poured him a cup of tea. Standing over him, she looked down on his tousled head with affection. "There's a stranger in your tea," she said.

She extracted the floating tea leaf with a spoon and putting it on the back of one hand, hit it hard with the back of the other.

"This year – no," she said, seeing that the tea leaf hadn't changed hands. "Next year – yes. There you are," she said triumphantly, "there'll be a stranger coming into your life next year."

"I don't want a stranger," he said.

"'Tisn't what you want, my boy. It's what's coming to you. That's what it is in this life. Oh damn," she said suddenly, "I wish I could be a parlour maid in Ronald Colman's house. I seen 'im last night in the Empire. Gor, d'you know, I couldn't *look* at the boy I was with after that. Wouldn't let 'im touch me – and he paid for me, too, poor dab." She brooded for a minute. "Like them sardines?" she asked moodily.

"Alright," he said greedily. "You have some, Maggie?"

"I've 'ad my tea, don't worry," she said, "I'll take one, though."

She picked a sardine from his plate, very delicately, holding it by the tail.

"I wonder what *she* thinks about Robert Colman," she said thoughtfully, nibbling the sardine. "She was in the front row upstairs. And 'im, too. Sitting like pokers. They seen me coming out, I know. Didn't acknowledge, though." She licked her fingers, "I bet she wouldn't mind a romance with Ronald Colman, I bet she wouldn't."

"She's married in any case," Morlais said scornfully.

"Married, indeed." Maggie sneered. "That don't signify."

She raised her arms high above her head, flinging them out in a vivid gesture of released life. Her eyes glowed.

"D'you ever see her look like this?" she asked, her lips parted and her nostrils opening with swift indrawn breath.

Morlais contracted, pressing his elbows and chin into his body, but he could not take his fascinated eyes off her face. She seemed to be everybody, somehow, enormous.

"No," she said. "You didn't." And then she was just Maggie again and she was saying "But what I'm saying it to a kid of fourteen for – and she's dotty on you, fair play for her –" and he was eating the last juicy lump of luke-warm toast and the fire was burning orange and the clock striking six.

"She ought to be back by now," Maggie said. "The shops will be shut now."

"What's she doing, then?" he asked, begging for some reassuring fact about her after the upheaval into which Maggie had cast her image.

"Shopping," she snapped. "And don't ask me what for, either, because she told me not to tell you."

"Alright," he said, getting up from the table and taking up a pile of his books.

"Aren't you going to finish your tea?" she asked.

"No," he said. "I don't want it."

"What's up?" she said. "What's the matter? You look shaky."

"Nothing," he said, crossly. "I'm alright. I'm going to work in my room."

"Don't you want to know what she's buying?" Maggie asked.

He hesitated.

"Well – what?" he said.

"Something for your birthday," she said. "You're fourteen day after tomorrow, aren't you?"

He thought for a moment.

"November the eighth," he said slowly. "Yes, that's it. Ooh, Maggie, what's she getting?"

She laughed.

"That's better," she said. "Don't want you looking like a dead flatfish, do we? Laugh a bit more now, 'cause I won't tell you 'cause I don't know. Now go on and do your old sums."

"Sums," he said scornfully. "We don't do *sums* in the county school, we do mathematics." He opened the door, then suddenly asked "When is *her* birthday, Maggie?"

"March the fifteenth," Maggie answered promptly.

"How d'you know?" he asked. "She never has a birthday tea, or presents, or anything. Nor he."

"P'r'aps they're not excited about being born," she said. "Or they don't think of each other like that, p'r'aps. It's only she likes to make a pet over you, that's all."

"But how d'you know when her birthday is?" he asked, frowning as if willing his mind to ignore the words she flung out so petulantly.

"Because her birth sustificate is in her drawer, that's why," she said sharply. "And her loveletters, too, if you want to know."

He slammed the door quickly against her words and carried his books down the silent passage, brooding under the soft fall of orange light that lapped the polished oak stand and the cedar floor and dropped as silently as his feet upon the plum-coloured stair carpet.

His room was at the end of the landing; David's old room, but so completely realtered that it was unrecognisable as the fresh green nursery of three years ago. The rocking horse and the train was gone; so were the paintings – the Ugly Duckling, the Blue Boy, and Reynold's child angels. The walls were now painted blue; she had let Morlais choose the colour; and the rocking horse's corner was occupied by a walnut book case containing novels by Henty, Ballantine, Scott, Stevenson, Dickens; there were a few fine editions, too, in which she had written Morlais's name – Peter Pan, Alice in Wonderland, Van Loon's Story of Mankind, and several of A.A. Milne's childrens' books. Where the train had been was now a neat little writing desk on which a reading lamp with decorated shade rested. A small single bed with a blue coverlet, a white chair by the bed head, and a fine oak wardrobe completed the furniture. The window looked down onto the garden.

Morlais shut the door behind him.

"Hallo, room," he said softly.

He turned the reading lamp on and after gazing down into the dim garden for a minute slowly drew the light green blinds across. Then he turned to his books.

First he learnt his French verbs, repeating them aloud with his hands over his eyes. "J'aimais, tu aimais, il aimait...."

Next, English. More learning. He rubbed his eyes with his knuckles and opened his Mount Helicon. For half an hour his voice stumbled irritatedly through Henry V's speech before Agincourt.

"Oh dash," he kept saying, "I'm forgetting it more and more."

Several times he stopped reciting or looking at the book and listened, with a dreamy intensity. Once a movement downstairs touched him in the middle of repeating a line as though it were a live wire. He jerked into a strained waiting for the sound to return, nearer, on the stairs. His body poised ready to spring towards the door. His face looked tensely at the door knob, his eyes seemed to have rushed into the passage, out of the room, while his hands fidgeted with his buttons, preparing the room for its guest. But the sound did not come again, and moodily he began drawing on his blotter.

That moment of waiting and disappointment had been an eternity; the flower had budded and flushed into ripeness and been blighted. His bottom lip trembled and he pushed his Mount Helicon off the desk. It fell crash to the floor. He kicked it with his toe.

He covered the blotter with scribbles, then pushed that away and dropped his pencil. For a while he sat doing nothing, his hands laid flat on the desk like unnecessary gloves. Then he went to the door, opened it, listened carefully, and hearing no sound in all the house, closed the door again and went back to his desk. He took a sheet of notepaper out of the drawer and carefully wrote the address
in the top right-hand corner.

> *The Elms,*
> *Glannant,*
> *Tredwr,*
> *Glam.*

Dear Hetty,

I am your brother Morlais and I am in a dungeon and I am thinking about you with my pen. I saw you once a month ago but you didnt see me you were with you're frends and had some flowers from the river. Are you all right? I thought you were grown a lot and I felt proud, you are a pretty girl Mrs Reames said one day when she saw you with our Mother. How is she? Are you working hard for scholarship, It's alright in the county school, you must go there, because if you dont you'll be like Doris or Maggie Thomas, nothing much, not like my Mums. I call her Mums now, Mrs Reames I mean. I didnt like to at first but I am glad Im writing to you this dungeon is full of giants, I mean grown-ups of course, and no children, or boys my age. And you mustnt tell

anyone this secret, because no one but you knows this is a dung-
eon and they wouldnt like it. And I wont send this letter to you, so
you'll keep the secret I know, like you always keep my secrets.
Have you got any new secrets. I expect so, in three years you will
have. How is your cough? Im never ill but sometimes I dont feel
well, like now, but Im not ill really —"

The door opened behind him. He heard the soft fall of her
foot on the rug and with betraying swiftness pulled the blotter
over the sheet of notepaper. Then her hands covered his eyes
and her presence was round him like music; but he was a hard
knot, undissolved, in the middle of her, and he pulled her
hands desperately off his eyes.

"Hallo, little scholar," she said, fond laughter mellowing
her tone. "Rabbi Ben Ezra wasn't as wise as you."

She sat on the edge of his bed, taking of her chamois gloves
and her grey fox fur, and looked at him as though she were
refreshing herself. He sat twitched up in his chair and
dropped his eyes before her gaze. "Have you finished your
homework?" she asked after a silence.

"It's English learning," he said, "and I can't remember it."

"You want some fresh air and a run in the open," she said.
"Take the dog for a race, or play ball with him on the lawn."

"I don't want to go out," he said, looking at her and the
warm intimacy of the lamplit furniture.

"And I didn't want to come in," she said, and then, with
forced jollity, "well, let's leave our homework for a little and
play the piano in the front room, shall we?"

"If I was sitting in the back row I'd be able to keep my
Mount Helicon open when we've got to say it aloud," he said,
getting up from his chair.

"You mustn't do that, Morlais," she said. "That's silly. Boys
who do that are letting themselves down, as well as the
master."

"It's old Bony's fault," he said. "He's too sleepy to notice anything. We can do what we like with *him*."

"I don't like you speaking like that about Mr Beddow," she said sharply. "He's had diabetes for years, and his wife is a cripple with rheumatism; it's cruel of you to take advantage of him."

Morlais looked anguished.

"He made me stand in front of the class in grammar today," he said in a thin painful voice. "Just because I was thinking when he asked me an answer. And he made them laugh at me."

She stroked his hair back gently.

"Never mind," she murmured. "Never mind. Perhaps he wasn't feeling very well. Come on. Let's go and play something."

"I *hate* grammar," he said bitterly, following her out of the room.

She drew the heavy curtains across the bow windows in the front room and switched on the lamp over the piano. Morlais turned the electric fire on and as he stood up caught a pale glimpse of his face in the frameless mirror over the cream-white mantelpiece. He started as though a stranger had flashed out of a hidden door in some stone corridor and got caught for one instant in the light, before the door closed. He turned round, and she was sitting with the light on her black hair, her coat laid aside and her arms like alabaster on the purple silk of her lap. He curled up on the soft arm-chair by the side of the piano and watched her fingers go like butter-flies along the black and white keys.

"D'you know what this is?" she said, playing, and not looking round to him.

"Cradle Song," he said.

She nodded confirmation. He felt a warm drop inside him, elixir in the cold vial.

"You don't know this one, though," she said.

He listened. Oh, the way the tunes ran along the maze of

lanes, in and out of the trees, criss-crossing, meeting with delight, with surprise, dipping down to little brooks whose waters tinkled with lumps of ice, and the whole wood so lovely, so green, you wanted to get lost in it, you wanted to run in it, climb the trees, smooth the plumage of the uncatch-able birds. And – yes, it's Hetty is running towards you, laughing with excitement, having found a new flower....

Then the crystal was shattered by a discord. Her fingers stopped dead.

"There you are," she said, "it's no good. We see the beauty for a moment, and then commit some horrible blunder...." She laughed, and turned to him with a quick impulsive movement. "Do you know what that sort of music is called? When one tune runs to meet another?"

"No," he said absently, not hearing much what she was saying.

"Counterpoint," she said. She laughed again – she always laughed to herself – *against* herself, it seemed sometimes, and he felt unhappy although her laughter was all kindness to *him*.

"You play now," she said, standing up. "You haven't practised for two whole days."

"No," he said, clinging to the chair arm. "Play some more, please."

A shadow of indecision crossed her eyes, putting their light out. Then she said more insistently than before, "No, it's no good if you don't practise. Come on, lazybones. Let me hear you."

Laughing she pulled him to his feet and with an ill grace he slumped down on the piano stool.

"Here you are," she said, putting his well-thumbed music book before him. "Play this little Schumann song you practised with me last week."

The black and white keys lying so pure, lilies on a marble altar, and his angry fingers clumsily desecrating their silence. White and black whirled up in wrath as his fingers crunched on them, and flung the outraged notes back, daunting his swimming eyes, which couldn't see flat from sharp, which couldn't find the proper key, but crashed into something hideously wrong, something waspish that stung his wretched fingertips, his hands groping forward in panic....

"That was quite good," she said. "You're still a bit heavy, but that's the cold weather. Keep on with it. You'll be glad of it one day."

"No, I won't," he said. "No I won't. I *can't* play."

He flung himself away and back into his chair.

"Don't be so silly," she said with asperity.

He winced.

"I *can't*," he said hopelessly, dully.

"Of course you can't, if you *won't*." she snapped.

He hid his face in the chair. A shudder jerked his shoulders up and his hands went up to hide his cheeks.

"Morlais darling," she gasped, on her knees instantly and passionately tearing his hands away from his face. He tossed his head away, his wet eyes, straining to be out of sight, twisting his neck.

"Morlais, oh Morlais." She still held his hands and her voice was like birds dashing themselves against a shut window. Then she let his hands go and for a long time there was only blackness and the hard wrenching of gear inside him, steel crowbars hacking at the living coal. Then her voice came again, a shaft of faint light.

"Aren't you happy here, Morlais?"

He tried to answer, to deny his misery. Yes, yes, yes, thought screamed she is the only goodness – something like that he yearned to say. Then he fell quiet, stopped sobbing, lay still, and listless. Her voice came from an immeasurable distance now, meaning nothing, and her hands stroking his head weren't stroking *his* head any more. Only hair on a head.

"I *have* tried," she said. "You're intelligent. One day you'll be able to understand, and judge. You may condemn me, I don't know."

Her voice was toneless, her hand automatic, like a hair-brush.

"I've been selfish," she went on; each word came alone, slowly. "I can't help it. Some day you'll understand. In music and poetry you'll understand. Selfish is in us, *in us*. It's the same with children as with lovers. We play our theme on them, improvise when the theme gets lost. And then at the end we have to read the garbled manuscript of it all, read it to them, and say this is what we made of them." Her hands just lay on his head. When she noticed them she took them away.

"You'd better go and have a hot bath," she said. "There's plenty of hot water in the boiler. You can use my bath salts tonight, if you like."

He turned his head towards her and shamefully sought her. He understood what she said about bathing. He would be glad of a bath, and thankful, for it wasn't his bathnight. It was her water. He looked at her, and something leaped violently inside him. He couldn't bear her eyes looking at him like that. He went hot and hurt and angry, angry. With himself, with her, with... with... But it was too hard to roll away, too heavy on him. He accepted it, and so was able to look at her again without flinching.

The door opened.

"Ah, here you are, are you?" Mr Reames said.

She got up swiftly.

"I thought you were all out," he said hurriedly. "I was hoping you were well wrapped up. It's freezing."

He shook his great shoulders like a dog shaking the frost off its fur.

"We've been practising the piano," she said with unnatural firmness, turning from him to adjust her hair slide in the mirror.

"Morlais coming on at it alright?" he asked, stiffly.

"Yes," she answered, more lightly. "He's really very good,

if he only kept at it instead of getting all hoity toity."

"Too impatient, are you, Morlais?" he asked, looking unsteadily at Morlais and smiling as much as he could manage.

Morlais faltered.

"Youth has all life ahead of it, and yet it's never got time to do anything properly," he said. "Only middle age finds time long, when really it's almost all gone." He laughed. "I thought for a second that I'd thought that out for myself.... I wonder where I read it?"

"Any poem by any poet," she said.

There was a pause.

"Did your shopping expedition prove a success?" he said.

"What a formal speech!" she replied quickly. She laughed and rubbed her forehead with a quick nervous gesture. "I think we're all a bit stagey tonight, for some reason."

"Not a bit of it," he said forcibly. "If *you'd* spent three hours examining plans in that icebox of an office, and then received a deputation of uncompromising colliers, you wouldn't think life at all unreal, my dear."

"No, no," she said, her voice rising. "Of course I wouldn't. If I were a man, doing a man's job, I'd *know* what's what and what isn't, wouldn't I? But as it is I just get lost in my morbid fancies, don't I?"

"Edith –" he began.

She waved his remonstrance away in her growing excitement.

"Edith nothing," she said, "Do you still believe that? That nonsense? D'you think I'm just a 'case'?"

"Edith," he said, loudly.

She stopped.

"Well?" she said.

"Well, don't go over all that again," he said.

She rubbed her whole face, like a tired animal.

"I'll believe you're right in the end," she said.

He looked at her.

"You've spoilt your eyebrows, darling," he said.

He smoothed the thin bow back.

Then he turned to Morlais, who was still sitting in the chair, looking from one to the other.

"Well, Mr Morlais," he said. "We are a tedious couple, aren't we? Talking all this shop. Come on, sonny, off to bed with you if you're going to do your lessons properly tomorrow."

He picked Morlais up.

"Get onto my back," he said.

"Just a minute, dear," she said. "I'd forgotten. It occurred to me in town this afternoon. Would you like to invite Hetty to your birthday tea on Friday, Morlais?"

Morlais was climbing onto Mr Reames's back. They wouldn't notice him start, guiltily. She'd seen who he was writing to? Had she?

" You could send her a proper invitation card," she said. "Morlais Jenkins requests the pleasure of Miss Hetty Jenkins's company at The Elms, Glannant, on the occasion of his fourteenth birthday. How would that be?"

"Oh, yes," he said, jubilant. "Can I paint it? Before I get into bed?"

Hetty was waiting for him at five past five just as he'd asked her to in his invitation. In the back lane of Glannant Street. He wanted to run towards her up the empty lane when he rounded the corner and actually saw her. But something stopped him running. He walked, things tingling under his skin and making his voice want to shout. And she stood there, not coming towards him, just standing there. She had a little straw hat with turned up brim, and there were yellow waxy primroses on the band. And she had white socks, and her shoes were polished and polished. She was smiling, he could see, in a serious sort of way; and when he was a few yards from her, only then did she take a hesitant-eager step towards him.

"Hallo, Hetty," he said,

"Hallo, Morlais," she replied.

They walked on slowly.

"I got your card," she said.

"I was hoping you would," he replied.

"Dilwyn said, you didn't do it yourself, but I said you did."

"It was a mess, wasn't it?" he said. "All the wrong colours."

"I liked it," she replied.

She looked at him from the corner of her eye.

"You been quick getting to fourteen," she said. "I'm only ten so far."

"Well, don't you be in a hurry to grow up," he said. "Everything gets harder, that's all it is."

"How?" she asked.

"Well, we do algebra, and Latin, f'r instance," he said.

"Goo," she marvelled.

"I got lots of things to show you," he said. "I got a room for myself, to work in; and I got a part of the garden for my flowers; and a cabinet for birds' eggs..."

"I got a purse, too," she replied. "Look. A proper, growed-up one."

She had, too. A leather purse with a penny and a hanky in it.

"Our Doris give it me," she said. "She 'ad it off a boy, she said, for a present, and she give it me when she got engaged to James the Grocer, week ago."

"It's a proper purse," he admitted. "It fits you alright, too."

"She's going to 'ave a veil and orange blossom," Hetty went on, "and a minister from away to marry them in chapel. She's full of it. She was asking Mam should she invite your – you know – Mrs – Reames.

Mam said not to ask *her*, and Doris said well, she would then, just to see the look on her face. The icebug Doris calls her, I don't know why, only that's what she calls her."

"This is our gate," Morlais said loudly.

Hetty stopped in front of the prim green and white wicket as Morlais had once done, three years back.

"Can I come in?" she asked dubiously, suddenly self conscious.

"Course," he said, "course you can. Only watch what you're saying, see?"

She didn't know why he was cross with her, and sounded so threatening.

"Yes," she said, crest-fallen, pulling her yellow coat tidy and stepping onto the gravel path as carefully as if it were a flower bed.

"Are you hungry?" he asked gruffly.

"Not very," she said. "Mam gave me some bre'm butter 'fore coming out so's I shouldn't be greedy."

"There's plenty to eat here," he said grandly. "All cakes and things, too. We never have bre'm butter on birthdays."

"Go on," she said incredulously. "What is there?"

"More'n you can think of," he said. "Eclairs, sausage rolls, tartlets and some things with French names she ordered specially, too."

"Oh no," she said, ravished.

"I got a present for you, too," he said. "It's in silver paper, on your plate."

"Oh no," she repeated. "Oh, Mor."

After a pause, when they had almost reached the french windows, she said perplexedly, "Why don't we have birthdays in our house?"

"Look through the window," he said. "See the table?"

Hetty looked on Paradise, through glass.

Mrs Reames said that if Hetty stayed after dark Margaret would have to take her home. If Morlais was to take her by himself they must go before nightfall. Holding Hetty's hot hand firmly, then, Morlais led her down the gravel drive to the gate, through the cold dusk.

"Did you like it?" he said.

"Oh, yes," she breathed ecstatically, and in rapt silence recollected the wonderful happenings.

"Them candles in coloured lanterns," she sighed.

"The crackers I like best," he said stolidly.

"The first one frightened me," she said.

"You were a daft one, screaming like that," he said.

"Well, it frightened me," she said stubbornly.

After a pause she said definitely, "It was nicer than Sunday School tea party."

"I was hoping you'd like it," he said.

He began whistling.

Suddenly he asked, "How is Mrs Rabbit, Het?"

"She's alright," she replied.

"Did she have them little ones alright?"

"What little ones?" she asked.

"You know. Dad said she was having them just before –" he hesitated – "you know, just before I went to live with –"

"Oh, then," she said. "That's ages, now. She've 'ad lots since then. She's always 'aving them. We don't hardly pay no notice to her now. She got a peddlegree now, Dad says."

"I never seen her having babies," Morlais said, morosely.

"They can't see, the babies can't," she said omnisciently.

"I got a nice room for myself, haven't I?" he said, consoling himself.

"Yes," she replied. "I can't think!"

"I won't come any more with you," he said.

They were at the bottom of the back lane. The street lights shed a cold immature blur over the grimy square. A train whistled desolately down the valley. Steel clattered testily from the pithead, away across the rack of sidings.

"Solong, then," she said, starting to go.

"Don't go, yet, Het," he passionately begged her.

She stopped in the middle of a run, poised, held by the

fierceness of his entreaty.

"There's something I forgot to say," he said. "Don't go."

"Well, it's getting cold," she said.

"Yes, but don't go," he insisted.

"Mam will be waiting, too," she said.

"Alright then, go, Go if you want to."

He shooed her with his hands. She stood indecisively.

"Go then," he shouted, his voice high. His eyes brimmed tears.

"What did you want?" she asked,

"I don't know," he said miserably. He picked at a broken nail, not looking up at her. At last he stammered, "Did Mam say I could bring you all the way to the house?"

She hesitated. "No," she said. "She didn't say. Dad said for me to find my way home by myself, though."

"Dad did?"

"Yes, Dad did. He never says nothing about you. He stops us speaking about you. Only with Mam we –"

"Alright," he interjected. "Go on, then. You'll be coughing again if you don't watch."

"Solong then," she said.

"Look, Het," he said suddenly, gripping her sleeve as she turned away and speaking with a tense whisper. "If we could write letters, say, us two, and put them somewhere. You know the wall of the allotments on top of the ash tip?"

"Which one?" she said eagerly.

"By where we found a blackbird's nest once," he said.

"Yes," she said.

He looked up and down the lane.

"Right," he said. "Well, listen carefully now. I'll steal a cocoa tin, see? And put letters in it and hide it where the nest was, see?

"Right," she hissed.

"Every Saturday," he went on hurriedly, low-voiced. "And you'll write to me?"

"Yes," she said breathlessly.

"Criss cross?"

"Drop dead."

"Solong, then."

"So long."

He ran home. He didn't want to cry now. He didn't know why the tears were coming when he felt so happy. He didn't even feel guilty, yet...

From the Cocoa Tin.

> *The Elms,*
> *Glannant,*
> *Tredwr.*
> *Oct. 27th.1928.*

Dear Hetty,

I am writing the address this time just to show you the proper way to write a letter as your letter wasn't proper, and it was written in pencil and some water had got in and I couldn't read some of it. It was annoying but then I made up what I couldn't read and it was nice. But please *write in ink if you can I know you must be careful and you got to write in the coal cwtch but if you can you will, won't you, write in ink? And I'll put a piece of turf over the hole next time. Perhaps we can write in code, like secret service, if I can find a code somewhere. It would be safer, because Ive got to write in secret, too, and I don't know what Id do if she caught me. It would be all up.*

I scored a try today in our house match and they all patted me on the back. I won't mind games now. I used to be afraid to kick the ball at first. Dont you feel cross with yourself when you think what a fool you used to be? You will when you grow up, anyway. I would like to be really grown up, like the head prefect in school. He says grace at dinner and he got a stinker in Higher and he can play Rugger alright, too. He plays wing. Higher is a hard exam you sit when you are grown up and after it you leave school, you go to College. I cant sleep sometimes when I start thinking if I'll get all that way. Mums came in one night. I dont know what she came in for. She was in her bed-things and she was surprised I was awake. And I said I was thinking how to get better marks than I did in the exams and she said "You go to sleep." And then she said "Dont worry about your marks now, because you are the sort that does better in Higher." She said "Good wine tastes better when it has been kept in the cellar. She's always saying things like that. I wish I knew what she means. I was hoping you'd say if you liked her after my birthday. She read a story to me that night she came in till I slept and it was funny waking up at first because I thought she was still there but it was Maggie. Well, its dinner time. We have dinner at seven in the dining room. I can smell it. So solong and dont forget about the ink.

> *Lots of Love from*
> *Your brother,*
> *Morlais.*

> *October 30th.*
> *Our coal cutch.*

Deer Morlais,

I am riting ink, but its harder. the ink comes off on my cloths. Its the nibs fault. when I get a hapenny next Ill biy a nib. there are some in granny tomsons with colured handles like outside the barbers only smaller of coarse. I dont like writing, its slower than drawing and I can say what I want to better if I draw. I cant biy a nib for a bit because I am puting my mony to the sunday school outing its to Barry Island like last year. I still got a balloon and a bag full of sand from it last year. Mam kept me behind in chaple last Sunday because Doris was out with James the grocer and I was the only not grown up in chaple. And Mam started preying out loud and they was all quiet watching her but I didnt. I squeezed my eyes till I could see black and hot culurs and after chaple she huried me home and then she hugged me in the back lane, Doris says Ben James cant get married yet because his mother is better again. she was very bad and the amblans came for her and they were going to live in her house. But now Doris says she dont know when it will be. Well its getting dark and uncumfy now so solong.

    Lots of love from your Sister, hetty.

                             November 4th,
                             My bedroom.

Dear Hetty,

    You are a hero writing in the coal cwtch. I wish I could make some sacrifice, not have everything like I have. It is so lonely, I cant explain. Its so quiet the air moves round and round you and it whispers but I cant hear it, only I must listen. They are letting off squibs in the back lane. I can hear them. We had a guy in the garden last year but you remember it rained and were not having one this year. I dont like to ask why and I tried telepathy to get one but it wasnt any use. Telepathy is silent religion but it doesnt matter about I explaining it because I must be working it wrong somewhere. She says telepathy is real. You can talk to people that are somewhere else, in heaven for instance. I heard her saying to him that she vowed the child had spoken to her. She was speaking loud otherwise I couldnt have heard because I was upstairs. He said something and she said "I wish to god it was mear dremes." I didnt hear any more because I put my hands over my ears You mustnt tell this to anyone, only I want to tell you. Its great being able to tell you, not keep it all inside me. Youll be having squibs I expect like we used to, cathrin wheels and things. I wont write any more now because I feel sorry. I want to do something only I dont know what. When you write next time tell me Is Dad alright in the pit? I saw Bob Linton today, he stops to talk to me always, I wish I was working underground when I see him instead of school school school. He said the men were getting ugly and Dad was going on a deputation to ask about a district with water in it the men working there work in deep water. So tellme. I dont like to ask here.

Goodbye, dear Hetty,

Your loving Brother, Morlais.

P.S. I wish I could come to Barry with you when you go. We never go away for holidays. I dont know why because he's always telling her she ought to go away for a change, but she wont. I would like to discover an island where there are wild birds nobody has discovered.

Dear Morlais,

We didnt have a guy forks. Dad said who was to pay for the squibs when theres not enough bread. He was cross, it wasnt any use argewing. so we watched them letting them off two doors down, and Mam gave me a halfpenny on the quiet for not having squibs. she said dad is worrid these days about the pit, and hes not the same, hes out in the nights, and Doris said she saw him speaking in the park in Tredwr where we play on saturday there are men in the kitchen every nite neerly now. Mrs Rabbit is gone now. she tasted a bit hard, we had her for dinner three days ago now. I berried her skin in the garden. I go to bed after tea now. theres nobody to play with now. I got moved up in class because I made a good composition about pigs. I wrote about the pig in the alotment, and it was alright except I said it had too many tits. the polisman came asking where was Dilwyn last night, but he was in bed. somebody smashed a window in the playground. This is a secret, like yours. He told me not to say. It was he did it, Dilwyn. I wont say. The dog next door found Mrs Rabbits skin. You cant keep anything from him. Dilwyn doesnt mind me now. he doesnt hit me or pinch, and he told me that secret about the window, so I told him one. I only had one. about writing to you, so I said that one. My finger is aking now so solong, Hetty.

Dear Hetty,

I dont know the date but it's Friday night. They are in the pictures. *I said I didn't want to go. I dont like going with the two of them together much. I dont know which one to speak to and they both speak to me at the same time and I dont know which to answer.You know I didnt like him much at first but I do like him now more and more. He digs the garden with me and he made a box with a glass top for me to keep ants in but the ants got out all over the floor of my room. And his voice is always the same, too. Not like hers. She can play the piano. She doesnt play it now, though. Only when shes by herself she plays a lot, Maggie said. Maggie says silly things. I wish we didnt have a maid. I dont like maids. I like it like in your house, Hetty dear. Oh, I would like to smash something, its quiet again, and Ive been trying that telepathy but I couldnt decide who I wanted, and I could see lots of faces in one. So I must do my homework now. Im sitting Senior in July and the masters are always telling us we wont pass and I* must *pass. I* must. *She would be cross with me if I didnt. But its so quiet Im afraid to open my school bag. I expect youre in bed. Its very dark tonight.Why did you tell Dilwyn that? But perhaps he's a better sport now. I often think of the rows we used to have, fighting in bed. Its very quiet here, and I can see big cracks in the wall and fire running up the curtain. And a white rabbit, I made a duck shadow on the wall then with my hand and it frightened the rabbit. Now I'm scratching the desk and the rabbit is cocking his ears.Well, I must do my homework. I dont know what I want to be yet. Can you suggest something for me to be?You can come and live with me then. Not here, but somewhere where we haven't been yet. So Goodnight now, Hetty. I say your name to God before I go into bed, and Mam's name, and Dads sometimes. Then I wait a minute and I says hers and ask him to pardon my iniquities.*

Your brother for ever and ever,
Morlais.

Dear Morlais,
I can't send you any more letters, you got to stop too. Dad said.

he was very cross. Dilwyn clecked on us because I wouldnt play with him. Mam said to tell you and she said to send her love. So I wont see you again ever. Im going to town with Doris tomorrow. shes going to buy things for her wedding; ben James the grocer his mother's very bad again, Doris said. Fancy going to town to all the shops, furniture and coop; ben James is paying for us. Solong, your sister, Hetty.

Morlais woke slowly, dragging himself up from the muddy dregs of his grey sleep-phantasies. His eyes opened sullenly, hurt and offended at the harsh summons of the light. Thin and impersonal a cock trumpeted in vainglory, high on the hills beyond his sight and outside his imagining; the sun struck its white palm fiercely on his cheek.

He jumped out of bed and went to the window, pushed it down and looked out at the garden all green and unaware with a thrush in the heart of it and its apple trees in white, like the wedding of a virginal choir. Like the Lady of Shalott, only not sad nor tired. Like being born....

He got soap in his eyes when he washed; when he shaved his gooseberry chin the skin blotched painfully as the razor scraped over it. When he put on his clean shirt the starched cleanness covered his limbs like communion wine on a cold Sunday. When he took out his best suit from the wardrobe his fingers tingled to touch the rough well-pressed serge. He was happy in the well-being of his body, in being awake before the day became the property of people, in the simple actions of clothing himself cleanly for his sister's wedding.

Thinking of the wedding his face grew solemn in the mirror, and for a moment he was once again sitting entangled in the arduous thicket of a Latin prose in his lamp-lit room. Maggie had come in so quietly...

"Your Doris is by the back door," she said, lowering her voice. "She wants to speak to you. She won't come in, though. Don't want the missus to see her. Step on it; don't look so twp."

Maggie's conspiratorial hoarseness hypnotised him. Still perplexed with subjunctives and ablative absolutes he followed her downstairs, going with instinctive caution past the closed door of the drawing room, trembling slightly at the sound of Chopin and the silence of voices. Through the kitchen, and the scullery, Maggie's comfortable domain smelling of hot water and crumbs and carbolic soap, to the back door.

"Hallo, Morlais!"

His heart jumped. It was too dusky to see her face, except as a pale blur on the dark velvet of the rose bower. But he could see her body wrapped in a loose mackintosh, and he knew it was Doris, his sister.

"Hallo, Doris," he replied.

He held out his hands but she did not see them. He withdrew them, feeling suddenly dejected, as though he had tried to reach an apple on a high branch that was hopelessly out of his reach. He felt his hands misshapen and clumsy hanging heavily at his side.

"How are you?" she asked, moving her face into the light of the slightly open door.

How handsome she was, so suddenly revealed in the thin shaft of light, smiling eagerly with white teeth and blackberry eyes and animal affection.

"Alright," he said ineffectually.

"You look tall," she said, and taking his sleeve in her hand she moved him into the light. "Gosh. I'd never have known you, Morlais. What is it? Five years since you left us, isn't it?"

"Yes, about that," he said.

"What are you now? Sixteen?"

"Yes."

"My, you are different."

Her wonder restored him, exciting a warmness inside him,

an immediacy that made him glad, glad, and intensely aware of himself being there with his sister, actually his sister.

"I was hoping you wouldn't mind me calling like this," she said. "I asked Maggie when it would be best to call without being seen. She said about ten would be the best time. It's a big garden, isn't it?"

"Yes," he said.

"Bigger'n our little chicken run," she laughed.

"Have you still got chickens?" he asked.

"Not in the back," she replied. "Dad's got an allotment now on the mountain – least, half on the mountain, half ash-tip. Keeps them up there now. And a pig."

"And rabbits?" he asked.

She laughed.

"You ought to come and see," she said.

"I'd like to," he answered.

"Well, why don't you? Mam would go over the moon to see you, I know."

"No," he said, turning away from her. "I *can't.*"

She was silent for a long moment.

"That's what I called for," she said at last.

He waited, still with his back to her.

"It's my wedding tomorrow," she said, "and it didn't seem right, somehow, you not being there. Well, I know Dad wouldn't be a-willing if I asked him first. But it's *my* wedding, isn't it, not his? And I want you to come for a special reason. You will come, won't you, Mor?" She sensed a tautness in his averted body, in his silence.

"Say you will, Mor." she asked quietly.

"But I can't, Doris. How can I?"

"Look," she said impetuously, lowering her voice and catching his sleeve in an excited grip. "Listen now," She drew in her breath sharply. He turned to her, inexplicably frightened.

"I'm marrying Ben James, see?" she said. "Well, never mind about that now, except that I'm not all I might be. But never mind about that now." Her voice was alive with strange undertones of inarticulate longing. The silences between her hectic words struggled to say something, something. "Well, I'll be leaving the house, won't I?" she went on. "That's certain, anyway. And I don't know. Mam isn't right. I don't like the look of her. And Hetty's going on her second year in the County – little bit of a thing with skinny legs in black stockings and her bag of books just as big as she is. Well, Dilwyn, you can't say what about him. He's taking groceries round for Ben. Well, Ben's gone shares in the greyhound track in town – p'r'aps you didn't know – and that's all Dilwyn talks about now, is greyhounds... Oh, it's no good talking. You see, I'm not easy, and you're the eldest after me. You're sixteen, and I've always thought you had it in you. I didn't bother with you much, I know, when you was a kid. But I didn't miss seeing that much, anyroads. I always ask Maggie about you, see?" She paused, waiting for him to speak.

"I'll come to the wedding," he said.

She kissed him.

He took her down to the gate.

"I don't suppose there'll be a chance to speak to you on Wednesday," she said. "Ebenezer the wedding's to be in. Eight a.m. Then we'll be catching the nine train to London. I don't know what we'll do up there. We're going to stay in a proper hotel."

"You'll enjoy that, I bet," he said, trying to say something.

"Well, you won't forget, will you?" she said. She moved away from him. "You won't decide I'm asking too much, will you?"

Something came over him, choking back his words.

"What d'you mean?" he said at last.

"I'll be crying in a minute," she said. "Solong."

She was gone; the warm mist of summer evenings, of all summer evenings since the first sun fell behind the first garden, took her away, and he stayed at the gate, waiting for some releasing touch. Then, in the end, he went back to finish his Latin prose.

He hadn't been inside Ebenezer since he had left home. It was in a grubby cul-de-sac side street behind the Co-op warehouse. On Sunday nights he used to listen to the train going past while the minister chanted to God, the yellow gas bracket going plop-plop as it shed a soft radiance over the puckered eyes and shining bald head. One night the minister had begged God to succour all lost souls, and the train had gone past in the half distance, streaming past with the echo of wheels and a cold blast of sound. And Morlais heard it hurling itself into the ravine of the valley, and he knew that God was pursuing it. And he wanted it to get free, to win the race to the lost land, for he was driving it, and he was stoking it, and it was himself that God wanted, he knew. He never shut his eyes in chapel, for the darkness was potent and full of strange images of dragons with blue scales, and great bats with dead skins. So he kept his eyes opened and watched the white heads of the deacons in the big pew. And when they muttered "Ie, Ie," at the minister's words he felt himself guarded by a circle of holy men who nodded to God and kept Him away. He hadn't been inside Ebenezer since he had left home.

He was early. There was nobody there except the cleaner, Mrs Jones Working-clothes they called her. He knew her alright. She came charing to the Elms on Mondays, and the school week began with a good morning to Mrs Jones as he hurried out after breakfast to catch the bus and passed her whacking carpets with her fat red arms.

She was wearing a man's cap flat over her grey bun.

"Good morning, Mr Reames," she said, ducking humbly. "Just tidying up I am for the wedding."

She picked up a pail of dirty water and a mop and waddled down the aisle. She stopped by him.

"Take a front pew, you," she said. "First come, first served I say."

She hooked her shoulder up and rubbed her ear against it.

"Rheumatics all over," she said. "If I do stay still, I can't move again indeed. Washing too much it is; paying for my wages I am. However I won't be grumbling so long as the Lord don't take me away before my proper three score and ten."

She had never spoken so freely to him before, this yellow old woman whose personality was always obscured by her perpetual environment of mangle and tub and mop. He had been mortified that she did not remember that he was Jenkins the deacon's son, but now her unexpected tongue put him at ease in the chapel and in the wandering channels of her cracked brain he felt anonymously secure.

"Yes, indeed," she sighed. "There's many that go before their time. Many a good corpse I washed and dressed in my day, and I do always feel thankful it isn't myself that I'm tidying up for the last time." She straightened her cap and pushed an iron-grey wisp of her scraggy hair away from her wrinkled forehead.

"Yes indeed," she said. "Give me a good fun'ral 'fore a wedding any day. Specially a wedding no good won't come out of, like this one today."

"Why won't good come out of it?" he said slowly.

She stared at him with her almond eyes, confidentially, and her withered lips opened over her gums.

"It isn't what the minister says that do count," she said, grinning.

"'E can't mend a broken cup by praying over it, I know."

Morlais wrenched his eyes away from her and walked along the pew to the centre of the chapel. He sat down by the pillar supporting the balcony and bowed his head against it. It was cold against his skull. His fingers inter-locked and he bit his teeth together and in the dowdy little chapel he prayed till sweat broke out under his arms and the roots of his hair prickled with heat.

When he looked up he saw his mother and Hetty. They had come in through the vestry and hadn't seen him. Hetty was putting a bowl of flowers on the red-carpeted platform. Marigolds and violas from the garden. His mother was kneeling on the steps below the organ. Hetty waited until her mother had finished praying. Morlais watched them all the time. He could see Hetty's new pink coat and old straw hat with waxy primroses, and his mother's bowed head and bony shoulders under her black coat. Looking became too intense and he dropped his eyes to the pillar. And scratched on the pillar he saw the initials M.J. But it wasn't Morlais Jenkins that was there now. His thumping heart and twisted hands proved that. The initials of a dead child, he said to himself, essaying to steel himself to this meeting that was too imminent. He didn't know, didn't know.... Only to be away from this place, to unwind the ceremony that was about to begin. There was Doris, too, somewhere, powdering herself in the glass while the taxi waited, and looking at herself and saying over in her mind the things of the future she couldn't say aloud. And Ben James divested of his white apron with its margarine stains, with no pencil stuck into his hair, coming here too. He covered his eyes in his hand.

"Morlais."

He looked up and smiled to his mother and dropped his eyes again.

She came along the pew and sat down by him. Hetty followed her.

"I thought I said I wasn't going to see you ever again," Hetty said.

He smiled and the health came back to him.

His mother was looking at him all the time.

"How are you then, Mam?" he asked.

"You're looking a fine boy," she said. "She's done you

good."

He laughed.

"I wasn't thinking to see you here," she said slowly. "You'll all be here again, now then. In our own chapel."

"I got a bag of rice to throw over them," Hetty said, holding up a brown paper bag full almost to bursting. "I'm going to wait by the door while they sign the book."

Her eyes were dancing.

"Want some to throw yourself?" she asked.

"If you've got any to spare," he laughed.

"Yes," she replied thoughtfully. "I can let you have a handful."

"You don't look as happy as you should, Mam," he said, "your eldest daughter getting married."

She smiled. The smile trembled on her grey face like uncertain sun in wet winter. Her skin was hard and lustreless, fretted into long furrows, and her eyes were quiet as though something had left her, left her dismayed. And as he looked at her for that moment her face entered into him, making his body troubled. She was his mother, her face was hers only – her frown, her mouth sunken at the corners and indrawn because her teeth were gone and she had no false teeth, wouldn't put down the money for them; hers the brown mole on the shrunk neck; his mother's.

"Sometimes things goes against you," she said, "no matter if you pray, they won't change the way they're going. This marriage is coming too late, I'm thinking."

"Go on," he said. "You're tired, that's all; Doris is only twenty. She's young enough."

"They're coming," Hetty said, excitedly tugging her mother's coat.

Steps on the stone, in the porch. Ben James and his best man, a suave young Jew who worked in his father's hat shop in town. He had a topper and tails, and a white carnation; his hair was glossy and waved.

Ben James followed him down the aisle, both of them smiling at Mrs Jenkins. Ben walked on the soles of his shoes, softly, as though the empty chapel had warned him to be humble. They both sat down in the front pew, the young Jew smoothing his hair back with an elegant thin hand, Ben shifting about and fingering his bow tie self-consciously. Morlais looked round at the empty pews and the cracked green plaster of the walls and the grimy windows along the empty balcony. The place was really small and drab, and not at all the chapel he had in his mind, the chapel of gas-light and murmuring grey heads and times without number. There was a hole in the roof, covered clumsily with felting over a trellis of laths. The walls were faded and stained. The empty pulpit had a wooden vacant air. It was just a building, bare and ugly, this chapel. Cold and dead, sucking the life out of ceremony, freezing the passion out of vows.

A car drew up outside; there were steps and a voice; and turning his head he stared at the side door which someone was pushing open. His sister, Doris, with scared eyes glancing round the empty building. No murmur of excited crowds, no music. Her face moved Morlais suddenly. The powder and rouge couldn't hide her naked self-abasement at the coldness of the place. She carried a sheaf of shop lilies against her white silk dress. He stood up and went out of the pew and down the aisle. They all watched him. He smiled to Doris, feeling his face twitch with the effort. His smile encountered the neutral countenance of his father, who had entered behind her. He saw his father's eyes start, fire, die, in a flash and his cold body responded to that flicker of recognition. He crossed the small space in front of the deacons' pew and sat down on the chair in front of the yellow-keyed harmonium. His hands poised a moment. Then he played the Wedding March from Mendelsohn's Dream music.

The chapel came warmly to life and glowed. The minister came out of the vestry, smilingly acknowledging the bride who, flushed and agitated, had taken her place on the stone steps beside the groom. The music died under the minister's uplifted hand. Morlais turned round in his chair and could not isolate himself now, from this wedding. Ben James shifting his weight from one flat foot to the other, Doris crushing the lilies with hands that trembled, his father standing strong and upright in his Sunday suit, and behind him his mother and Hetty and Mrs Jones Working-clothes, all like him held by the minister's hands and the bond of words, creating and being created by the single all-divining inevitable Act. In that moment of oneness, of one blood and one past and one present being, Morlais felt himself heave in ferment. And he became for that instant aware that God and the Devil were there at that wedding in the fullness under Doris's girdle....

"I don't think I can manage it, Dor," he said. "I've got to catch the 8.50 bus to school. I've only got half an hour."

"Never mind," she said, brushing off the rice from her veil and breast and hugging Hetty against her thighs, "if you only come up for ten minutes that's all I want."

"Yes, come on, Mor," Hetty said, tugging at his coat. "You can come up in the taxi, look. Have a ride in the taxi,"

"Yes," Doris said. "You *got* to come."

The fierce insistence of her eyes forced him to yield. He got into the taxi after her. Ragged children held a rope out to stop the taxi at the end of the street. Women dishevelled with sleep watched from their doorsteps, Ben James sat on the folding seat with his back to the driver and his knees pulled up under his chin. He wiped the sweat off his face with a big white handkerchief and smiled at Doris and Morlais and Hetty with one big smile. He had heliotrope socks.

"Give some money to those kids, Ben," Doris said.

Ben leaned forward, nearly overbalancing and pushed his fat hand into his back pocket. His face fell.

"Oh Jewks," he said. "I been and left it at home. I had a pile of coppers ready on the dresser, too. Oh Jewks."

Doris laughed.

"Well, we can't go then, can we?" she said – to Morlais she seemed to be speaking not in the present but in some deep past or somewhere yet to come, some moment the future threw back to her – "We can't go; we're stalled."

The taxi driver waited impassively; the children held the rope taut and shouted a wedding box.

"Oh, Diws," Ben James said. Then he wound the window down and stuck his red face out.

"You come to James the grocer's next Friday, there's good children, and you shall 'ave an orange each," he shouted.

The children wavered in silent consideration for a moment.

"We want a copper," a scraggy boy in long black stockings shouted hoarsely, "gi's a copper now, you old Jew."

"Friday," shouted Ben, beetroot-colour. "You sh'll 'ave it Friday."

"Go on," he said to the driver. "Start 'er up, for God's sake."

The driver grinned and shot the car forward, yanking the rope from the truculent child hands. Yells of derision and anger and the smirking of dishevelled women were their send-off.

On the way home through the grey anonymous streets Doris squeezed Morlais's hand. He looked at her a moment; her eyes were distended and hot. He knew she was thanking him for playing the harmonium. He returned her look and she quivered, seeing that he knew the intolerable falseness of her situation.

Mrs Jenkins was waiting at the front door when the taxi drew up. She opened the taxi door and took Doris's hand to help her out. Morlais followed, stretching his cramped legs and standing for the first time for five years on the threshold of their house. His mother was smiling, and people were coming up the street from all the houses to partake in the Act, the rejoicing of the grey street making doors open and fat old women quicken their waddle to an ungainly trot, while children on their way to school stopped a minute and stared. Morlais went into the passage, Doris stayed outside to be gazed upon and kissed.

His father was standing at the foot of the stairs. Morlais stopped still. His father faced him with his grey eyes and impassive features. Morlais stared back, his sight blurring and swelling painfully as he struggled forward to bridge the few feet of cold passage along which the grey eyes smouldered. But all his effort failed to move his body forward, only swaying it on the balls of his feet, like a tree rooted against the storm. Then his father smiled, slowly and fixedly.

"Good morning, Mr Reames," he said, pushing the parlour door open, "the breakfast is ready laid if you'll go in there."

Morlais clenched his hands to crush the black spasm that seized on him, and with bent head went into the parlour.

"In there, Mr Bernstein; in the parlour, Ben," he heard his father say in the same stony voice.

The table was laid with a white cloth and the best blue crockery, the Swansea set. Eight plates of cold ham, eight glasses, a bottle of port and a white iced cake with pink lettering, a heart and an arrow transfixing it. The parlour was cold and spotless, conveying nothing of life.

"Didn't know you could play the organ," Ben James said, rubbing his hands together heartily. "Bit of luck, wasn't it, for us?"

Morlais flushed.

"Jolly good presence of mind I call it," Mr Bernstein said easily, looking at himself in the gilt-edged mirror which the damp had spotted.

He looked round the parlour.

"So this is where you did your courting, eh Ben?" he said.

Ben grinned and put his finger to his lips.

"Less of that," he said. "You watch what you're saying, Moisie."

Hetty flew in.

"Morlais," she said gleefully, and then, seeing the other two, she stopped abruptly. "I got a garden of my own out the back," she said quietly. "Come and see it with me."

"After breakfast I will," he said, putting his hands on her shoulders and feeling her thin shoulder blades against his palms.

"Hetty," said Mr Jenkins at the door. "Come on out."

The wedding breakfast began with a speech by Mr Bernstein, who proposed the toast. He said he was sure the young couple were ideally matched and he made a little joke about them not needing a hot water bottle and he drank his glass of port in one mouthful. Then Ben James said he'd rather not say anything as he wasn't a good public speaker but he was sure they'd be very happy together. Then they sat down and ate the cold ham while Mrs Jenkins poured out the tea; but Mr Bernstein said he'd rather have a second glass of port, and Ben James said what was good enough for Moisie was good enough for him, and Doris said if they were going to make pigs of themselves she would, too. So three cups of tea got cold. But Mr Bernstein laughed so loudly at his own jokes about weddings that the coldness didn't spread, but crept off to the faded oleographs on the wall and the china dogs in the fire place and the strained faces of Mr and Mrs Jenkins and their son. Then Morlais spoke for the first time, saying he'd have to go.

"But you've only pecked at your plate," his mother said.

"I know," he replied, looking at her imploringly. Her voice had the note in it he remembered from the times when he was sick, and she had put her hand on his forehead to feel whether it was flushed and the burning feeling had turned instantly sweet and cool. "But I had breakfast before coming out, and I'll be late for school if I don't hurry."

His words sounded thin and ineffectual. There seemed no way of getting out from the parlour, no way out. His face seemed to have starched and stiffened against his cheek bones. He had to force a smile. Doris stood up too. She was flushed with the port wine.

"Just a minute, Morlais," she said.

He stood still, fiddling with his chair.

"Gi'me your note case, Ben," she said.

"What for?" said Ben, fishing in his breast pocket.

"There's one thing I want to do," she said, taking the case from him.

She took out a crisp green pound note.

"This is what's wrong with South Wales," she said. "And with this town, and this house, and with us." She held the note over the table.

She was smiling in a way, but her face was stone-serious.

"Seems to me it's the only thing right with us," Bernstein tittered.

"Sit down and finish your food," her father said, "and stop this nonsense."

His voice was hard with anger.

She ripped the note into pieces swiftly, and flung it into the air. Shreds of green paper, some falling into the tea, some on the uncut wedding cake.

"That's my confetti, anyway," she said.

She sat down.

She had done it all in a flash, in a gasp of their breath. She laughed.

"You're like a lot of ghosts," she said, and laughed again. "If I die of starvation I won't care."

"You want the strap on you," her father said.

But Morlais saw in the toss of her head a revolt that split the wall behind her wide open, leaving a jagged crack that widened, widened, till all the houses in the street fell apart and the inhabitants ran naked and helpless into the road, beating their fists on their temples ludicrously, their property lost. He didn't understand. But it was easy now to go, for no one was there to stop him. Not even himself.

In the street he took his school cap out of his pocket and put it on his head and at the corner he waved goodbye to Doris, and ran.

When he came up the drive at tea-time Morlais saw her bending by the flower bed to the left of the French window picking violas and wall-flowers and asters. He hesitated, wondering whether to go round to the back door, or go up and speak to her. He felt dirty and insipid and he wanted a cold bath to cleanse him through and through. She was wearing a soft voile frock and the sun was on her hair which she wore long, like a young girl. A fine glowing fold of it mesmerising the gold light. He went towards her, uneasily, thinking he must say how nice the flowers were, and how the violas would float about the dining room like spindrift on the subdued tide of curtained light; and it wasn't so today. Flowers were silly today, meaningless ineffectual things that made no difference. He felt exasperated that she should be picking flowers and thinking of their tones and scents and of how they would merge into and symbolise the thoughtfulness of the quiet rooms. What was it all about?

She heard his step and looked up swiftly. Her smile was so spontaneous that his heart jumped, scattering his humours. Flowers were all forgotten.

"Hallo, chips," she said, and with the long scissors she pretended to cut off his ear. "How's school?"

"School?" he said, and laughed. He dropped his satchel on the lawn.

"D'you really want to know about school?"

"Of course," she said. "I want to know about everything

you do."

"Well," he said, "Old Bones said my essay on Keats's Ode to a Grecian Urn was very fresh. He said he expected me to get a distinction in Higher English next month."

"So do I," she said, looking levelly at him. "I'm not worrying about your result. It's whether you'll get a State Scholarship or not that worries me. You should get it in English and History. It's your Latin I'm doubtful about."

"Latin," he said. "Oh, never mind about Latin. It's such a cold old subject."

"It isn't cold if it gets you a State Schol," she said. "Because that means Oxford, or London. Wouldn't it be marvellous?"

She embarrassed him, the way she grew so happy and her eyes so sort of light, like fresh water, when she talked about his future like that.

He felt himself grow serious and arid again.

"Think of the things you'd have to tell me when you came home for vacation from Oxford," she said. She laughed and touched his sleeve. "Don't you think it was nice of old Bones to say your essay was *fresh*?" she said. "It's the nicest quality in the world, I think."

He pulled his arm away with a curt gesture.

"That was about Keats," he said, turning away and picking up his bag, "You can say things about Keats because his poems are – oh, I don't know, – they're *different* from every day."

She watched him and then in her cool voice said quietly, "It's because you half realise that difference that I think you'll get a State Schol, Morlais."

"I don't know what you mean," he said, palely.

"What's happened today, then?" she said.

He looked at her for a long moment, and he knew his eyes were daring her, defying her, to probe again with a closer question. She met his look and her face flickered with anxiety, her eyes darkened and she turned away.

"Well, you'd better go and have a bath," she said. "The rim of your collar is soiled as if you've been sweating."

"I thought of having a bath," he said. "Is there time before tea?"

"Yes, if you hurry. I'll put these flowers in the vases. They fade so quickly in this dry weather."

Tea was indoors, for the wind was chilly to sit about in. She was reading his dog-eared school text of Keats' Poems of 1820 when he came down. He felt strong and hungry, his flesh tingling with the cold water and the rough towel.

"D'you know what happened in Latin today?" he said.

She put the book down and took the cosy off the silver teapot.

"No idea," she said.

He watched her pour the tea, a fluted arching rod of fluid bronze. There was a little bone pressing against the white smoothness of her wrist when she held the pot up like that. He took a scone.

"Well, I had a free period and I was nearly sleeping, so I decided to do something nasty to keep awake," he said. "Don't put any milk in, Mums, it spoils the colour. So I started going over Lucretius for Higher. And d'you know, that cold dead old Latin, all hard words and meanings you can't get at, d'you know what I found"

"What?" she said eagerly, catching his mood.

"Two lines all about the spring. Today's spring, you know. Just like our garden. It said that spring comes in sweetly with sap in the trees and paints the green grass with flowers. I never thought old Lucretius saw the green grass like that. I didn't think there would be green grass then, somehow."

"Oh, there've always been poets," she said.

"Yes, but it's such a long time ago, isn't it?"

"Time?" she said after a pause. "Time is what the clocks tick, and what our bodies feel getting a grip on them. That's all. It isn't the real spring of life, though."

" Well, you wouldn't think a moment like that could have lived all the centuries it has, and then actually happened again," he said, not really following her thought. "It *did* happen, in that stuffy sixth form room. I *felt* it."

"Yes, I know you did," she said. "You're growing up now. You will feel things that are past from now on."

Her words pierced him with a hot deep thrill, as though something had happened, changing him – not clarifying, but in an obscure and frightening way complicating his being; as though he had come into an inheritance that he couldn't renounce.

He stirred his teacup, watching the leaves swirl in the submerged autumn, the spoon gleaming like an archangel's sword.

"Do things matter when they've finished, then?" he asked. She laughed.

"Yes," she said abruptly.

"For everybody?"

"Everybody."

"Supposing you forget them – they can't matter, then, can they?"

"Sometimes they matter more if you forget them," she said.

"But how? If you forget them, they're gone, aren't they?"

"If you forget a thing it means that you didn't live that thing, didn't understand it, didn't let it become part of yourself," she said, slowly. "And if the thing you've forgotten was an important thing, well, it's like forgetting to eat – you get thin and anaemic and –"

"You forget a lot of things, don't you?" he said suddenly. She winced.

"Why d'you say that?" she asked.

"You don't talk about when you were a girl, or about your mother and father, do you?"

She laughed.

"Don't I? Well, when your own life becomes so boring that we're tired of talking about it, and a day comes when nothing happens at all, I'll tell you about my mother and my father," she said.

She poured herself a second cup of tea.

"I was thinking what they looked like," he said, frowning at his teacup

"Did they look, – did your mother look thin like mine?"

"I've only seen a faded photograph of her," she said.

"I expect she was very pretty," he said suddenly. And then, as if his words had caught him unawares, he stood up and put his cup back on the tea wagon. "Well, I'm going to do some homework," he said, flushing.

She didn't look up.

"Yes," she said. "Don't let that State schol slip out of your hands."

"Oh that," he said impatiently. The clock chimed six mellow notes, softly, like the violas on the deal reading table.

"Your foster-father's very late this evening," she said, looking out through the window at the yellow-saturated lawn, the sunset caught between the grass and the threat of fine rain.

The kitchen door clicked across the house and they both turned to face the door by which he would enter.

"Hallo," said Mr Reames, walking in so that the quiet swirled round his oil-stained mackintosh. "Still at tea, you two?"

She stood up with a silk rustle of stockings and frock and thighs and Morlais felt himself forgotten for that instant as she tilted her head back and his mouth brushed against her closed lips.

She was holding him by the lapels of his mackintosh and standing back from him a little.

"Yes, I know," he said. "I'll be ruining your polished floor with my hobnails. Never mind just this once. Is the tea cold?"

"I'll get you a fresh pot," she said.

"No, don't go," he said. "Morlais will fetch it."

Morlais took the silver teapot from the wagon. As he was going out he saw a long blue bruise under Mr Reames's eye, raw skin and discoloured cheek.

"What have you done to your cheek?" Morlais asked.

"Oh, Denis," she said. "What is it? I hadn't seen." He hesitated. Morlais stood stock still, teapot in hand.

"Have you banged it against something?" she asked.

"No," he said. He wiped his forehead wearily with his dirty hand.

"A man was killed by a fall an hour ago," he said. He paused. "One of the rescue party hit me with his fist, when we'd put the body into the ambulance."

"Oh," she breathed, shuddering and seeming to dwindle, to crumple.

"Fetch that tea, Morlais," he said. "Put three teaspoonfuls in."

His face was working; the bruise glowed against his dead white.

Morlais didn't move for a second. They all three stood woodenly and the room was still, all heavy and sick, as if what he had just said had embalmed movement in a locked intensity. Then the clock whirred softly, a flutter of wings, and the quarter stroke was released. The moment touched time, the invisible harp resolving the tension by dissolving them in a single chord. Morlais walked to the door, opened it, and went down the quiet passage to the kitchen. A rustle of silk behind him as she felt for her chair and sat down in it; Maggie's voice crooning and muffled by the closed kitchen door ahead of him; he feeling nothing.

He opened the kitchen door and Maggie turned round quickly, her mouth open in the middle of a note.

"Oh, it's only you," she said, and grinned, and went on singing. "The moon was new, but Love was old –"

"Oh shut up," he said sharply.

"What's the matter with you, Lord Muck?" she said with lazy tolerance. "Can't I sing in my own kitchen if I want to?"

"Make a fresh pot of tea," he said.

"Oh alright," she pouted. "Anything to oblige, I'm sure? What's up? Been 'aving a row or what?"

"No," he said.

"Feeling bad, then?"

"No, for God's sake."

She stopped grinning.

"What's the matter, say?" she asked.

"A man's been killed underground."

The shoe she was cleaning dropped from her hand. To prevent that horrible moment of immobility recurring, he spoke quickly.

"Will you take the teapot in?" he said. "I'm going out."

"Who was it?" she asked.

Her mouth was still open. He looked at the fillings in her teeth.

"I don't know," he said. "You'd better ask him yourself."

The kettle bubbled its brass lid up and dribbled boiling water with a hiss onto the fire.

"Damn you," she said, springing up and snatching the kettle off the fire, "spoiling my clean fender. Wonder who it was."

She sat down again.

"Hurry up and take him that tea," he said.

"Oh *alright*," she flashed. She emptied the dregs from the pot. "Let him wait a bit. It's the third death in twelve months. Fetch 'is own tea."

Morlais left her and went quietly past the half-open door of the front room and tiptoed upstairs. In his own room, with the door closed behind him, his body lost its tension. His shoulders dropped, his mouth went lax, his hands hung limply. He stood still, swaying slightly, the books in front of him a red blur. Lifting his eyes he caught sight of himself in the gleaming wardrobe mirror. The sun was on his face, streaming through the window. In the ivy sparrows were insensately chattering.

"Shut up," he said. He walked to the mirror and stared at himself.

"You fool," he said.

The dull face twisted its mouth scornfully. He considered its brown eyes.

"What the hell are you here for?" he said.

"Oh God, stop it."

He flung himself away from the icy contemplation and dropped onto his bed. He shut his face into the blue quilt.

"Oh, stop it," he said thickly.

He turned onto his side and seeing a Palgrave's Golden Treasury by his bedside picked it up and opened it at random.

"Like as the waves make toward the pebbled shore,
Since it must be, come, let us kiss and part.
Nay, I have done.."
"Fair daffodils, we weep to see
You haste away so soon..."
"Thee, sitting careless on the granary floor,
Thy hair soft-lifted by the winnowing wind,
Or on a half-reaped furrow..."
"Thy sweet child Sleep, the filmy-eyed,
Murmuring like a noon-tide bee...."

He slammed the book shut and dropped it onto the floor.

"Oh God," he said, and standing up suddenly he pulled his coat tidy and pressed his face against the window. The garden glowed below and all about him, neat and familiar and untroubled, the boles of the apple-trees daubed with lime, the potato rows touched with blue flowers, the figs a swollen hard green against the mellowing wall. And beyond the garden the swoop of mountain, an unfaltering curve like a newly whetted scythe, like a swallow's flight carved out in black immovable rock. And the evening sky pouring down on it in green foam. He watched a flight of sea gulls sail with steady wings into the clear sparkle of that distance, seeing them grow black and dwindle and disappear, leaving the sky and the distance for his mood to resolve itself into. The taut contradictions disintegrated, fell apart, and as he gazed and gazed at the pellucid reach they took flight one by one, without sound, and he watched the second flight of gulls dwindle and vanish away, seeking the sea and a calm season.

He went out through the garden door without anyone seeing him, and crossed the field behind the house. It was so quiet, everything. An engine shunting, the clank of couplings, disconnected sounds, a blackbird running between the hawthorns, children shouting from a long distance. He crossed the meadow, taking care first of all that the farmer wasn't about. He felt strange and new, sneaking through these coverts of childhood, past the chestnut tree where conkers were to be found in autumn. His senses thrilled, his fingers delighting in the touch of rough bole and veined leaf and wire fence. Soon he was across the river, and the asphalt path where they walked on Sundays, and striking through the gorse for the high crest of rocks on the mountain. He was laughing and breathless when he reached them, and sprawled on his belly in the whins. It was too early for the berries...

After a while he stood up and began strolling along the brow of the hill, walking down towards Glannant, the way the river was flowing the way the valley fell.

Morlais followed a sheep track along the crest, his shoes crackling against the lusty short grass. The track skirted a broken stone wall enclosing the high field where the children played football on Saturdays; and, remembering the distant

Christmas when he had been given a football and had immediately run out into the street before breakfast to arrange with the gang for a game after dinner on the mountain, he was tempted to cross the wall and kick an imaginary football there again. Instead he walked on, wondering why there should be a wall on the mountain when there was no pasture land to fence in and the whins had wasted the whole stretch of upland. He wondered at the wall, and at the other walls on the sheer reaches across the valley. And then he remembered the chapter in the Welsh History book they did for Senior which described Welsh farming in the Eighteenth Century. It said something there – something boring it had been, something to be tediously learned and reproduced, something dead and dry – about Enclosures, enclosing land for pasturing sheep in order to get more wool. The great landowners had enclosed their land, he thought. He tried to recall the page, or the notes he had made for homework. Dimly it came back: *Effects of Enclosure Movement*: small tenant farmers lost their right to common pasture and so could not keep their own sheep, etc. Forced to leave the land and find employment in the coal and iron mines then being developed in Merthyr, etc. He stood still, breathing deeply the air of the mountain and stretching his arms back to inflate his chest. And he saw this valley in which he had always lived in a way he had never seen it before. His eyes saw it intensely and the sight of it made his heart pound. It was so narrow and deep; the mountains possessed it, overpowered it. It was theirs, this narrow valley with its straggle of grey streets, its ruck of railway sidings where the timber was stacked and the coal trucks waited, its tips and its colliery whose great wheel seemed so tiny. The mountains had mastery, the vast power of silence, the huge upward sweep of fern and rock and swart grass. Scanty pasture they gave to the skinny sheep and the wild ponies; great silent misers hoarding their silence through the centuries. Build walls on their tremendous flanks; the walls crumble. Scar and pock their sides, quarrying coal and sinking pits; let men come like flies about the dark wound and clip the torn flesh with steel, make it fester with their picks and drills and streets; no matter. The farm down there, halfway up the mountain; that was older than the pit or the village. Yet how insecure its tenure, clinging with its white-washed cowsheds and muddy yard in poverty to the mountain. And the perpetual flux of people, coming, going, meaning less than the farm, less than the pit, less even than the sheep that found shelter among the green rocks in wild weather – he began running, leaping from tuft to tuft, and laughing and sobbing for breath. If he wanted to he could have leaped across the valley, landing on the crest of the opposite range. He had found the three league boots of the giant who inhabited the mountains; he had pulled them on and they fitted him. He stretched his arms back as he leaped, tilting his head back so that the sky came down softly in veils and perfumes and opened, half opened its azure lips and smiled, and the sunset brushed against his mouth. So he found that the mountains held in their silence the secret of love, and their love was for the blue sky, the infinite, intangible feminine, the termagant of winter. He flung his arms round the twisted bole of a thorn that squatted on the very brim of the mountain. And he saw how dwarfish and stunted it was, all its branches bent in the direction the wind blew, the wind that was the temper of the silent strife of mountain and sky, the gusty passions of eternity. He felt the scars and knots in the broken bark and ran his hand along the bowed branches, testing their strength, pricking his finger on their stubborn thorns. And he thought of his father. And then he thought of the children going to school in winter, and remembering his mother warning him against the bitter wind. Before he left the house she buttoned his overcoat round him, fastened his gaiters with the button hook he couldn't manipulate, and told him to run all the way and save his knees chapping. But this thorn stood alone against all the long assault, and put its leaves out in spring and held its silence. That was his father. He tried to tear a branch off, but it wouldn't give. So he left it and followed the path through an ancient upheaval of rocks, down the steep side of the valley towards the farm and the row of mining cottages that ran from the farm to the village. And as soon as he had begun descending the slope he lost himself, being once more in Glannant, going down into it again and no longer immune to the power it had to hurt.

The path he was descending went past the yard of Ffynnon Wen farm and ended where Mountain Row began. Mountain Row consisted of twenty miner's cottages with walls of wood and roofs of corrugated iron covered with felting. They were inhabited by the poorest families in Glannant; two of them were empty and windowless, the others rickety and in disrepair, their occupants for the most part old people or improvidents. The fronts faced on to a rough lane of ashes which was continually reinforced by the daily emptying of yesterday's fires. The backs were against the mountain and the scanty gardens whose rocky soil afforded little opportunity for cultivation sloped steeply up the hillside to the lane, from which it was separated by a tumbledown wall embattlemented with lavatories which were for the most part doorless. The cottages were on the land of Ffynon Wen, the farm which supplied milk to most of the villagers. Mountain Row was a favourite place for the children, who climbed the stony track from the village and played endless games in the stream that bubbled out of the rock just above the row. It was also the trysting place of the gamblers who assembled every Sunday to play an afternoon's crap or poker in the quarry while one of the small boys stood on watch for the police. But the decent people never went that way. Their Sunday walks followed the river level, along the asphalt path that ran alongside the river to the top of the valley. So Mountain Row lived quietly alone and exalted on the stony hillside, and its occupants were known as a mixed lot – a couple of the boys were good footballers; they were O.K.; – a few of the elders were respectable chapel-goers; nothing against them; – as for the rest, they were Mountain Row. If they broke their legs going home after the pubs shut that was their own lookout. And if they whistled after the lovers who went that way in search of the heather, well, no decent boy would take his girl that way. But Morlais had always dreamed of living up there on the mountain. In the elementary school he had regarded Nan Blackmore with constant envy because she lived in Ffynnon Wen. As if living on the mountain wasn't enough, she had a real farm to live in as well, with cows, real cows, and ducks and a mare and sometimes a grey little foal that never let him feed it but came placidly to her hand and nuzzled at the lump of sugar in her palm. She used to take him to see the foal every time they had a new one, and she didn't half lord it over him when he nearly popped out of his skin with vain wheedling of the lanky little beast and then had to stand and feel vicariously the soft tickle of the sensitive nostrils and wet mouth in her hand. Nan wasn't like the rest of them in school. Living on a farm made her different somehow. She never played games in the playground and she hadn't got a gang for the nights to meet in the back lanes and play scotch. But she was at home on the farm and Morlais loved following her around the sheds and asking endless questions which she patiently answered. She was in the County School now, doing Higher as he was. The boys' and girls' schools were at opposite ends of the town, but the Glannant children travelled home on the same bus sometimes. Morlais never spoke to her, and both of them avoided each other's looks. He didn't know why, but somehow they did. She was mostly reading in the bus coming home and going to school. She must be still the same, not mixing up.

Swinging down the path towards Ffynnnn Wen Morlais wondered whether Nan would be in the farm yard. The cows were grazing in the pale green field below the farm; probably they'd been milked already. In that case Nan might be taking milk down to the village, or sitting at her books. Most likely swotting at her books, as he ought to be doing, with Higher only three weeks ahead, and so much depending upon the result – Oxford even, perhaps. No, he wouldn't see her; didn't want to see her, either. He only went hot and sticky when he bumped past her and fumbled clumsily with his hands. Oxford, perhaps.

When he was about two hundred yards away from the farm something silent about it made him stop. He had been looking at it all the way down; it seemed dead; no sound or motion, none of the life that a farm always has. He felt apprehensive, and all the more so because there was no reason for the cold feeling under his skin. It was probably because it was a house, and he had been high up on the mountain beyond life, and coming back to it like an outcast forced to seek re-admittance – but it was so cold, the sun gone from it and the whitewashed walls grey and neutral, repellent. He began to run, stumbling on the piled flints of the path and twisting his ankle in a sudden water rut. He certainly had better get home and do some work before supper; he hadn't even told Mums he was going out. She'd probably be a bit distant with him; she took everything so *personally* somehow. And then, just opposite the farm with the lane overlooking the open kitchen door, he saw – and stopped as if a hand had caught hold of him – the legs of a man laid out on the table in the big stone-flagged kitchen. Oh God. He saw the ugly bruise under Mr Reames's eye, and felt the cold thud inside him that a man had been killed. And here it was, this time unavoidable. Not her father, for he worked on the farm since he touched sixty. Her brother it would be, Luther, who sang at the chapel Eisteddfodau and had won all those cups they had in the parlour.

At that moment Nan Blackmore came out through the kitchen door and there was such a bounding in him that for a moment he couldn't breathe. She was in her navy blue gym slip and white school blouse, her slim legs black-stockinged. Because of the smallness of her face and the shortness of her skirt and the floating out of her wavy hair her legs seemed lanky, like a foal's legs. She walked in a dazed automatic way, but when she saw him standing in the lane above her she looked at him with a slow and unembarrassed recognition, and smiled. He stared seriously back. She had begun to walk towards the cowsheds, but turned and crossed the yard towards him, walking through the slushy dung, not picking her way from white stone to white stone at all. He came down off the lane and unlatched the five-barred gate and entered the yard,

"Hallo, Morlais."

He looked at her and looked at her and turned his head away, seeing beyond her in a mist her dim eyes.

"Luther's dead," she said. Her voice was tiny.

He looked at the badges on her blouse – Head Girl, Hockey Eleven, L.N.U., the pretty blue badge with a delightful quintet of continents framed within its old-fashioned oval, like a locket.

He swallowed the shiver that hacked at his throat.

"He was dead when they brought him," she said.

"Oh –" he put out his hand to touch hers. His hand stopped halfway and was like a monkey's paw begging and then dropped to his side out of sight.

"He said his district was dangerous," she said, "and I wanted him to come out and work on the farm. There's enough work here for him,"

"I'm sorry, Nan."

"Will you come in and see him?"

"Yes," he replied, sweating.

He walked by her side across the yard, through all the muck. At the kitchen porch he wiped his shoes on the iron scraper. She walked straight in. A girl passing through the clarity of a dream to the darkness in which the dream both ended and began. He followed her into the kitchen. Mrs Jones Working-clothes was there, in a white apron with sleeves rolled up. An enamel bowl of water now luke and dirty was in her red hands. She puffed breath out with a contented whistle, her work well done. Two other women were there, wrapped in black shawls of loosely knitted wool, sitting with long faces by the fire, warming their worn-out soles; and the mother standing by the table, gaunt and grey with a long thin face and fallen hands. Morlais stood by the door.

"Come in," Nan said. "Morlais Jenkins, Mam."

She lifted her dull eyes and said "Come on in, Morlais."

He remembered her on a cold winter day washing a great wooden vat in the yard with quick knotted hands and singing a bit here and there in contralto part while Luther's tenor made the kitchen merry inside the raw day. Her hair was grey then, and she was lean; she didn't seem to notice the winter.

Luther was washed and in pyjamas, his head pitted in a white soft pillow, his eyes closed.

Morlais took a step into the room, just entering the dusk under the heavy-raftered ceiling.

"Come on in, bach," Mrs Jones Working-clothes said, "there's nothing to be afraid of, for certain."

She put the bowl onto the settle.

"I'll tip the water out now," she said. "only take off this pinny first."

"Aye, indeed," said one of the middle-aged women by the fire, rocking to and fro in the deep old chair, "'tis the Lord God Jehovah 'ave willed it and only bow our 'eads we can."

She dabbed her eyes with the corner of a cloth she was using as a handkerchief. She was one of the Chapel people from down the Row, Mrs Tomos Carmarthen, a decent respectable body doing the least she could do.

"Oh, 'tis a terrible thing, a young man taken like that," she said, rocking herself, "a lovely voice on 'im and all."

"Aye, a champion voice," Mrs Jones Working-clothes said, taking the bowl of dirty water from the settle and shuffling towards the door.

"To 'ear 'im singing them choraleys."

She clucked her tongue like a duck prodding the mud at the pond's edge with its bill.

"It's a scandal and a sin," the third woman said loudly, standing up and pulling her shawl closer round her shrivelled bosom. "They do put up pitprops no better than matchsticks and rotting in the damp down there, our Will do say. And it's a cruel shame for a fine boy like Luther by there to be kilt along of their meanness. It is, indeed."

She crossed to the table, dragging her feet; and standing over him like a pillar of salt and then nodding her head slowly.

"It's wicked," she said, and then, "there's a beautiful face it is, too."

She put out her hand to touch his hair. Mrs Blackmore suddenly swept that hand away.

"Get back, Moriah Griffiths," she said, "and leave 'im be. And keep quiet. You'd be quiet enough if it was your own son was there."

Mrs Griffiths stepped back with a jump, offended but silent, and sat down in her chair again, and looked into the fire.

Mrs Blackmore went to the wooden settle and sat down. She sat very stiffly, then sagged a little, and gasped sharply, clutching at herself and crumpling.

"Oh, merched," Mrs Tomos Carmarthen exclaimed, jumping out of her chair and bending over her.

"Leave 'er 'ave it out, poor thing," sighed Mrs Griffiths. "It's what she needs. It will better 'er condition, always."

Nan looked at her mother bewildered and walked to the door, putting both hands against the doorpost and laying her cheek on it.

Morlais stepped to her and stood a moment in the

doorway.

"I'm going now, Nan," he said. He touched her sleeve. "God bless you."

Then he saw she was weeping soundlessly and he stood there not knowing what in his agony to do.

"Nan bach," his mother said, suddenly standing there in her best black coat and shiny Sunday hat and seeing him with a single look as she put her hand gently on the girl's shoulder. "Don't you break yourself now, there's a good girl."

"But he won't speak any more," Nan said in a thin incredulous voice, and turning into Mrs Jenkins's arms blindly gave herself to her grief.

Mrs Jenkins let her rest there, and when her shoulders shook only convulsively in a deep stillness led her into the kitchen while Morlais waited outside. He leaned against the wall, forehead almost touching the whitewash, pressing his uplifted knee against it and his hooked knuckles.

After a few minutes his mother came out from the kitchen and he stood up to face her.

She put her hand on his sleeve and looked at him.

"Better get down from here now," she said. "It's no use doing anything now, only leave them be. Coming down Mountain Row?"

"Yes," he said.

He turned and accompanied her down the rocky path towards the first houses, falling into her slow pace.

"My feet 'ave gone soft a bit underneath," she apologised. "I got to walk careful."

"What is it, Mam?" he said anxiously.

"Oh, it's nothing to complain about," she said. "Standing on them too much, I 'spect, and this hot weather we been 'aving."

"You ought to stay in bed for a few days," he said.

"Likely," she laughed. "With Doris gone and your father and Dilwyn coming 'ome 'ungry as bears every tea time, and

Hetty wolfing it, too – fine row they'd make if their dinner wasn't on the table for them."

"Well, you ought to stay in bed," he said stubbornly.

"Oh, poof," she said. "What are we talking about a little thing like bad feet for, with that poor boy up there?"

After a silence Morlais said, "Is it right that the pitprops aren't safe, Mam?"

She lifted her foot carefully over a jagged stone, peering at the path which the dusk was slowly blurring.

"Luther was kilt by a fall, whatever," she said.

"But surely, Mam, the company wouldn't do a thing like that?"

"I don't know what," she said. "The men is all grumbling, anyroads. The pit is getting wet and they getting rheumatics. And not working their full turns neither, for the sidings are full of loaded trucks with no buyer."

"Well, they ought to be glad of a rest. I wouldn't mind an afternoon off from school once a week."

"Neither would they, I don't doubt, if they was paid the minimum wage. But it's only the shifts they work or the coal they cut that they get paid for these days."

Her voice was bitter, like a stain of lemon in the gathering darkness.

"But they can ask for their minimum, can't they?"

"Aye, they can ask. They'll get it, too. And the sack with it."

He stopped, catching her loose sleeve tightly.

"It isn't true, Mam," he said, "it isn't true. You don't know. Really, Mam, Mr Reames is always at the colliery. It's his *life*. He'd never treat the men like that. I know he wouldn't. He isn't like that."

"Alright, bach," she said, patting his taut hand. "Leave it be now. We don't neither of us know for certain anything, do we? Come on, it's getting too dark to see, and Hetty'll be getting frightened by herself in the kitchen."

"But it's terrible," he said.

"Yes, it's bad, indeed. Pity this thing should 'appen just now. It's putting the tin 'at on it. Dad gulped 'is dinner down today too much in a hurry to say two sentences, all because of a meeting the men are 'aving with the Federation leaders tonight in the Lesser Hall."

"I wish I was working underground," he said passionately.

"Don't talk so silly," she said. "What d'you want to live a pig's life for, mun? You get out of it with all your might, my boy."

"Get out of it?" he said, and walked on a few paces without saying any more.

"You got a fine chance," she said. "It's the only reason I'm not sorry you're living in the big 'ouse. You got a chance to get out of it all."

"No, I haven't," he said, clenching his teeth with the strife that was in him. "I'm here, *here*."

"No, you're not; not for good," she said sharply, stamping her foot. "Ooh, my foot, I forgot. No, you keep at your lessons now, and go to College, see?" She stood in his path and commanded his eyes with her burning ones. "You go on, see? You'll be a teacher, or a minister, something where you can be yourself, see?"

"I want to come home with you, that's all I want," he said quietly.

She caught her breath; he sensed her hardening.

"Don't be daft," she said curtly. "We don't want you."

"No, I know that," he said bitterly. "That was plain enough at the wedding this morning."

"Don't talk about that now," she said, her voice shaking. "Come on, Mor, let's get off this old mountain. I don't see you enough to waste time quarreling with you. Come on, there's a good boy. Hetty'll be getting frantic."

She pulled his sleeve gently and he went obediently with her, slowly descending the steep track to the dark village.

He left her at the bottom of Glannant Street and took his

usual way home along the back lane, which was all in dusk and silence, except for the sound of a gramophone coming tinnily from a back kitchen and the clatter of an empty meat tin overturned by a cat seeking scraps among the ash buckets. He walked slowly up the drive and entered through the slightly opened French window from which a swathe of light fell upon the foam of the hydrangeas.

"Hallo," he said abruptly, standing blinking in the light.

She put her sewing aside and looked up quickly.

"Hallo," she said, pale and serious although she smiled. "You're late, Morlais."

"I'm sixteen," he said shortly.

She bent her head to her sewing.

Her silence flustered him.

"Where's Dad?" he asked.

"Underground," she replied. "The mines inspector came up. He happened to be in Tredwr."

"He's got the wind up then," he said cruelly.

She whipped in a sharp breath and lifted her head slowly.

"What did you say?" she asked.

He felt something inside him inflating, in his head, in his lungs, and his hands began to quiver.

"D'you know what they say?" he began, tight-lipped. "They say the pit is a death trap and the management ought to be summoned for not putting good props in and draining it properly. They say *that*."

"Who?"

He hesitated, then snapped, "My mother."

She turned again to her sowing, but only stuck the needle in the hem of the silk frock she was altering and did not complete the stitch.

He looked at her and he went all black, great bubbles of black coming up into his head, making him whirl feverishly.

"The company won't allow any more money for repairs," she said. "They say the pit isn't paying, that they can't get orders for the coal, that the coal is too stony, and that we've got to use the props that have been stacked in the sidings for the last three years – you remember they got a huge consignment in when they thought of opening a new seam, and then decided not to, because of the general strike."

He listened to the end of her quiet statement and then turned away from her and walked towards the window.

"It isn't Denis's fault, Morlais," she said. "He hates it. He worries and worries, half the night he doesn't sleep –"

He turned to face her.

"He ought to resign," he said.

She returned his stare.

"Life isn't as easy as that," she answered levelly.

He spoke with a wrench of words, out of intense knowledge.

"I saw the dead man."

His lip trembled and then his face broke and he put his wet forehead against the milk-veined black marble mantelpiece.

In the dark and the silence he spoke: "The men are right. They are right."

She hadn't moved. She said "It isn't a question of right or wrong. It's a question of what some people have got to do, and of what others refuse to do. Business, organisation, capital and labour."

"It isn't," he shouted, brushing away the words he didn't understand.

"It's murder, that's what it is. Murder."

"Morlais," she said, standing up. "Please do this for me. Don't think about this till tomorrow. Or till after your exams."

"Exams?" he said feverishly. "Exams. I've finished with exams. They're daft. I don't want to pass exams. Nor go to college, I don't want to –" he waved his hand in the air hysterically.

"Morlais, Morlais," she took the lapels of his coat and made him look at her close to, "Don't talk about it now, dear.

Go to bed and sleep."

"I don't want to," he said, gasping for breath, "I want to go."

"Go where?" she asked softly.

"Home," he said, then screwed his eyes tight and in the same breath said "No, I don't know where. Nowhere – there's nobody wants me."

"Oh, dear, dear. You silly little boy." She had pulled his head into her breast and smoothed the high crown of his head with her palm.

"How many times would youth throw away its life if doing so was as easy as wishing to do so, I want you, don't I? I want you to do well, and grow up to a true life. And I know you're made of the right stuff, too. Let's make a cup of cocoa each and go to bed, shall we?"

"But I can't go," he said, his voice almost a scream despite its quietness. "I *can't*."

She could feel the tautness of his body, its knotting.

"Listen," she said. "You say you can't because you feel how hard it is. You're sensitive, more than most. Did you know that?"

"I don't know," he said, more calmly.

She waited a moment.

"Some people call it weakness," she continued, very slowly, speaking from deep in herself. "And it is weakness, too, if you haven't got the courage to endure it and turn it to profit. But without it nobody would do anything worth while. It's the power of understanding, a terrible power. As long as you're not brittle, and don't snap, or sneak away from people because it hurts you too much to love them, or be loved by them; as long as you've got the power to love in your flesh, in your blood and body, then you'll be doing good all the time; even when you think you've failed you'll be doing good."

The cool scent of lavender upon silk, the quiet of the room, the stillness of her voice and the power of her quiet words which lived their own life soothed him, calmed him.

"Well, don't bother about finding another bed tonight when there's an empty one upstairs you might as well use," she said, laughter colouring her voice. "Nobody else will use it."

He moved away from her, and as he let her hands go he squeezed them.

"Goodnight," he said, trying to smile and feeling his skin tight.

"Don't you want some cocoa?"

"No, I think I'll go and sleep."

"Alright, dear. I'll wait for Denis. Goodnight."

As he was opening the door she called him.

"Morlais. Where does that boy live? The one who was –"

"Ffynnon Wen farm, above Mountain Row. Blackmore. Why?"

"I'd like to call there."

He fiddled the glass door knob round.

"If you wait till after school I'll come with you," he said after a long pause. "I know one of them well. At least, not well, but –"

She was radiant.

"If you would come –" she said.

He frowned again.

"Luther his name is," he said. "Well, goodnight."

"Goodnight."

The last sight of her, standing with the sweet lamp light moulding her look into lasting marble, remained clearly transferred to his mind, even when his eyes closed in prayer for sleep, and in the darkness of his mind's house she moved among other people with the soft rustle of silk, till she became identified with a girl in black stockings and gym slip and a frail wasted woman in a black coat and shiny hat, and they in their turn became a man lying upon a kitchen table, and that man was himself, asleep.

Three weeks later Morlais came down over the rock outcrop above the village with the sun tingling his cheek. He breathed great exalted gulps of the mountain air and his mind was washed clean after the walk home alone from school along the mile of green track whence nothing but the wheeling rims of sunlit mountains and wave after wave of cloud-patched green could be seen. His satchel slung across his back hung lightly; there was no need for books in the evenings any more, now he had sat his last exam paper in the Higher Certificate. Over-work and relief and the upland brightness all combined to make him light-headed and exultant. Exams finished, and freedom to let the high summer flow in through the rocky inlets of his being, and the grass springy and strong under his rubber soles.

He had bought a block of chocolate in town and eaten it as he climbed through the alder groves up the mountain side. Now he didn't feel like going straight home to the Elms to eat the dinner that was waiting him in the oven – warmed up steak or perhaps a fresh green salad in a cut glass bowl and celery in the green vase. Anyway he didn't want to go indoors, and go over his answers to the literature questions with her and argue about Wordsworth's nature poems or Shelley's contribution to the Romantics. Shelley had a boat, and went sailing, didn't he? And sat among the Euganean Hills? Well, then, here was his great schooner, the black prow of rock and the thistle-down sails. And the lovers, as he remembered them that last-first walk of three weeks past, mountain and sky together lying, Zephyr with Aurora playing, and the sky larks too high to be discerned, eyes dazzled with seeking the black point of song.

So he sat down on the sun-ripened rock, quiet in the hope of seeing a fox trot past, a streak of autumn through the green uncurled ferns; and quietly he saw the grey streets in the lower reach of the valley, the sun flashing from the cheap ferro-concrete council houses above the park where the gramophone blared the Desert Song, the long ruck of sidings and stacked pitprops that looked no bigger than matchsticks, the turning wheel above the pitshaft bringing the men up to the surface, and at the top of Glannant Street the red gables of the Elms standing haughtily in their private greenery. He could see Nan Blackmore's white-washed farm, spare and clean in its oasis of watery green, and his father's house where Hetty would be revising for terminals. And he went happily down the steep path that cut a zig-zag scar of red flint from tip to toe of the sun-steeped slope and ended at the gate of Ffynnon Wen, which in English means White Well.

Nan was carrying a pail of milk across the yard. She put the pail down and smiled when he whistled from the path. He waited by the gate, his blood pulsing at the temerity of his whistle, and pulled a long white splinter out of the top bar.

"Hallo," she said, "walked home from school?"

His eyes were abashed as if the sun's glare were beating them down. She too lowered her eyes and rubbed an inkstain off her fingers with her handkerchief.

"Yes," he replied. "You ought to walk home these afternoons, too. It's marvellous."

"I don't feel like walking much," she said. "Besides, I've got to get home quickly and help Mam with the milk. Dad's gone back underground again, since – since our Luther died."

He dug his thumbnail into the white wound of the splintered bar, and blood spurted under his nail.

"It's terrible," he said.

She stretched her handkerchief out between her fine hands.

"There was a fine crowd at his funeral, wasn't there?"

He shuddered, wondered how she could sound almost pleased.

"All the colliers, and the president of the Federation, and all the chapels, and all our relations. My uncle came from

Cardigan, 'specially'," she said. "Mam and I were cutting bread and boiling water all night."

He wanted to overwhelm her with salt and swollen pity, but some effulgence, some serenity lighting her delicate features quietly, baffled and abashed him. He felt angry with himself, uneasy to be there talking to her.

"Everybody liked our Luther," she said. "It cost us over £20."

"Did it?" he said, stonily. And then half-heartedly he asked, "How have you done in Higher exams?"

She shrugged her shoulders and smiled.

"So-so. I didn't like the English lit. paper, though."

"Didn't you?" he said. "I thought it was the best of the lot."

"Oh well, it would be for you. You're brainy. Your poem in the school magazine last term, about spring, I thought it was heaps better than all that stuff Wordsworth and those wrote."

He flushed, at once pleased and embarrassed and slightly contemptuous.

"Go on," he said, "I'm brainy, indeed. I'm thick."

"Alright, Mr Modest," she teased, laughing at him with her velvety eyes. "Have it your own way."

Her words came so freely, warmly, smilingly, that he dropped his gaze.

"Your – you know, Mrs Reames, she called here the day after the accident," she said.

"Did she?"

"I think she's awfully sweet. Doesn't she dress in perfect taste?"

He laughed.

"I don't know, I'm sure. Yes, I suppose so," he said, flushing at the sudden thought of how different his mother looked. "She does dress nicely." He paused. "She can afford to."

"I wonder, did you choose that herring bone tweed of your sports coat, or did she?" Nan said.

He laugher clumsily and looked at his jacket.

"This thing?" he said, grinning self-consciously.

"It's a lovely colour," she said. And she actually put her fingers on his sleeve and ran them down his forearm to get the feel of the cloth. "I hate the flashy navy suite the collier boys dress in. Like dancing partners I always think."

"What college are you going to?" he asked.

"Me?" She opened her eyes wide and shrugged her slim shoulders deprecatingly. "I'm not going to any college."

"What?" he gasped. "But of course you are. After doing Higher you wouldn't throw it all away."

"What d'you mean, throw it away? I've been six years in school. That's enough studying for one lifetime, I say. Anyway, what's the use of me going to college? It would be too hard for me."

"But you've got to try. If you try with all your might you're bound to do alright, understand the problems, and learn all about things."

He was stammering with the difficulty of articulating his confused and struggling feelings.

"It's terribly important to go to college," he said, "it's the only way you can learn to live life fully, to understand it, instead of being narrow and ignorant and tied down where you were born."

She looked very serious.

"Mrs Reames has been to college, hasn't she?" she asked.

"Yes, she's got a B.A. in London, in English. Why?"

She pondered a moment, then tossed her head back impatiently.

"Oh well, what's the use?" she said sharply. "Dad says I've got to leave, and find a job in an office, or help on the farm."

"But if you get a scholarship on your Higher result?" he entreated. "He's got no right to deprive you of your future, then."

She stood up to him with a flash almost of anger.

"I don't want to go to college. I'm sick of swotting for

exams. It doesn't help you at all. I'd rather earn a living."

"But you learn," he insisted, impotently.

"I don't want to learn," she retorted. "It only gives me a headache. P'r'aps it's alright for you, or Mrs Reames, – though she looks out of place cooped up in a colliery village. No wonder they say she'd be better out of the place altogether –"

"What d'you mean?" he asked painfully.

"Oh, it's only talk," she answered, colouring up.

He also flushed.

"That's all it is in this place," he said, turning away and looking down on the morbid grey of slate and wall, "talking behind people's backs. What have they got against her?"

She jumped nervously at the passion of that last whipped question.

"I thought she was awfully nice," she said. "She was so gentle to Mam, and she told me about you, and asked whether I liked English too and was going to college –"

"But what do they say?" he insisted, his face white.

"They say it's because of her that her husband makes the men work like niggers underground," she said in a shamed voice.

"Oh God!" he breathed.

"Ssh, Morlais, for shame," she said.

"Oh," he gasped, looking piteously at her, his christian name coming from her lips, in her voice that gave words wings and sent them arrowing to home in his heart, his name her possession and he impelled to her, having pawned his name for her pity.

"It's only talk," she said. "I shouldn't have lowered myself –"

"But, Nan, it's a lie, that is," he stammered.

"Yes, I know it is," she soothed him. "It was wicked of me to repeat such filth."

She looked at him a moment.

"Why don't you join the Welfare Tennis club?" she asked.

"We'd be able to have some fine games now exams are over. We could make up a four with Tom Matthews and Margery Morse, couldn't we?"

"I don't know," he said. "I don't like hitting a ball about much."

He flushed foolishly. He did like tennis, really. Only serving faults in front of other people made him feel despicable, and Mrs Reames had said that once when her husband asked her to join the golf club in town – now he was falsely echoing it.

"It's alright," he added quickly. "But I like walking better."

He looked round, sweeping his eyes across the wave of mountain and taking a deep breath as though it were a physical effort to recapture the vanished rapture of being aiming the mountains.

"Why don't you come for walks instead?" he asked.

He stopped at his boldness.

"Oh, I don't know. There's nobody to go with," she said. "Margery doesn't like walking. It *is* a bit dull, isn't it?"

"It isn't *really*," he insisted. "There are heaps of things, really."

"Here's Dad," she said rapidly, catching sight of her father coming out of Mountain Row in his working clothes, a block of wood under his arm. "I've got to get his bath ready in the kitchen. Solong."

"Solong."

She was gone in a flash, leaving him bewildered. His legs knew their job, however, and took him on towards Mr Blackmore, who had been one of the gigantic figures in his child world – the man who came every morning before school and poured milk out of a tin gill into the china jug with a garland of roses round its scolloped neck. Mr Blackmore began the day. The lamp lighter with the long pole in which fire mysteriously lived brought it to an end. Atlas and Samson.

"Good evening, Mr Blackmore."

"'Owbe, young Jenkins. Taking a stroll, is it?"

"Yes, it's lovely now, isn't it?"

"Rain it is the grass is needing. Pity we didn't 'ave some of the water there is in that pit to wet these 'ere fields a bit."

Morlais saw that his working boots were soaked to a grey mildew, and his trousers had a tide mark just under his knees, below his straps.

"Is it very wet underground?"

Mr Blackmore laughed.

"Wet enough to grow melons," he answered. "That step-father of yours will 'ave something to answer for before long, the way the men are talking."

Again. Everybody was against him.

Morlais flashed his eyes back.

"He can't help it if the company won't pay for repairs," he said.

"He'll damned well 'ave to 'elp it if the Unions come in on our side," Mr Blackmore said. "Anyroads, I didn't ought to tell you what's going on. No doubt 'e sent you out to find what's doing, eh?"

Morlais went black, and then stopped himself. This man wet and grimy and strong as old rock, a hard day's work reinforcing years and years of the same labour, stood over him and cowed him. He was bitterly concious of his tweed jacket and well-polished brogues and creased grey trousers. If he had huge black hands, blue-pocked with old coal-cuts, then he could reply in the same deep ring. But now –

"Good afternoon," he said, turning away without looking up and stumbling over an out-crop as he hurried down the path behind Mountain Row.

Half-way down the hill he stopped to watch two children damming the thin trickle of water that came down from the quarry and in winter time spat and bubbled with tremendous energy. His mother used to say the old man was dribbling again when she took the children for a walk that way after a rainy spell. The children were cutting turf with a knife – a bread-knife by the look of it and a row for them when they got back home – and laying it across a narrow part of the course.

"What you're doing, mate?" Morlais asked.

"Makin' a lagoon," one of them replied busily.

He had blue woollen knickers and a green jersey; his hair aggressively red.

"Get a move on, Dai," the child snapped to his mate. "It's time she got under way; they finished loading 'er."

Morlais smiled, the children having hit on the combination of impulses inside him that released the deadlock and reintegrated him. He saw the sun shining on him, and there was Nan saying softly "Morlais," and he was alive, on the mountainside, exams finished and holidays ahead, and after that, oh after that, where the horizon became most beautiful and merged with its invisible antipodes, College.

"Better hurry if you're going to finish it before the rain," he said, and as the child looked up at the sky with a mariner's eye he said, "And your bum's in the water too, boy."

It was this secret exuberance that dared him to go straight down the hill to the heart of the village instead of turning off as he invariably did and going home by the deserted back lanes that ran below the hillside allotments. So down Bryn Road, his feet ringing against the paving stones, delighting himself with glimpses through the spotless windows at the still-life interiors, parlour after parlour, aspidistra, stuffed fox, dark armchairs with red cushions and antimacassars, oak dresser, framed Sunday School certificates. One parlour was actually inhabited – a small girl perched on a piano stool hammering at her Czerny while a lady in loose black stood over her with a long pencil ready to rap careless fingers. Miss Florrie Evans that was, just fancy her still teaching the piano. Heavens, it must be six whole years since she had rapped his own knuckles and told him with exasperation that he wasn't trying to keep time with that hateful metronome. And her sitting room, as she called it, always smelt of bacon and fried bread, stalely.

"Ai," a woman shouted from a doorstep across the road. He started. He hadn't thought, he was looking into somebody's house. He flushed and hurried on.

Well, exams were over after all. That was something worth celebrating. If he bought a packet of five Players he'd smoke two tonight, one in the back lane on the way home, one through his bedroom window. He could sell the remaining three for 1½d. to the bus conductor. Safer than keeping them on you.

To make the occasion really daring, really Elizabethan, he went right down the hill, across the level crossing, past the ironmonger's on the Square and into the Bracchi's – the Italian sweet-and-tobacco shop frequented by none but the riff-raff adolescents, whose proprietor was unprincipled enough to open his shop on Sundays and do nothing but open his fat hands palm upwards when a deputation of deacons from the chapels had asked him respectably enough to show some common decency.

There was a great mirror in the entrance to the little shop. Morlais saw himself suddenly there, and in that instant faltered inside his abandon. Sports coat in rich autumn tweed, brogues, middle-grey trousers, brilliantined hair. And his face. He went into the shop, momentarily derided by some inner mockery.

The shop shone with great bottles of sweets in phalanx on the polished counter. The steam from the coffee machine did not dim its spotless glimmer. The stout black-glossy-haired Italian in a white coat was polishing the green-tiled tables with a chamois cloth. The room had a curled odour of old cigarette smoke and evaporated coffee.

"Yes, sir," said Leo, smiling obligingly and hurrying to serve, "what can I do for you, sir?"

"Five Players," said Morlais, fixing his eyes on a bottle of barley sugar. He was sweating; the hot room droned with unseen flies.

"Five Players, sir? Certainly, sir," Leo beamed, producing the packet with a flourish as though he were planking a white rabbit onto the counter by sleight of hand. "Anything else you require, sir? Matches, Sen-Sen, Sarsparilla, sir?"

"No thanks," Morlais said, "thank you."

He turned to go out, thankfully, thankful the shop was empty, when he collided with Bob Linton, who was entering.

"Well, if it isn't *Morlais!*" Bob exclaimed.

To that spontaneous welcome Morlais responded with a deep smile.

"Hallo, Bobbie," he grinned, taking the proffered hand.

"You're not going?" Bob said, still holding his hand.

"I've got to get home," Morlais replied indecisively.

"Aw, stay a mo, mun; get home easy. Come an' 'ave a game of football on Leo's machine there."

"Alright," Morlais replied, gladly.

"'A's the style," beamed Bob. "'Ave an iced soda on me?"

"No. You have one on me. I've finished my exams today. I must do something to celebrate, mun."

"Finished your exams, eh? I bet you swiped them, too. Tommy Matthews was saying the other night you're about the best at his books in the County School."

"Aw, go on, don't talk so daft," Morlais demurred. "Come on, Bob, let's see if I can beat you at this."

"I've 'ad a lot of practice, mind you," Bob said. "I very near live here in the winter, don't I, Leo?"

"Wha's that?" beamed Leo. "Two Sarsparillas, you say, Mister Linton?"

Bob laughed.

"Yes, that's right, you old codger. Bit deaf, Leo is at times, Mor; but it don't do no harm to his business."

Leo's football game consisted of a fourlegged case with a glass top; under the glass a cardboard football field with twenty-two tin players whose legs could be worked by wires. You paid a penny in the slot to release the football. Bob took the Reds, Morlais the Greens, after they had duly tossed up.

"I never win with the Reds," Bob said.

Bob was dressed in his particular suit, a double-breasted pin-stripe with slim waist, padded shoulders and wide trousers. His face looked pallid against the rich navy, and despite his spirit, his eyes had a yellow look. His eyelashes were black, as all colliers' are for the first few years underground. He wore pointed patent leather shoes, his hair was thoroughly greased; a white carnation decorated his buttonhole.

"Damn, you're good at this game," he said ungrudgingly as Morlais potted a second goal.

"Pull your socks up, then," Morlais said.

"Oh, I don't mind losing to a better man," Bob said, grinning. "It would be different with some of them here. I wouldn't be licked by some of the wasters in this place not for a fortune. Not in billiards, nor cards, nor dominoes."

His teeth flashed with a fleeting smile that was half shame, half pride. Morlais wanted him to say more. He had a craving to know about this life Bob hinted at. And Bob seemed somehow to be apologising.

"You don't never come down this way, do you?" Bob said after his shot.

Morlais shrugged his shoulders.

"I'm afraid I don't," he said diffidently.

"Afraid?" Bob echoed. For a moment Morlais thought he was taunting him – with snobbism, perhaps – but he was mistaken.

"You ought to be glad you don't waste your time the way I been," Bob said. "You wouldn't believe, honest. Some of them – I'm not saying all of them mind you; there's damn good boys, I won't say – But some of them – Jesus, the filth they talk, and do, too – with girls and that. Look here." He turned to see whether anyone was in the shop. Only Leo the impersonal polishing his gleaming counter-rail. "They talk about giving the working class a square deal and that. Alright. I daresay we got to put up with a lot of sweating. But I'd throttle him if one of them chaps came into my kitchen. I would."

Morlais was put out. It wasn't this that he wanted to know.

"Why do you bother with them, then?" he asked, unaccountably peevish.

"Because I only just found out that they make me sick," Bob said. "The whole damn place makes me sick, if you want to know. I been working down under since I was fourteen and I'm not much different from a pit pony. And it's always the same, sickening. The men are alright, mind you, specially a few of them. That Luther Blackmore was a decent bugger before the Company killed 'im. 'E used to sing for us after the drams was all filled, or eating our dinner. We used to 'ave proper concerts in our district – five of the boys are in the Male Voice choir."

"Is the pit dangerous, Bob?" Morlais's guilt was awake again.

"I'll say," Bob said, boasting a little, though. "It's a scandal. You go down Dr Brown's surgery, you'll see. Cuts, and rheumatics with the water coming in from the old working, that's what they're all complaining of. I'm with the ones that want to smash the offices up."

"What?" Morlais blanched.

Bob stopped sharp, realising he had been indiscreet.

"Oh, it's only talk, don't pay attention," he said. "Anyroads we wouldn't do nothing without the men's committee being agreeable. Your father's chairman of the committee, too." He smiled as though he were glad to say this. "Everybody stands by him."

"Do they?" Morlais felt a tremor go through him. His father!

"Look here," Bob said. "There's a meeting of the men now in half an hour. Like to hear 'im speak?"

"Where is the meeting?"

"On the ashtip by the river, they're deciding tonight."

"Deciding?"

"Aye. Shilly-shallying they been for weeks, what with the Federation officials considering the case and insisting we get the non-unionists to join first by show of cards –"

"What d'you mean, show of cards?"

"Well, when they're going down for the shift there's men at the top of the lane asking for you to show your membership card. It's no good striking, see, if all the men won't come out. We ducked one chap in the river by the rocks last week 'cause 'e wouldn't join, the bloody skinflint. And now they say the Union won't back us if we strike – no strike pay or nothing – because the Company told the Federation the pit wasn't paying; and if the men struck they wouldn't get work again because the pit would be closed down for keeps."

"What are you going to do, then?" Morlais asked excitedly. Bob's voice, moody and fiery, aroused a conflict in him and a craving for action, for reality.

"God knows," Bob said, suddenly despondent. "There's a few of the younger ones want to smash the offices, and the engine-house, too, maybe. They're danted, see? They don't see no other way. The older ones say no, though. They got their families, they say, boots and clothes to buy and sons going in for the ministry and that."

He balanced his empty Sarsparilla glass on his thumb.

"What does my father say?" Morlais asked, his small voice seeking an answer which subconsciously he had already accepted, the answer of his father to his childish hag-ridden doubt.

"He's beat, I reckon, though he won't own it," Bob said slowly. "It's Reds or blacklegs; he's got to choose." He dropped his glass on the floor, failing in his convulsive attempt to regain it.

"Damn," he snapped, looking moodily at the splintered

glass. "Oh, hell and damn it all."

"Trupence that will cost you, Mister Linton," said Leo with his smooth business-like smile. "Trupence, I'm afraid."

Bob felt in his pocket, and flushed.

"Let me pay," Morlais said, holding a half-crown out. "And two more of the same, please."

"No, you don't pay," Bob said.

Morlais didn't know what to say, feeling Bob's embarrassed and self conscious pride. Leo turned up his palms the way he'd done to the deputation of deacons.

"Trupence, anyway," his grin said.

"Chalk it up for me," Bob said. "I'll pay you on Friday when I get my packet. Come on, Morlais, let's go to the meeting; if you're coming," he threw out.

"Have a drink first, then."

"Oh, alright," he agreed, his scowl changing to a smile as he returned Morlais's troubled look. He grinned and sat down again and they sat silently while Leo mixed their drinks. The silence was their tacit acceptance of each other, as somehow, henceforth, friends.

"D'you know Nan Blackmore?" Bob asked. "Thanks, Leo."

Morlais took his glass thankfully and sipped it before he answered.

"A bit."

"She goes to our chapel," Bob said slowly, the words coming from a long way inside him, heavy with memory. "If she was a-willing I'd be on the mountain now, not going to any old meeting."

Morlais felt his packet of Players in his pocket and clumsily pulled them out, his hands shaking a little.

"Have a fag?" he said, catching a quick glimpse of Bob's pale moody face, his grey distant eyes and black sooty lashes. Then he saw the green table-top only.

"She's too good for me, though. Thanks. Players, eh? Woodbines is my dap. Thanks." He struck a match on his sole. "I could 'ave pulled her hair out in a handful one time, on the path jest below Mountain Row. I asked her if she'd come to the pictures. She said, 'Not with you.' I could 'ave killed 'er." The match burnt out and dropped onto the table. Have you felt that about a girl?"

Morlais lit a match and held it to Bob's cigarette.

"I don't know," he said unsteadily. "I haven't had much to do with them."

"Like Nan," Bob said moodily. "She don't bother with boys." He inhaled his cigarette till the end glowed, and blew a thin fan of smoke over the table. "Different from some of the girls that was in our standard in school. Snips, that's what they are. I wish I'd never 'ad anything to do with that lot. Makes you sick."

Morlais felt the cold sweat burst out of his forehead and under his arms and round his loins. His body cramped with sudden nausea and a wheel spun round behind his eyes.

"Remember Winnie Morse?" Bob said sickly, probing away at his own wound. "She had a squint and a short leg? Remember?"

Morlais stood up.

"She's one of the worst," Bob said.

Morlais stubbed the cigarette he couldn't smoke any more.

"We'll be late if we don't go," he said.

"Oh, what's the odds?" Bob said, nipping his cigarette and putting it behind his ear. "The old uns will win and we'll just 'ave to go on and on." He stretched his arms up. "I wish to God I was one of them long greyhounds your brother Dilwyn takes up the mountain in the mornings. Solong, Leo. Don't forget the trupence."

They crossed the road and went down the rough path beside the Workmen's Hall whose cemented pine end was cracked from top to bottom by subsidence and the constant rattle of the nearby pithead. The path fell steeply past a row of small

cottages invested with ragged black children and two
withered old women sitting on chairs outside the doors of
their kitchens. Most of the doors had scrubbing boards
wedged between the uprights, half-naked babies squirming
over them. Pleasant View was the name of the row. It
commanded the steep gorge down whose sides the tipped
slag dribbled in smoking steamlets into the poisoned river.

Below the two boys, on the ashtip where the U.D.C. carts
tipped the village's daily refuse, a crowd of men stood about
in shifting groups.

They all wore cloth caps and dark suits; most of them had
mufflers round their necks. Morlais and Bob watched them
from the top of the incline. In one of the kitchens behind
them there was a row going on. A woman in a high rasping
voice was cursing a child; her voice cut through the slickly
circling jazz music coming from the next house; she sounded
danted.

"I've told you till I'm sick not to come in this kitchen with
them filthy boots on..."

"But Mam-oh, don't-oh...," the child's reply a screaming
treble.

"Get out on the street till its time for your bed, you little
bitch."

"Here they're coming," Bob said excitedly.

Three men came down the lane, one of them Morlais's
father, the other two strangers, one stubby and spectacled
carrying a portfolio, the other gaunt and loose, a red birth-
mark down his cheek. They were arguing; the little fatty
waving his portfolio, Mr Jenkins shrugging his shoulders; the
third man spat considerately. The loose groups of colliers on
the tip below stirred and tautened with a sudden quick
murmur of expectation, as if a spoon had stirred a black
sediment in some old pot black with use. Morlais, feeling the
tenseness below him and knowing his father was approaching
him, knowing with his body the gradual approach of his

father, like a giant stalking down the dark lane of a dream, cast about him for some means of obliterating himself.

"Come on," Bob said. "Let's go down to the tip."

Five yards further on a narrow alley cut up between the houses towards the main street of the village. Morlais saw it suddenly as they were walking down towards the tip.

"I'm going," he said quickly and before Bob could say a word he turned swiftly and ran from him through the narrow alley, across the back lane which the alley intersected, and out into the Square.

He crossed the Square and climbed the hill, then made his way home along the back lane. It was his usual way home; he took it without thinking; and he hurried, stepping it out along the ash-strewn uneven lane so hastily that he began perspiring. Children playing scotch yelled after him, "Reames's pet," and it made no difference to him, although generally he winced terribly with the hurt of it. He broke into a run when he turned into the open space by the river, and instead of following the bank to the bridge he slithered down the slope to the stream, a cloud of ash settling on his grey trousers, and splashed across, leaping from stone to stone and slipping sometimes up to his ankles in the polluted water. Up the other side, through ashes and salmon tins and jampots, he scrambled, and ran up the lane behind Glannant Street. He was aching for breath, his lungs dry and raw, his eyes swimming. The Elms was there. Yes, still there. From the outside it looked just the same. But he must get inside, quickly, oh urgent, urgent, to stop it. Stop it. He didn't know what he must stop; and so imperative was the intuition compelling his body that he didn't need to know what. Only get inside.

He ran up the gravel drive, a thrush bursting out of the bushes and chattering with alarm at his loud invasion of its quiet.

The French windows were open; the sitting room empty and quiet. Nothing out of place, the furniture polished, the mirror a calm sheet of glazed light, the piano with the keyboard unlocked and music on the holder. A book open on the reading table beside her easy chair, a nail file keeping the page. He stood in the centre of the room, panting and looking about him distractedly. Then he wiped his face and looked at the sweat on his hand. His shoulders sagged and he crossed slowly to her chair. Kneeling on it he put his hand out to look at the book. It was her morocco edition of Keats. The house was silent through and through, dead-empty. He seemed to be held in a vacuum. The book was open at the sonnets; as he stared at it, not seeing the words at first but only thinking he was a fool, running all the way in a panic that was only an excuse for his flight from the miners' meeting, the type slowly clarified. It was very odd, watching the blur slowly resolve into perfect letters, neat black groupings of letters in straight ranks and then the groups developed a meaning, a message; and then actually a voice, a frantic deadly earnest voice. The words were concentrating all their slowly-accumulated intensity upon him. He saw them; two lines.

When I have fears that I may cease to be,
Before this pen has gleaned my teeming brain.

In a bound he was pulling the door open; the dining room was empty, the hall, kitchen, scullery. The silence tried to thrust him back as he ran up the stairs. The bathroom door open, empty; her own door shut. He ran to it down the short landing and knocked. No answer.

"Mums," he called.

Her reply made his flesh leap convulsively, as though his blood had suddenly reversed its circulation.

"Alright," she said. It was her voice; it must have been; but utterly unlike her; strangled, forced, croaking.

He pushed the door open, so much did he need to see her, and went in. She jumped up and tried to thrust the chamber under the bed, at the same time putting one hand behind her back. She was a sallow white and it flashed into his mind that her face was haggard and plain.

"Get out," she said.

"Oh, Mums," he said, holding his hands out beseechingly to her.

Very slowly she sagged to a sitting posture on the edge of the bed. Her hand came hopelessly from its hiding and let the drinking glass tip from her lax fingers. The thick whitish liquid spilled over the silk counterpane.

"You haven't taken any of it?" he said urgently.

She nodded a weak no, looking dully at him. He saw her face for the first time weary and ugly, pouches of loose skin under her eyes, crows-feet and wrinkles, and her hair unclipped. A hand closed round his heart, squeezed it, making him sob and sprawl with his head against her knees and his hands clutching at her skirt.

"Why didn't you leave me alone?" she said tonelessly over his head.

"I *knew*," he said, his throat quivering with the great knot of pain that was forcing its way up.

He felt her collapse over him, her breast and head slumping forward in a soft dead weight upon his crown and neck. He put his hands up and gently lifted her back. He put a pillow under her head and ran to the door. He stopped at the door, looked at her, went back and lifted her feet off the floor and straightened her heavy limp body on the bed. Her ashen features were rigid and frightening, clammy and terrible to touch. He smoothed her hair back and then ran to the bathroom for the smelling salts....

Bathed and reclothed in her dark green frock and cool with lavender scent she sipped the china tea he had brewed for her. She looked round the sitting room; her fingers felt along the arm of the chair.

"It's funny being back here," she said. "I can't grasp the fact."

She sipped her tea.

"The tea leaves look pretty," she said. "The tea, too."

Then she looked up and he had to meet her eyes.

"I ought to thank you, I suppose, for fetching me back," she said slowly. Her voice was intense, yet somehow vague also, bewildered.

"It's the second time you've made me change my mind," she said.

She smiled.

"I wonder why I don't hate you," she said, her smile become something too profoundly simple for him to look at any longer. He picked his own cup up.

"I don't want you to tell Denis," she said after a minute. "It would have been better in the long run for him.... But as it is, he's got enough worry with the colliers. You won't tell him?"

"Of course not."

"He's been trying to persuade me to go away for a holiday for ages. I think perhaps I will go, for a fortnight or so." She paused. "If you'll come with me. Will you?"

He looked up, troubled.

"It would be more of a change if you got right away from us all," he said. "Wouldn't it?"

"You stopped me doing that," she said.

He winced.

"No, that isn't true. No, that's wrong," she said. "That wasn't why I... You will come, won't you, Morlais? You've finished your exams now. And you haven't been out of the place once. Wouldn't you like a holiday?"

He frowned, staring at his thumbnail.

"I won't keep you on a lead," she said. "And I won't want you to wheel me about in a bath chair,"

"It isn't that, Mums," he said, "don't be silly."

"What is it, then?" her voice came with a soft out-breath of relief.

He was a long time answering.

"I'd love to have a holiday," he said. "But – well, it's this trouble about the pit. You see –"

"Denis can manage it better with me out of the way."

"No, it isn't that, either. You see, my father, he's the men's representative. There was a meeting tonight, and –"

"Yes, I see, dear," she said quietly. "But it won't do you any good, will it, if you hang about here brooding about it. You can't *do* anything, can you?"

"No," he said, fretting bitterly. "Not even decide which side I belong to."

She sat up and leaning forward took hold of his sleeve.

"You don't belong to any side at bottom," she said. "Your struggle must be first to find yourself. Don't you understand? You must become yourself first of all. It will take all your courage and sweat to do that. You've got to go to college. That's the next step. You've earned the right to go there. You've worked hard all these years for it."

"No," he said. "That's nothing. That wasn't anything."

"Oh, Morlais," she said, "If you could only see."

"I know what I feel," he said.

She let go his sleeve,

"You feel tired, by the look of you," she said. "Please come away with me. Only for a week. That won't make any difference. It'll go before you can say nonsense even. We'll go to Aberystwyth and stay with Nora there. Shall we? I had a letter from her this morning. She's staying in digs there for a month, she's got some books she wants to read in the National Library. Shall we?"

Nora was her niece; she often talked about Nora. She was doing an M.A. degree; her photograph was on the dining room mantelpiece.

"When shall we go, then?" he asked.

"Tomorrow?"

He laughed, excited suddenly.

"Yes, yes." He stood up. "Shall I go down to the station and find the times of the trains?"

She laughed too, as gladly as he.

"Yes, go on. And copy the times down. I'm sure you'll never be able to remember them."

He slipped out through the French window. The lawn was dim with the indefinite haze of evening. The thrushes were silent.

A blackbird chuttered out of the rhododendrons as he crossed the lawn and scattered its song like apple blossoms down the path. He laughed.

"I'm going away, too," he said, to the vanished bird.

From that moment, when he spoke to the ecstatic blackbird, till the dull thundery evening when the taxi slid round outside the Elms and they climbed out, stiff and anxious and travel-sick to return Mr Reames's troubled and pre-occupied welcome-home, four swift days of delight elapsed.

For Morlais the delight began immediately. Going down the lane in the dusk; crossing the desolate waste ground to the grimy station; going up the grey station yard past the ragged boys who were kicking a tin about while they waited for the train to bring the evening papers they hawked round the streets for a halfpenny a dozen sold; knocking at the door of the booking office and leaning over the counter in the gaslight while the prematurely bald clerk fingered the time table and he jotted down the train times on the back of an envelope, every event of it prickled his body with pleasure. The rows of green tickets in the rack, the empty chair drawn up by the fire, the shiny elbows and Oxford accent of the booking clerk whose business was to arrange for the liberation of people while he himself remained a prisoner in the frowsy room at the top of a sombre valley, a hill-bound cul-de-sac, all, all delightful, exciting, energising, an exquisite release. Then the frenzied packing and the half-tasted supper and Mr Reames saying he was glad they'd have a change, the two of them, and wishing he could get away as well; and the restless tossing in bed, not even wanting to sleep; and, in good time, the early rising and cold washing and hasty dressing and the walk with heavy handbag down the deserted streets, past the milkman clicking his sleepy mare along and the ash-cart and a few colliers and clerks waiting along the road for the early bus. Oh, and waiting for the train in the damp misty air, tasting its rawness and looking down the valley every now and again, not so that anyone could see you were excited, though, and thinking all the time you could hear the train in the distance and see its white smoke billow in the whirling mist. And the porters whistling and rolling the churns along the wet stone flags. And then the signal dropping and the wire under the platform rattling, and this time there could be no mistaking the onward-surging beat of pistons and the rhythmic drumming of huge wheels, and the tremendous arrival of the train. And so away.

"Thank Heavens," she said, peeling off her gloves and taking the corner seat with her back to the engine. "Put the heater on full, Morlais. Let's be aisy."

He turned the little handle to ON, feeling as he did it as though he were driving the engine himself; then let the window down to half and gave his face to be skinned by the wind's razor edge.

She took the smut out of his eye for him with her lavender-scented handkerchief and rubbed his cheeks warm and told him to sit down and act like a commercial traveller even if he wasn't one.

"We've got six whole hours of travelling," he said, stupe-fied with amazement at the extravagance of the gods.

"Yes," she laughed. "And we won't even know the names of the stations until we see them painted in big white letters on the indicators. Even that seems more than I deserve – not to hear the conductor calling out the names of the streets at every halt between Glannant Street and the Co-operative Stores in Tredwr."

There was such sourness in the ends of her words that he was jolted by a sudden depression. He hadn't realised before that she disliked Tredwr like that.

"What sort of people shall we let into our compartment?" she asked, exuberant again. "What about a navvy? Or an old woman taking a jant to market?"

"Like the one who had a duck under her coat when you were in France – and when it quacked you screamed?" he asked.

She laughed so quickly she was like a young girl.

"Yes, we'll let *her* in anyway," she said. "But I propose we keep open house today. Let's fill the compartment plumb-full, everybody squeezed together, children and pets on the racks. Agreed?"

"Yes," he said. "Only we must reserve the corner seats for the punch-and-judy man and the organ grinder and his monkey."

"That's only fair," she said.

Well, there were too many things to remember on that journey. One little girl ate a huge stick of rock without once taking it out of her mouth. It just stayed there and got smaller and smaller while pink sugar trickled down her chin. Then she was very sick. Once Morlais saw a kingfisher; it seemed to be moving backwards along the bright green beck whose water broke in hasty waves against mossy rocks so rapidly did the urgent train out-distance it. There was no time to show it to her because she was separated from him by the sick child snoring on its mother's capacious belly. Once a servant girl got in and kissed a young man who was seeing her off and sobbed and sobbed for miles and miles. And you couldn't feel sorry for her because her tear-stained face was radiantly happy all the time and it was like seeing the sun through a dazzle of thin rain. And there were waterfalls and foundries, market carts and children waving from back gardens, and leagues of meadows with grazing cattle, and always the Welsh hills wheeling away and behind while the train raced on, the hub of it all, browbeating the hills to open and let it pass. Morlais saw a thousand horizons, and all the time he heard with delight the thrilling obbligato of rocking carriages and whirring wheels.

There were wonderful new names, too, when the train stopped. Derry Ormond, painted in white against a background of green fields and a distant rookery. Strata Florida, surrounded eternally by a brown marsh of peaty land, pathless and unploughed, not even fit for sheep to pasture on. And Welsh names that slipped from his mind as soon as the train had recommenced its journey away from and towards.... In the early afternoon they swung down a flat meadow beside a full brown river with sandy banks. There was a black cormorant fishing there, or sleeping. And he knew without her telling him that for the first time, the first time in his life, he was about to see the sea. And he did. From the carriage window to the misty end of vision the flat grey-green sea stretched on and on.

"D'you like it?" she said.

"Oh, yes," he breathed.

She ruffled his hair.

"Good," she said. "I was afraid you'd be disappointed."

Then along the harbour and over the mudflats, past the football field and the empty cattle mart, into the subdued light of the station. Nora was waiting for them at the barrier.

"I'm so sorry, Auntie," she said, kissing and laughing. "It isn't that I'm mean. I just hadn't got a penny in my purse to get a platform ticket."

"I could lend you one," Mrs Reames said. "It's a bit late now, though. How are you, dear?"

"How are *you*? Did you have a good journey?"

"Ask Morlais. This is Morlais."

"Hallo, Morlais. I thought it was you, but I didn't say anything in case you were somebody Auntie was eloping with."

"Your mind seems to have become very low, Nora, to harbour such base suspicions," Mrs Reames laughed. She looked at Morlais who had flushed uncomfortably. "If we two would only shut up for a minute I think Morlais is trying to say something."

Morlais laughed.

"Only hullo," he said.

"He's just seen the sea for the first time," Mrs Reames said. "You can't expect much in the way of speech after that, can you?"

"But for the first time?" Nora was astounded. "Where have you been keeping then?"

"Oh, the tide was always out before," Morlais said.

Chattering and bustling, hand bags and paper bags, they went through the arch past the fruit stall and the Enquiry Office into the street.

"If you come to my digs you will only have some burnt toast and a cheap brand of sardines," Nora said. "So I propose you repair your famished selves at one of our innumerable eating establishments. They concern themselves almost solely with the inner man in this town."

Morlais drifted like waste paper in a wind of talk, along a busy pavement, through a door, up some stairs; suddenly he had stopped drifting and was hanging part of himself on a peg – his burberry, in fact.

"They're very observant people in Aberystwyth," Nora was incessantly saying. "Keen psychologists of the behaviourist school. They condition your reflexes very cunningly. It's quite irresistible. Before you've been here a week you do everything automatically – walk down the prom before lunch, quicken your step when you hear the municipal orchestra open its shoulders, clap from the depths of a deck chair when they've blown Brahms to pieces, eat rice and stewed prunes daily as naturally as a sheep eats grass. Yes, really, Auntie."

"D'you want a wash, Morlais?" Mrs Reames asked. "There's a place over there – that door on the right."

Morlais washed himself with hard water and carbolic soap and dried his face as well as he could with the slippery roller towel. Then he looked at his train-sick face in the uncertain mirror and combed his hair into its waves. The journey had made him light-headed, his thought whirling round a central vacuum. Nan Blackmore wasn't there so much now, he couldn't feel her all round and through him as he had done every time he saw some marvellous thing through the carriage window. She was so far away. And there had been the sea, which was now quite close to him, waiting for him, although he had ridiculously bolted himself into this lavatory and couldn't see it. How different from his old imaginings – when he saw it he would fling off his clothes and race into the swirl of white foam and tossed yellow sand – but later! And how different Nora was, too. At least not different. He hadn't thought of her speaking at all. She looked so quiet in that photograph, not at all off-handed and flippant and saying such odd things, seeing things somehow like a biologist dissecting animals. And he hadn't thought she was so short, either. She wasn't nearly as tall as he; he'd noticed that when she was walking beside him down the street. He rubbed his face until the colour came back to his cheeks. Then he did some arm exercises and a man came in as he was bending to touch his toes. Flushing, he pretended to be tieing up his shoe-lace. When he had untied it he went back to the table. Plaice and chips, and Nora holding the sugar tongs over his cup and smiling with raised eyebrows at him and saying "Three?" Always when he thought of her after that he saw her face looking up unembarrassed and clear-featured, asking him how many lumps he wanted. Her talk was like a lot of paper wrappings about that precise engraving. When she talked you didn't notice her face; there was a mist of words, an improvised bunting of ideas, and you couldn't get hold of *her*, really because she had diffused herself through all her quick comments and retorts. But catch her in some natural act, pouring out your tea, say, and she was quite clear, concentrated into one look, eyes, fine downward slanting brows, curly brown hair clipped back from a forehead that sharpened into two faint vertical lines above a slightly retrousse nose. And then she escaped again.

"I'm sure half the animals at the Zoo die of sugar diabetes, the amount trippers gorge them with....."

After tea they walked along the prom to the little street by the harbour where Nora was digging. She had fixed them up in the same house. The front sitting room and three bedrooms. Morlais to have the attic.

"I hope you don't mind being pushed under the roof like this," Nora said apologetically, standing at the door while he put his suit-case on the bed and looked at the tiny room. There was a single bed, iron bedstead painted green and a pink coverlet, pressed against the wall with the roof, white-washed, sloping down sharply to the foot of the bed. The window began at the roof and ended at the floor, a very small window.

"Oh no, it's lovely," he replied, genuinely delighted. Then quite suddenly he went serious. "It's like my bedroom at home." He hesitated, glancing at her to see whether she understood. "My real home," he added.

"Good," she said, relieved. "But don't catch cold here. Your feet will be sticking out of the window, remember."

"I'll have to wash them, then."

"Nobody minds in this street. And if you won't wake up when we knock on the door tomorrow morning I'll tie a feather onto a long pole and tickle your soles from the road."

"No need. I'll be up with the sun tomorrow." He paused. "Gosh. I can hear the sea from my bedroom. I'll never go to sleep."

"It makes a sleepy sound in the night. It's so dark and deep. You'll sleep alright."

They went downstairs. Nora started apologising for the sitting room next, laughing all the time and speaking quietly in case the landlady heard her.

"It's because you like flowers, Auntie," she said. "I told the old lady you had a lovely garden; so she put the aspidistra in the grate and made it look autumnal by putting that red tissue paper round it. I think it rather suits a draughty room like this, don't you?"

"Yes, one does get the feeling of leaves falling down," Mrs Reames replied.

Morlais disliked the room, coldly. It was like the parlour at home, with its antimacassars and its china firedogs and brass irons. The dogs had pink noses instead of yellow ones – that was the only difference. And a badger in the glass case instead of a fox. The paintings were different, of course. These people seemed to be seafarers. There were two paintings of a tramp ship, S.S. Erinna, one in calm, one in storm, in a style rather like the Bayeux tapestry. But there was one the very same – Sunrise in Sicily. It *was* draughty. He forced his thoughts away from the hard memory of his last visit to the parlour at home – that Jew, and Doris ripping up the pound note, and his father's silence and the nasty taste of port wine – and tried to get inside their conversation. He fancied he could hear the sea. But it wasn't. It was a refrigerator in a butcher's shop opposite. Outside the street was grey and squally; people passed hurriedly, wearing mackintoshes and scarves. And Mums and Nora talked on and on, like two skaters, about clothes and novels and relations he knew nothing about and foreign affairs which bored him; Nora smoked five cigarettes, the small ash tray on the arm of her chair piling up with stumps and dead matches.

She didn't offer him one, either; she had looked at him doubtfully when she lit the first one and then evidently decided he was too young. He felt crushed. She had a lot of books, four shelves full – heavy works of reference with library numbers on them, several Oxford volumes of the poets, Milton, Pope, Wordsworth, Shelley, Browning, a pretty volume of Yeats and some thin ones of W.H. Davies, T.S. Eliot and Walter de la Mare, and a pile of novels, among the authors being D.H. Lawrence, Gide, Dickens, Jane Austen, Aldous Huxley and Sterne. He looked along the rows for one at least that he had read, and failed to find one. Oh yes. There was one. Precious Bane. He felt a deep relief, a warm feeling as though a capsule of brandy had broken in his stomach. She had read about Prue Sarn. The books were no longer a forbidding phalanx of oppressive erudition. Did she love Prue Sarn? When she read the book, was she like Prue, heart and soul? But if *she was*, why sit in and smoke and talk the evening away – it was already difficult to see their faces; the whiteness had gone from the dusk – when she must know how passionately he wanted to see the sea in the darkness? He had read that the waves were white at night, phosphorescent. This cold room, furnished by somebody else with no taste at all; why should she choose this room to live in? To hide in? Had she a room of her own in some town, a room which he might visit one day and have tea with her on a winter evening sitting on the rug making toast and talking about College, or Hetty, or Mums?

"He's day dreaming. You mustn't expect an answer from Morlais the first time you knock," Mums said.

Morlais woke with a start.

"What? I'm sorry –"

"I didn't mean to interrupt, Morlais," Nora said. "I suppose I've spoilt a poem in the making now by asking a trite question. Have I?"

He flushed, feeling the barb under the gentleness of her voice.

"Of course not. I was woolgathering as usual. I'm sorry."

She bit her lip, bowing her head slightly, his humility

hurting her.

He was full of confusion at the sudden realisation that the words were alive in their passage between them, the casual sentences somehow charged with power to hurt.

"She only asked how you'd done in Higher?" Mrs Reames said.

"Oh, that," he replied, looking at Nora as though she had spoken last. "Oh, alright. Mums has taught me the tricks in answering questions."

"You've seen through one racket already, then?" Nora said, surprised. He felt foolishly proud of himself, then correspondingly ashamed.

"Mums explained the works, I didn't discover them," he said, snubbing himself.

"Rot," said Mrs Reames. "It's you're the cynic. I'm full of faith still."

He darted a look at her, unaccountably angry. Damn, damn, damn. Why did he know about last night, about her inner failure and bitterness? Everything she said now must taste like paper, everything happy anyway.

"Well, what about a walk before supper, people?"

"Oh, must we?" Mrs Reames said, ensconced in her chair. "There's such a lot of fresh air outside, and it's chilly enough here."

"Just as you like," Nora shrugged. "Morlais?"

"No, I don't feel like going out much," he lied, writhing inside him.

"We've had a pretty long day, I suppose." Oh hell.

So they went on talking, and had a boiled egg and cocoa for supper, and then went to bed. Morlais lay on his bed fully clothed for a long time, cheek on crooked arm, head by the window, listening to the sea till the sound became a coldness in his marrow and the darkness of it paralysed thought and action, demanding from him a great effort of the will to get up and undress and slide his shivering body between the cold new sheets. It was too cold for sleep, so he perforce lay awake, understanding what cold perspectives the night had, and how the dim corridor narrowed to a pin point of light, far off, farther than thought, the needle's eye opening onto the everlasting future, tomorrow's unapproachable dawn. Lonely, alone, not even hearing the sea's grey undersound – and when he woke up to a knocking at his door and a dazzle of sunlight in his bewildered eyes he could not remember what it had been. Only there was some dream, some cold thing inside him, some slimy sea serpent staring up from the dark crannies of the rocks.

Not until the afternoon did they leave the town and go where he desired – away from all houses and people, past the brewery and the oast houses he had seen from the train and along the far side of the muddy harbour to the utterly desolate sweep of shingle beyond the stone jetty. The great feel of the stone ringing under the feet, the massive green capstan, the white-painted flagstaff with tarry ropes for hauling up the lantern, the way the green waves broke into white against the blunt snout of the jetty from which blue boulders thrust out of the packing of cement, the seething and white boiling below and the pools of rain water where the stone had sunk or was dimpled, all in the wind's teeth, in the very scream of it lashing the long breakers like a frenzied Mazeppa, generated a mood of high elation in him, set his mind free to brave the weather from the bridge of the Cutty Sark. The stone jetty had a head like a whale. Perhaps it would dive.

"I feel rather like a slithy tove," Mums said. "Come on, Morlais. Let's go inland. The grass looks nice and warm."

"Alright," he said. "I'll come after you now."

"Come after the seventh wave then," she said, turning away with Nora, who had a silk scarf tied round her head.

Morlais was alone for a moment, and with none to see his face he flung his head back and breathed the biting air deep into him and laughed aloud, feeling the strength in him, and the freedom, and the power of life. Then he heard a scream and flashed round. Mums had fallen from the side of the jetty.

He ran with great strides, terrified.

She was lying on the wet boulders underneath, having tumbled five feet down the sloping side. He slithered down after her, took her by the shoulders and lifted her up, She smiled, shaken and pale.

"Oh, Mums," he said, trembling with tenderness. "Are you hurt?"

"No, dear. I'm alright. Help me up. My foot's got stuck between the rocks."

Nora helped him to lift her. She was dead-white and silent. It was a bit difficult to free the foot. Mums winced. Morlais saw her face twitch and felt his body contract sharply.

"That's alright," she said.

But she couldn't walk on that foot. Her ankle swelled up and Morlais bandaged it with his handkerchief. Then they went home slowly, one on each side of her. They were too shaken to speak much. They took her up to her bedroom and bathed the sprain and made her comfortable on the bed with a bolster behind her shoulders and a rug over her body.

"There, that's marvellous," she smiled. "Now you two go off and finish the walk like good children."

"No, we won't go out again," Nora said.

"Don't be silly, child. You can't imagine how foolish the two of you look, standing there as though you're determined to catch my last breath."

"But are you sure you're alright, Mums?" Morlais asked, touching her hand.

His touch brought warmth to her grey look.

"Of course I am. And I'll have a nice little nap if you'll go and leave me. Allez-vous-en."

"Well, we'll bring you some nice shell fish for tea, then," Nora said.

Morlais and Nora went out together, just the two of them. Morlais felt it strange, and exciting. There was the same vast reach, the same illimitable promise, the same strange coldness before them now as there had been that moment alone on the jetty. He didn't know what to say before it all. It dwarfed him and made him feel self-conscious, all bunions and nose. Nora was talking about Aberystwyth in her dispassionate satirical way, something about the architectural short-comings of the catering trade; and he could see the point of her sarcasm, and laughed with her; but it wasn't real, what she was saying about Birmingham baroque and parochial gothic; it wasn't *her*. He answered indifferently, annoyed at having to answer, annoyed at this feeling of irrelevance which swept away what she said. He felt himself waiting for her really to speak, to him, Morlais, for the first time. They went by the same path, across the harbour bridge and past the workhouse and the café and the isolation hospital. Morlais was moving towards the jetty, activated by a subconscious attraction.

"Don't let's go along that bleak thing again," she said.

Half-hurt, half-surprised he altered his step at once.

"Alright," he said, falling in with her and going along the path that ran parallel with the shore. The shingle formed a high bank, buttressing the path. The scream of the waves on the pebble ridge had all the wildness of ocean gales in its sounding.

"I'm sorry," she said, after walking a few paces. "You're dying to feel how cold the water is, aren't you?"

He laughed like a child.

"You should have told me to go to hell," she said. "Shall we go down to the shore?"

"Shall we?" he asked. And then, feeling awkward because he had asked her permission as though she was his nurse, he turned, poised a second like a stag sniffing the wind, and leaped down the concave bank of stones. When he reached the boulders across whose shoulders the waves were breaking he looked back. Nora was picking her high-heeled way carefully down to the sea. The wind flung her cape about, making her look like a spider whose bag of a body is being blown off a high ledge. He turned away, feeling embarrassed; as he did so a wave hit the boulders with a soft thud and spume slapped his cheek. All along the beach a veil of fine spray drifted inland over the blue-grey smoothness of the rocks. Watching it he suddenly perceived its poetry. Poetry is action in its most beautiful form, and here was all beauty, the earth having assumed strange perfection, smooth, round, oval, polished and as strong as the burnished armour of an Arthurian knight, pebbles and boulders steely-hued and dappled with green. And the sea was coming in naked and wild with music, washing away the roughness of the earth and casting its marriage veils over the bridal beach. Earth and sea, water and stone, eternally in intercourse, the thrust of the inward flow, the caress of the ebb, the renewal in whiteness of foam and smoothness of rock. And he perceiving it with all his life, like Shelley. He tossed his head back, tasting the salt on his lips, and for the first time felt his manhood respond to the attraction of being without at the same time being tormented with shame.

"It is bleak, isn't it?"

He turned round, hearing her speak by his side.

"I prefer reading about it," she said, picking up a pebble and squeezing it between her fingers. "I got much more kick out of D.H. Lawrence's description of the beach in Kangaroo than ever I've got from my own feeble observation. That's the worst of education. It develops the capacity for second-hand experience at the expense of immediate feeling. A shepherd knows more about Nature than any professor of poetry."

Morlais felt himself dragged into the cold operating theatre of her intellect, forced to resume life on a rational plane.

"You don't like this?" he said foolishly.

"Not much, I'm afraid. I don't know why. I suppose simply because I haven't got the necessary organs. Or perhaps you'd prefer a Freudian explanation. When we were children we used to spend August in Cornwall. There was a long stretch of sand, and rocks covered with honeycombs of hard sand full of worms and soft little crabs. One afternoon I and my brother had a competition in catching crabs. We killed nearly all of them in our haste, prodding them out of their holes with the edge of our spades. I was getting sicker and sicker, and more and more excited. I couldn't stop; it was too disgusting to contemplate; so I won by five crabs with smashed shells."

He looked at her in fascination, held by the hard vein in her quick voice. She was smiling, but fixedly and with a bitter sense of humour.

"I always develop the most morbid thoughts when I'm walking along the beach," she said. "Like listening-in to jazz, it always brings out the worst in me."

His serious attention disconcerted her.

"Have you read Kangaroo, Morlais?"

"No. I've read hardly anything."

"I should think you'd like it. You seem to have Lawrence's feeling for the vitality of things – sea and earth always in eruption, giving vent to their immortal urges. Wahah."

She flung up her arms as though she were forswearing the world as somebody else's business.

"If I'd been born a farmer's daughter I'd probably have found perfect happiness in hedging and ditching and rushing about to see the seeds sprouting madly all over the place. But alas, she was only a rector's daughter. Why do you look so disgusted with me?"

He started.

"I wasn't," he said. "I was only thinking you're different from the photograph we've got of you. I thought you'd be – oh, I don't know. I've never thought a person could *dislike* fields and rivers and things. Lots of people don't know about them, of course; but if you have *discovered* them, I don't know how you can dislike them."

She looked at him quizzically; her silk scarf fallen onto her shoulders and a cluster of rich curls blown over her steady eyes; the wind had flushed her cheeks to a subdued glow.

"I always associate *discover* with two ideas – piracy and research. One can hardly *discover* anything, properly speaking, except buried treasure or a mildewed medieval manuscript mouldering in well-merited must. Gosh, that was alliteration alright, wasn't it?" She laughed with delight, spontaneous for a moment. Then she slipped her hand in the crook of his arm. "Come on, Columbus. Let's get back to Europe. I don't like these damned Bahamas."

"What *do* you like?" he asked, stung by her elusive mockery, pressing his hand deeper into the pocket of his grey trousers so that his elbow held her hand captive. She was so near to him that he could see the down on her cheek and the slight twitch of her delicate nostrils as she breathed. Her eyes, too; there were little jet islands in the deep sea of the irises.

"I refuse to be made to stand and deliver, you bully," she laughed. "Come on, let's go up-river a bit and revive the circulation. Only a heman like Socrates can sit on the ice a whole day and go on thinking till somebody comes with a brazier to thaw him. When I get cold I automatically stop thinking. That's why I love being in digs. It's much too cold to indulge in morbid introspection. Of course it has its disadvantages, too. My thesis, for instance, has all the signs of being written by a complete dolt. Cold fingers, cold brain, that's the process. Everything has a physical cause."

They had climbed the pebble ridge and their feet fell softly on grass. Swifts flashed up and down the stream, white bellies and flickering wings, snapping at the flies. The water had a black sheen on it, cold and deep, a swirl and steady flow of ebony. Then the sun broke out of the melancholy sky and the water was molten silver, gushing against the stones like boiling liquid. Morlais kicked a lump of shale from the path into the stream, frowning and looking at the ground.

"Don't you like College, even?" he asked at last.

She was a long time in replying. They walked on, not looking at each other.

"I don't think it's much use," she said eventually. "It's pretty futile just to take down other people's conclusions in your notebook and them dish them up again at the end of three years. Knowledge doesn't do you any good unless you go through the process of acquiring it yourself."

"But you can learn by yourself if you want to."

"Of course. But why go to college if you can do it better outside? Anyway, I'm a misfit. Don't listen to me. I decided to do research because I thought it was real learning – discovering, if I may borrow your word. And also because I wanted to – oh, I can't explain it. I had a sort of belief that all life was one stream, a kind of bloodstream, Shaw's Life Force. Darwin didn't start the idea. Christ said the same thing. And so I thought I'd reach a feeling of continuity in life, and be able to experience life with the basic instincts and *share* in it, not he cut off from it all the time –"

Her voice had become somehow naked, divested of its respectability.

"D'you understand?" she asked, gripping his arm sharply and forcing him to look at her. Before the intensity of her eyes his own wavered.

"Don't you think you'll succeed?" he asked, clenching his fists in his pocket at the savageness of his question. He hadn't meant to ask her that. She *must* realise he wasn't prodding her wound callously. Only he had to say something, just for breathing space, to tide over the taut moment when she exposed her anguish to him, and he couldn't help but see her naked.

"I don't know," she said. "I don't know at all,"

They walked down the sandy path to the wicket gate; then they had to go in single file along the bank. Nora went first.

"They call this path Nannigoat's Walk," she said. "Nice, isn't it?"

Across the stream Pen Dinas lifted its mountainous bullet head over them.

"There's a pre-Roman camp on top of that brute of a hill," she said.

"Is there, really?" he asked, excitedly. "What a marvellous place to live on. Like an eagle's nest."

She laughed.

"A propos of our discussion on research," she said over her shoulder, "our archaeological society spent months excavating the camp. And we discovered one single relic, an amber bead the size of a pea."

"Well, if it was good quality, it doesn't matter about the quantity."

"We weren't digging for treasure, you noodle. We were digging for something which would enable us to *understand* those people. And a solitary bead won't open the gate to a person's mind any more than a necklace on the neck of a drowned girl will explain why she committed suicide."

The path widened enough for them to walk abreast. Morlais came level with her. People walking shoulder to shoulder are almost invisible to each other. He didn't want to go on looking at her. Every time she made a remark she had turned her head so that he must see her gentle profile, like a fine carving by an old Greek. And he didn't want to say that her face was like a slender sailing boat queening it down Life's stream, nor that when he looked at her he felt the onward joy of that current racing down his veins. Instead he felt a bitter distrust of words, a revulsion from complexity, a trapped feeling that must tear its way out of a tangle of nerves and recover the sea, the rocks, the sunlight on the water. To release himself, therefore, he moved up with her, and when they had walked silently together long enough to recover physical anonymity he ground out the hard words of his thought.

"Mums had a bad sprain, didn't she?"

"Yes. She had a nasty shaking. I don't think we should have left her, really. We'd better turn back soon."

"Yes, I think so, too."

"If we step on it we can go back along the road. There's a bridge ahead of us, and if we cross it I'll show you a lovely eighteenth century house. The sort of house that proves how sane and happy its first owner was. Like to see it? Its rooms must be full of the sound of water."

"Yes, please."

They quickened their pace. After a while Morlais spoke again.

"I wish I knew what to do to make her well."

"She'll be alright by tomorrow, boy. Her ankle only needs rest."

"I didn't mean her ankle. I mean herself."

She stopped abruptly and faced him, searching him with her suddenly apprehensive eyes.

"What d'you mean, Morlais?"

He looked down. The path was wet and swaying with bulrushes, peaty-brown in colour. He plucked the little plumes of seed from the dry spears.

"I don't know," he said slowly. "It's terrible. There's something all smashed up inside her. I know."

She was silent for a long time.

"Aren't she and Uncle Denis happy together?" she asked at last.

He made no reply.

"Let's walk on," she said.

They followed the sweep of the stream, picking their way over the muddy faults where the path had sagged through the tunneling of water rats and the perpetual sapping of the swirling river. Reaching the bridge they stopped again and leaned over the parapet to watch the icy detachment of the water seethe limpidly over the mossy bed of pebble and reef.

"Does she ever talk about David?" she asked.

"No," he replied moodily. The supports of the bridge were mildewed and banked up with drift, straw and sticks and sogged clothing thrown away by some upland farm-wife. "She never says anything about him. But I know she broods about him, I've heard her shouting his name out in her sleep in summer when we leave the bedroom doors open. It's terrible."

"Why?"

"I don't know. Because I feel we're poisoning each other, the three of us. In that big house. I hate it sometimes. Hate it."

"But, Morlais. You don't mean that; you know she's devoted to you."

"How d'you know?"

"The way she looks at you when you're reading or writing, for one thing. And what she says about you, too."

"Don't." He lifted his hand in a blind gesture, his face sharp with anguish.

"Aren't you happy living with them, Morlais?"

"No," he said, his voice trembling. "No. No."

The river gurgled icily round the groyne of refuse, the smooth sheet of water breaking into two diagonal currents. The bridge seemed to be moving upstream, its prow thrusting the current aside.

"I owe them so much," he said. "And they both want me to go to college next year, and it would be so marvellous to go to college. And I do love her. But I can't go on like this much longer, Nora. It hurts too much."

Her hand fell on his sleeve. It had the delicacy of a seashell, her knuckles whorled marble, too fine to touch.

"You're a bit run down after your exams, Morlais. Don't think about it for a month or two. Have a holiday. Take a leap into the pleasure of life. There's plenty to make you happy. Music, mountains, plenty."

"I thought, after what you said about yourself, by the sea just now, that you'd understand and wouldn't say Oh, it's nothing – try Horlicks," he said.

She winced.

"Alright," she said. "I take it all back. Other people's advice isn't much use, I know. Only I wanted to save you from pain. In self-defence mostly, I tried to minimise your trouble, I suppose."

Then she took hold of the lapel of his tweed jacket, making him look at her.

"I'm asking you to do something very hard. I've got no right to ask it of you. But may I?"

"Yes," he said, agitated by the intensity of her.

"Speak to Auntie about it before you do anything. Thrash it out together. Don't sneak away." She paused. "Will you?"

"I can't," he said, his eyes brimming up with tears.

"You must. Force her to speak. Get at the root of it. You're throwing so much away if you break off now. What would you do, anyway?"

He couldn't endure it, the compulsion of her look and the tautness of her lips and fingers. He twisted his coat loose and turned away. He wiped a silly tear off his cheek.

"Oh, Morlais, I'm sorry,"

He felt her hands on his shoulders, all solicitude.

When he made no reply she said "You're so young to have to make such a decision. Can't you let it slide? Just go to college. Take what's been put next on the agenda. Everybody's unhappy, more or less. Can't you accept it? You know you make Auntie happy, don't you?"

"No, I don't," he said through clenched teeth. "I think I'm strangling her."

"Don't be ridiculous," she said sharply. "She's a grown woman. If she's in trouble it's not your making. What harm have you done her?"

He turned round, his face white and heavy.

"It's too terrible to talk about. Let's go back for tea, shall we?"

"Alright." She shrugged her shoulders. "I'm sorry if I appeared to be inquisitive. Turn to the left. The house is just round the corner, under those poplars."

He didn't move.

"It isn't that, Nora. You've been so kind. Only I can't tell you. I *can't.*"

It was too much for him. His face contorted into a desperate grimace. And then it broke into weeping, into upheaval.

She stood still, her body brittle.

"Don't," she gasped.

He was sobbing into his folded arms, bent over the stone parapet, his shoulders shuddering.

She went slowly, reluctantly to him.

"Please, Morlais dear."

Her hand went out and stroked his head softly, smoothing his untidy hair back, lying quietly on his high crown.

Then, the storm abated, he looked up. His raw eyes made him look like a child, not grotesque and dishevelled like an older person weeping.

"I *am* happy, lots of times," he said, as if defying himself. "Only there's this tangle" – he put his fist angrily against his forehead – "in here."

"Never mind," she said. "Never mind now. Let's go back and have some tea and buttered toast."

"But why is it?" he insisted, his voice hoarse with baffled will.

"Why can't I mend it? I try and try and try, terribly hard."

"It will mend in time," she said. "Just as this river makes its way to the sea."

"But now. Now. I want it now."

He clenched his fists at the overpowering sense of urgency within him, the immediate agony and the intense ache to resolve it. Now. Only now.

"Oiae. Young lovers quarrelling, eh?"

They swung round to face an old tramp with creeping

beard and horny skin furrowed and grey with dirt and submission to life and time. He had a sack slung over his shoulders; his torn coat was tied round his waist by string; his boots were broken and unlaced. He had no stockings on; his trousers only half covered his dirty shins. He was laughing, black stubby teeth and clear blue eyes.

"There's only one thing they quarrel about when the apple trees is in blossom, I know. But you make 'im pay for 'is pleasure, young lady. Don't give 'im a baby till 'e've gave you a 'ouse. He-he-he," he dribbled down his yellow beard. "But don't go quarreling, my dears. Time enough for that when you're married."

"Thank you for your good advice," Nora replied, laughing.

"Aye, don't mention it, if it isn't worth a penny, miss."

He touched his cap with a withered brown hand when Morlais gave him a penny. "Good day and God bless you, little sparrows," he said. And he went on unsteadily across the bridge, breaking out in an old quavering voice into Danny Boy.

"There you are," she laughed. "That's all Father Time has got in the way of wisdom. Come on, Morlais. You're compromising my good name here, evidently."

"I can't imagine being his age," he replied. "It seems impossible."

So they went back to Aberystwyth, talking about old age and success and failure and the ruthlessness of society and the undying will to live. The sun came out as they went down the hill towards the town and all the mayflower and apple blossom began dancing. The finches left their nests to chatter and flash their wings in the river of gold. The tide came glittering up the harbour, lifting the yachts from the mudflats and rocking them gently in its lap.

"Isn't it lovely," he breathed, twitching at the freshness of it.

"Yes," she said, "let's run."

They raced down the hill like school children going to the sweetshop, simply excited with life.

As they crossed the bridge into town Nora stopped abruptly, checking him with her hand.

"What's up?" he asked. "Dropped something?"

"No," she replied. "Only I forgot to show you that house. Still, I don't suppose you feel like settling down just yet."

For some reason or other Morlais felt as fresh as dew on the grass from the moment they ran down the hill. They bought pikelets and muffins in a little front parlour shop with bottle glass windows and took them home to toast in front of the gas fire. Mrs Reames was so glad to see them again that her response made them also enjoy each other's company. It was nice to be together, and the swelling had gone down; she could walk if she stepped lightly. They even enjoyed being stinted of butter for the muffins. Landladies are very human.

Waking up the next morning was the same. A pellucid day, the little window framing the blue colour of joy; the rumble and clang of the fish barrows wheeled from the ketches in the harbour ringing crystal-clear, voices of children going to school bright with laughter. Some force inside him, some vivid impulse flung him out of bed, white sheet and pink quilt thrown topsy turvy, bare feet tingling with the white feel of scrubbed floor boards. He splashed the water out of the cracked jug into the yellowing bowl, and it was all good. New.

They went round the College. One moment he leaned alone over the stone balcony and stared down at the deep cold well of the empty quadrangle. And saw himself down there with gown and books, and heard the bell ring for lectures. There were other students there, all talking and flirting, and sometimes he lost sight of himself among them all. But their talk didn't interrupt his reverie any more than bees break summer silences. He could feel his heart pounding against

the cold stone. His body was all desire. Then he followed the
other two up the steps to the library, which had two great
doors of darkened wood. He tried to open one in vain. He
twisted the knob and pushed with his knee, but it stayed shut.
He felt small and jumpy and shut out from something; from
the envisaged room, the tiers of books rising dizzily to the
glass dome, and the people talking in whispers and looking
down through the bow windows at the blue sea, then turning
again to the books in their hands and turning the pages over,
forgetting him, forgetting all about him.

The other door opened from inside. Mums and Nora came
out. They both laughed, seeing him gripping the knob of the
locked door. He laughed too, mirthlessly, suddenly craving
the sunlight and the careless holiday crowd and an end to this
fluttering of wings inside him, this ranging round the cold
quadrangular tomb.

But outside it was all alive again, the stone flags of the
promenade blindingly white; the sea sparkling; frocks all
sharp colours like jagged rocks; skirts blown across the vision
like foam driven or excited butterflies; green lamps and
benches; upright old colonels; ladies with bottle-legs and
poms straining bad-temperedly at the leash; girls sitting on
the green railings with sand paper laughter at the antics of
their boys who must treat them to pink ices and answer them
back with red hands on their bare knees – "Love and litter,"
laughed Nora. "Let's go and sit in the castle grounds."

They bathed from the shingle after lunch. Morlais said it
was just like plunging into a huge glass of Andrew's Liver
Salts. Nora, floating on her back, said that was the nicest thing
she'd ever heard about the sea. Afterwards they lay on their
backs watching the seagulls squabble and stab each other in
the verminous tide wrack and suddenly take wing with swift
wing beats, shooting sharp angles of flight through the
breathless air. The heat burnt off the pebbles; a woman came
down with a basket of washing and laid, the white sheets on

the pebbles, fastening them at the corners with stones. The bathing pool was crowded with children no room to sail boats or sit down properly.

"Sunbathing is the only thing I can do perfectly," Nora sighed contentedly. "I have a marvellous feeling, as if I'm really fulfilling myself for once. Shall we go to the tea dance afterwards, Morlais?"

Morlais turned over, finding his arm cramped and his bare side raw with rough sand.

"I can't dance."

"Oh. Pity. Why haven't you taught him to dance, Auntie? It's very remiss of you. No young man can be considered eligible if he can't dance. It's a deformity. He might as well have his leg in irons. Really."

Mrs Reames took off her sun glasses and laid them down on her novel.

"You really are ungraciously decadent, Nora," she said, "considering the fine weather."

Nora flushed, digging her fingers into the sand.

"As a matter of fact I think he can dance," Mrs Reames added. "Margaret our maid taught him in the kitchen. Didn't she, Morlais? Own up."

"Yes, twice, that's all."

"Well, three times for a Welshman," Nora said. "Come on. Put some clothes on. Coming, Auntie?"

"No, I don't think so, dear. I think I'll just sit. You two go, though. That is, if Morlais is as restless as you."

So they went along the promenade to the Pier and took a table behind the band.

"You don't need any sugar in your tea with the crooner so near," Nora said. "He's more cloying than Tennyson, even."

The tables had glass tops; through the glass windows they could see the sea; the pleasure boat coming in like an obese porpoise covered with shrimps. They had peach melbas, icy cold, tall glasses.

"When are you going to go on with your work?" Morlais said, fumbling amid all the sensations of being in a thé dansant with a girl whom the loungers at the next table were eyeing for her good looks.

"Oh dear. Why drag that up?" She tasted the iced peach. "I don't know. When you go back, I expect. Unless my moral cowardice drives me there tomorrow."

"What d'you mean?"

"Well, it's easy to hide oneself in an alcove and worm one's way through a pile of tomes. But it doesn't mean anything." She looked up with a sudden challenge. "Or does it?"

He coloured at her look.

"When you do something real you should feel it in your guts," she said.

He was holding the ice-cream wafer in his fingers. Some unconscious pressure snapped it. It was like something in his head breaking. Something brittle, like a tiny shell of mother-of-pearl. He didn't dare say anything in reply. Words would fall like boulders through the fine ice, leaving a jagged hole, and blackness.

"No, Luce. I 'aven't been out with 'im at all, tell you the truth. 'E do live next door but one to us. It don't seem worth it, some'ow, going out sparking when you're neighbours. It's different with a student or a visitor. You never know, like, then, do you?"

Two girls had come to the next table. The one who was speaking was powdering her face at the same time. The other one was contemplating the bunch of young men in grey bags and plain navy blazers standing by the dance floor.

"I think I'll give 'im a try," she said. "Don't like them sideboards, though."

"They won't show in the dark, gal. Don't bother."

Nora laughed, mostly at Morlais's confusion.

"I do lead you into the most vulgar predicaments, don't I?" she teased. "Shall we dance?"

She stood up, pushing her chair back. Flushed with the afternoon's sun, and animated with her detached amusement, and strong and light in her low-necked voile frock, she gave him a floating sensation as he walked along the soft carpet with her to the waxed floor. He was nervous again as soon as he held her ready. Like an old lady waiting for a likely step on the escalator he waited to catch the beat of the slow foxtrot. Then, he didn't know whether she led him into the rhythmic maze or whether their two bodies felt the dance and floated into it like a boat lifted off the mud bank by the inflowing tide – they were dancing. Tall mirrors in the white panelled walls had their image gliding past. It was a fact. It *was*.

It was a thistledown walk home, perspiring and careless, full of chatter. Morlais was too happy to think. So Mrs Reames's pale and frightened face in the stodgy parlour of Nora's digs jabbed him like an iron pick.

He said "What' s the matter?"

Nora said, "Auntie!"

She said, swallowing and going a shade paler, ashy, "I'm afraid we'll have to go home, Morlais."

"What's happened, Mums?" he said, drawn to her and kneeling on the shabby carpet beside her chair.

"I listened to the wireless news – the door was open and it was on full blast in the kitchen. It said there was rioting at a pit in Tredwr following the dismissal of one of the colliers. The police had to make a baton charge. Three men are in hospital and some of the machinery has been damaged."

"Oh," he said, sickening and shaking all over like a distempered dog.

"I'm afraid for Denis," she said. "I'm going home tomorrow. You can stay, though."

The little clock whirred, then dropped a tinny chime. The silence of the parlour formed into a whirlpool, dragging them round and round. The street seemed remote, a street in

Murmansk. The sea broke round rocky cliffs in the Faroes. Nora lit a cigarette after Mrs Reames had waved away her proferred packet of twenty. She let the match burn, watching the flame.

"Can we catch a train tonight?" Morlais asked, stammering and dry-lipped. He was sweating profusely.

"No. The last one left at five," she said. "We'll have to wait till tomorrow morning. You're perspiring."

"I'm sure it'll be alright," Nora said, "Anyway, how about going to the first house at the Coliseum? The Marx Brothers are there."

She looked at Morlais as hard as she could. He had stood up, leaning now against the sideboard with the light from the street on his uncertain features. There was a pimple at the corner of his mouth; his whole face drooped, his bottom lip sagging open a little and showing his white uneven teeth.

"Come on," she said when she caught his vague gaze, holding his troubled eyes and forcing him to obey. "It's no good getting panicky. Go and wash the salt off your eyebrows, Morlais."

It was a relief to do something. Washing, wiping, parting his hair – each action had the power of motion and reality. He took a long time over them, towelling his face with unnecessary vigour and pulling the fluff off his chin afterwards with careful slowness. On the way to the cinema he was aware of his legs walking, of his shoes and the tarry surface of the road. In the cinema was darkness and scent of Jeyes and the luxury of plush seats and the laughter of a full house. Groucho and Harpo enthralled him and he laughed hysterically out of his profound uneasiness.

Even in bed he felt nothing except, a blurred indecisive pain. Bed was darkness and a flattened body between sheets. Turning the hot pillow over produced coldness against his cheek. Sleep perpetuated the emotions' deadlock, heavy and dreamless. Only when they were leaning out of the compartment window next morning with their suitcases on the rack and Nora hurrying along the platform with an Illustrated Weekly and TitBits did the two ends meet. The spark spurted into flame inside him and he could have shouted at the driver to stop chatting with the porter and smoking his clay pipe and get going, get up steam at once to break the agony of being stationary in the grey neutral station. To do something he stepped down onto the platform and walked to meet Nora.

"Be careful, Morlais," Mrs Reames said, seeing the guard coming up with his leather box and furled flags.

"Alright," he said, and started running.

"Here you are," Nora said, giving him the papers.

"How much was it?" he replied fumbling in his pocket.

"Nothing, silly," she said, holding his wrist.

"But yes –" he insisted.

"Quick, don't waste time," she said. "Listen." He was still facing her, close up, and she still held his wrist. "Write to me when you've got time, will you?" She gave a little laugh, half apology. "Life's a bit thin up here."

"Oh yes. May I?" he breathed.

"The guard's ready. Come on. Auntie'll be having D.T.s."

He got into the compartment, leaning over Mrs Reames. Nora moved from one foot to the other. The train started moving. Puff – heavy puff – like a fat man feeling the heat.

"Goodbye, Nora. Thank you so much for your hospitality. You'll be able to get some work done now."

"Write, won't you, Auntie? So glad you came. Goodbye. Goodbye, Morlais."

The platform dwindling, the clink of points crossed. "Goodbye...." The platform ended, running down swiftly to the clinker walk. Nora was still standing, getting doll-like; a toy porter wheeled an empty barrow past her. Mums was waving. The train swung round the bend. He felt his heart contract as the station vanished.

"Goodbye," he shouted, leaning out of the window, still standing on the seat. As if she could hear.

Then it was just he and Mums. They were silent for that flat hiatus of feeling, sitting and regarding each other blankly, as though somebody had swept past them, ignoring them. She crushed her handkerchief into a ball.

"Better take a last look at the sea, Morlais," she said.

For a long long moment the sea was in sight. Then they swung inland. On the other side of the river was Nannigoat's Walk. He saw it with a jerk; it ripped and parched him violently. They had been along that little green track; they weren't there now. He looked out through the other window and glimpsed between sycamore and elms an old slate roof and a grey porch, wistaria and a frieze of poplars. The house.

Then they were in unknown land, going through a cutting with a roar, and he felt the dead weight of himself.

It must have gripped her, too, the same necessity to surrender. "Well, we're going home, then," she said slowly, half to herself.

It was a bad journey, a dream impossible to alter or dispel. The names of the stations repeated themselves in reverse order, like a spool of negatives unrolling in the mind. Caradog Falls, poverty stricken stone cottages clinging to the brink of a wild fall of white river, ashes and tins and tyres on the spurs of the cliff. Strata Florida grey and listless and lost in its brown swamps, letting them go without a nod, without a valediction. Derry Ormond, too, in rain misted and bemused. They stayed a long time in Lampeter, nothing happening, no passengers alighting or entering. There was a yellow tin advertisement fastened to the railings outside their window.

"Would you like to try one of Duck, Son and Pinker's pianos, of Bath, Bristol and the West of England?" she asked, reading the black words. "Or do you favour the flute as a means of expression?"

"I prefer the saxophone," he replied. "Would you like me

to slip out and buy a bottle of Stephen's Ink? I expect they sell what they advertise."

"If you must buy me a present I'd like some Jeyes Fluid. Or better still, wait till we get to Carmarthen and get me a cup and saucer full of tea."

Forced jokes, forced laughter, long intervals of looking out through the rain-blurred window; so the slow journey went on. They talked about Aberystwyth, the dance, the college, the accents of Lancashire. But disconnectedly, the topics snapping off, drying up, their thoughts sucked back into themselves again. Neither of them mentioned Nora. When marketing farmers came into the carriage they silently welcomed the incursion of an alien presence which released them from the need for conversation and gave their eyes and nostrils occupation.

They reached Carmarthen after three hours of this.

Now they had to change trains. They had difficulty in finding a seat; it was a main line train. Eventually they squeezed into a smoking compartment, blue with smoke. The windows were misted with steam inside; outside they were slashed with horizontal sabre cuts of rain. There were six men in the compartment when they entered, all of them smoking. Two of them moved up ungraciously, swirling the blue smoke. They sat down in as short space as possible, keeping their elbows in to their sides, one on each seat, facing each other in the middle of the compartment.

"Would you like to change? Sit with your back to the engine?" he asked.

A man in a bowler hat looked over his paper with severe eyes and bushy eyebrows, sombrely sucking his pipe. Morlais shouldn't have spoken as loud as that. Damn it all.

A few stations further on three railwaymen got in, standing. They filled the floor space. Morlais felt his feet getting cramped. He was sweating under his armpits; wishing he'd taken his mackintosh off.

The strain tightened; he wanted to speak. Must speak. Knowing that speech on the matter he had in mind was impossible here.

He wanted to go to the lavatory, too.

He stayed there, neither speaking nor moving, only perspiring with the tension on his thoughts and his bladder.

When at last they did get out, changing for the third and last time into a small local train only twenty minutes from Tredwr, two stops only, he had lost the will to speak. He was just ragged and amorphous and morbidly aware that it was no good speaking. Not even if she broached the subject. Watching her covertly as she wiped and powdered her hot face in the mirror of her shell flap-jack he wondered whether she had said anything to Nora – about him, or about the trouble at the pit.

Oh, who was it had been hurt? Who'd had the sack? And why?

No. He didn't want to know; didn't want to think about it. Not yet. She was pulling on her yellow gloves, looking down thoughtfully. No, she wouldn't have told Nora much; certainly nothing about herself. She was too complete for that, somehow, like ice, compounded of innumerable crystals and facets, a unity.

She was a great lady, wonderful. All these years close around him, and always unfolding new things naturally for him, books of stories and reproductions of great paintings, poetry, music, the flowers in her garden, which she planted and watered and pruned and cut for the great bowls of frosted glass. There were distant snows she knew of; she could transport him there with the silken swish of her skirt and her carefully chosen words, estimating the worth of a poet, of an artist, expansively, constructively. And to find her in her bedroom dragged down, degraded at being seen incomplete, unfinished, beaten. Only four days ago. Oh, Mums.

She looked up suddenly out of her thoughts and caught his

eyes red-handed regarding her. His body jerked guiltily; hastily he yawned.

"Sleepy, dear?" she asked gently, seeing his wet eyes.

"It *is* hot."

"I'll open the window. Rainy weather in July is always oppressive."

She spoke off-handedly, far away. She let the window drop. Rain scurried in, hitting her in the face.

"Oh," she gasped, wakened. She laughed. "That one got me."

She moved away from the window.

"Uch," she said, her shoulders huffing in sudden revulsion. "Look."

A colliery straddled across the narrow gorge of the valley. And a great slag tip sprawling down the mountain, a journey of trams crawling up the black vertebrae of it, bedraggled refugees taking their badness to untenanted high places to vomit the defiling stuff among the ferns, and return empty to the pithead, to be once more and unremittingly corrupted. The sharp rock shoulder of the mountain held the valley breathless, hunched over it, ignorant of the misery of rain. Damp clothes, sodden working boots, washed underclothes and Welsh flannel shirts drying by the kitchen fire, sweat, boredom. Children with broken shoes, water squelching through cracked soles, sitting in wet stockings in the coalhouse at the top of the garden, playing house and carving swords from old laths, too engrossed to wipe their noses after sneezing or feel the cramp beset their bony dirty legs.

The train steamed stoically up the valley, swung onto the viaduct, rumbled slowly over the eight arches of dripping stone, and plunged with a scream into the tunnel. It emerged in Tredwr and stopped shudderingly, as though it had over-run itself.

"Tredwr," shouted a porter unnecessarily.

"He ought to know," she said. "He's been on this platform

ever since I came to live here."

"He was born here," Morlais said, yanking her suitcase off the rack.

"He lives three doors down from us. I mean –" he flushed, – "from my father's house."

"You're well up in local physiognomy, dear," she said.

"Yes. Whatever that means."

"The science of love at first sight," she laughed.

So they were back in Tredwr. And he'd said nothing, despite his promise. The broken pledge was real, like a bad nerve in him. But the promise itself and Nora and the afternoon along Nannigoat's Walk were as remote and unapproachable as Hans Andersen's Land.

They had wired from Carmarthen. But Mr Reames wasn't there. A taxi driver touched his shiny-peaked cap.

"Mrs Reames?"

"Yes."

She held the umbrella, Morlais carried one suitcase, the taxi driver the other. Morlais had refused to give him both.

"No, please. It's quite alright," Morlais said. "I can carry one."

The man was as embarrassed as he, but didn't insist. Let him, if he wants to be a man....

They sat back, deep in the corners of the back seat. There was room to make a bed on the floor of the taxi with the bucket seats up. The confetti hadn't been swept out, either. Had they had confetti at Doris's wedding? Doris.... He hadn't heard anything about her since.

"Woolworth's," she said gloomily, looking through the window. "Smith's. The Square. The cenotaph. Co-operative Stores. Ricci's for coffee. The Duke's Hotel." The taxi purred on, no sound except the spurt of water as the tyres slid through the shining wet streets. "The National School. Playtime already? Three-thirty. The train was ten minutes late. Oh dear. Isn't it hideous, Morlais?"

She was nervously moving her knuckles under her chin, her eyes blue with fright.

Then the waste ground below the grimy station where the train stopped, forced to retrace itself because of the impassible mountains, and the black river in spate with muddy froth. Then Glannant Street, same as ever, pavements empty because of the wet, children squirming over the scrubbing boards wedged in open doorways. To a standstill by the green gate. And they climbed out, stiff and anxious and travel-sick, to return Mr Reames's troubled and pre-occupied welcome-home, four days after saying goodbye.

They left the suitcases in the hall and went into the dining room. There was a fire, just nicely burning through, and the table was laid with a clean starched cloth and the best cutlery and crockery.

"How thoughtful of you, Denis," she said, looking round the room and sensing the prepared welcome. "My hands *are* a bit cold."

"All the same," he said, smiling at her as she bent over the fire, "I wish you'd had a decent holiday while you were at it, instead of running back as soon as you got there. Couldn't you keep her there a little longer, Morlais?"

Standing in the door in his raincoat, Morlais shuffled his feet and grinned unsteadily.

"We both wanted to come back," he said.

Mr Reames was looking at him. There was some kind of breadth in his direct glance, some power of bluntness in his square shoulders and hewn features that made it difficult to return his look without feeling a diminution of one's own stature. Morlais felt like a guilty child silently arraigned by his father, dropped his eyes and flushed with anger. He wasn't in the wrong. He'd done nothing, And yet he felt ashamed. Ashamed to ask who'd been sacked, and why, and what had happened. And angry because Mr Reames wouldn't tell him and because there was something in that look that impelled him to go away.

"So you're back again then," Mr Reames said, settling the matter.

He picked up the paper. Morlais, thwarted in his urgent wish to know, went into the hall, hung up his raincoat and went upstairs. He knew what it was. They were waiting for him to get out of the way before they talked about the trouble, they kept him outside; always had done. When he entered the front room in the evenings after finishing his homework they became two other people. Not husband and wife, but host and hostess. He could hear the undertone of the previous conversation flowing along in their minds while they talked to him about school. Sometimes, in the gaps between sentences, the undertone became a drumming in his ears. Well, he didn't want to hear their secrets; he didn't want to pry. But this time he must be told. This time their secret was his secret, too. The sealed envelope must be opened, not locked away from him. In it was the letter instructing him what to do.

He took his own suitcase into his bedroom and dropped it onto the bed. For a minute he sat on the blue coverlet. Dear room; books lying about untouched since he left, a sheaf of school notes beside his bed – last minute swotting before turning the light out. And the sheaf of notes, thumbed and dirty, struck into him with a pang.

All that was over and done with. All over for good.

Dear room.

It was as if the fixed scheme had been smelted, all the familiar faces and objects reduced to their original amorphous matter, and now slowly, with intense pain, recast.

He jumped up from the bed. The room, and the silence, it was too painful to feel both those mingling; blood and acid.

He washed and combed his hair in the bathroom. He felt hot, and inside him was all molten liquid, black and burning. He could smell boiling tar in his mouth, like a whiff from a road-making machine. Oh God.

He stood at the top of the stairs, wanting to go down to the dining room, open the closed door, and demand the truth.

He stood there a minute, clenching the bannister head, then picked up her suitcase and carried it along the landing to her bedroom.

He put it at the foot of the bed, turned quickly from himself in the long glass of the wardrobe, and stood by the bow window, staring vacantly down at the garden, now grey with the shadow of the mountain mist. Nothing moved out there, neither the rhododendron bushes nor the tall elms nor the great chestnut with its pagodas of flower buttressed by the blackness under the thick spread of leaf clusters. And the path was empty.

If something would only happen, something to shatter this thin glass globe of standing still, the remoteness of this tormenting ignorance.

It was.

It was. Instinctively he jumped back and stooped, in case he should be seen.

He was trembling.

It was his father, coming up the path.

Carefully he watched. It was him. His cloth cap and old grey raincoat. Through the closed window he could hear his heavy boots crunching the gravel. Holding his breath he heard the doorbell tinkle in the kitchen, faint through closed doors. And then there was a pause, during which life lapsed into eternity. And life flooded back in action again with Maggie opening the kitchen door and her footsteps sounding in the hall.

"Hallo, Mr Jenkins," she said, a note of incredulity in her voice.

Familiarity, too. He was one of her class.

"Is the boss in, Mag?" – his virile voice sounded raw, roughened.

"Yes, he's *in*," she said doubtfully. "Said he wouldn't see anybody for an hour, though."

"Tell 'im it's me. And that I'm leg-sore with looking for work," he replied with short temper.

"O.K.," she said, "'E said 'e wouldn't, though."

Morlais, standing on the landing, scarcely breathing, heard Maggie knock at the dining room door and a moment later announce the caller.

A slight pause, then Mr Reames came into the hall.

"Want to see me, Jenkins?"

"Yes, sir, matter of fact."

"What is it you want?"

"Nothing I'd care to say in public."

"Will you go in there, then? I've got some work to finish, I'll be with you in two minutes."

Morlais heard his father go into the sitting room, Mr Reames went back to the dining room.

"It's Morlais's father, dear," he said.

Her voice was quick with apprehension.

"What does he want?" she said.

The door closed.

So it was all round him now. All in the house. Under his feet there.

And he locked away in the garret, gnawed by guesses.

Mr Reames came out of the dining room, crossed the hall and went into the front room, closing the door after him. Then she came out. Morlais slipped into the bathroom and noiselessly shot the bolt. He heard her go into his bedroom. Then she went into her own, passing the lavatory door. A moment later she was trying the door, pushing it.

"Morlais?" she said softly. "Are you there?"

"Yes," he said, and then, ridiculously, "Are you in a hurry?"

"No. Only come into my bedroom when you've finished."

"Right."

He hesitated for a time before knocking the catch off the frosted glass window and pushing it up. His bedroom on the right and the sitting room on the left both projected beyond the lavatory. If he slid down the drain pipe to the garden nobody would see him.

He squeezed through the small window with difficulty. The pipe was clamped to the wall; sliding down it his hands bruised against the rough facing of cement. If somebody came he'd look a fool, climbing out of his own bogs. He reached the ground, shaking all over, knuckles bleeding, and ran on tip toe round the front of the house. He thought he'd noticed the French windows were open when they came from the taxi. He was right. Standing against the wall between the window and the porch, trying not to trample the flowers, he heard their voices with alarming distinctness. They sounded so close that he felt they must know he was there. He stayed there like a frightened little cutpurse, frightened of being caught, frightened of what they were saying, on edge for any sound.

"I wouldn't 'ave come of myself," his father was saying. "But my missus said if I didn't, she would. She's not going to let the children starve out of pride,"

"But you're qualified for the dole, Jenkins. There's no talk of starving, man. You were dismissed. Officially because we are cutting down staff. You're alright."

"Alright." His father's voice was lined with lead. "The only time I 'aven't earned my bread with my own 'ands was during the '26 strike. I'm not the one to live on the dole."

"Well, you're an experienced haulier. I shouldn't think you'll have much difficulty in finding a new job."

There was a pause.

"I've always 'ad a liking for you, Mr Reames. Not liking, p'r'aps. Respect. I thought you were straight with the men. Downright. Now I think my missus said right. She said you've stole my 'ands from me same as you stole my eldest boy."

Morlais tensed himself, pressing his shoulders and the back of his head against the wall. The room was silent. Then somebody struck a match. Then silence.

"It's not much use apologising, Jenkins, I know," Mr Reames said slowly, very quiet, "I've treated you shabbily. It's clear. It's not worthwhile saying that I feel not only bitterly sorry, but also contemptible, shameful. I'd rather this should have happened to anyone else. Not simply because of Morlais, but also because you're a thoroughbred yourself. Otherwise you wouldn't have asked for your rights when you knew what the result would be. I'm sorry. Very sorry. I acted on orders from head office. It was my job or yours."

"It's not that I'm 'olding against you so much," Mr Jenkins replied.

"It's what took place today."

"What?"

"Well, I didn't 'ave a reference, or nothing, and I wasn't going to ask you for one, neither. So I tramped to every colliery within five miles of Tredwr and asked for work as an ordinary collier. 'You're the Jenkins they sacked at the top pit yesterday?' they asked. 'Sorry. We've got no use for you 'ere.' Every office the same."

After a pause Mr Reames said. "I suppose that's my doing, too. I had to send your name in to head office. They've circularised the other pits, though. Not me."

"Oh well, what's the odds?" Mr Jenkins said, his voice fallen flat. "It's a dead end. There you are. No good getting your moss off."

"I doubt whether I can do anything Jenkins. If you're thinking of moving from the district – there's good work for Welsh colliers in the Midlands, you know; I'd be only too pleased to help you to move – financially."

Mr Jenkins laughed. His voice was strong again.

"I wouldn't borrow or beg from you nor no man," he said.

"Work is what I want. And I'm not going out of this district till I've fought your damned company and beat it. Don't think you can manage me as easy as you did Morlais, Mister bloody Reames,"

"Very well. If you will misinterpret my motives, Jenkins, it's not much use us continuing this talk. Is there anything else?"

"I came to ask you for a reference. It's my due, after all."

Mr Jenkins sounded defiant and debased.

"I'll post you one tomorrow. Is there anything besides?"

A tense silence in Morlais's head and taut body, waiting the reply.

"No. Only –" he faltered – "there's Morlais. If you could tell us whether 'e was satisfied with 'is exams. We'd like to know."

Something crumpled up inside the boy, softly like a blown egg shell or a floating mass of thistledown suddenly crushed in a hand. It snatched his breath in and he leaned forward, putting his hand to the pit of his stomach, as though he had stitch. He couldn't see, except dazedly. He didn't hear Mr Reames's reply.

But he did hear her bedroom window go up behind him. The sash rattled like the knife of the guillotine on his neck, cutting right through him.

He caught a quick glimpse of her standing at the window watching him as he ran.

He didn't even realise how silly it was to return by the way he had come. He did it unthinkingly, running to earth. He slipped down the pipe once, climbed again three feet up, slipped back, made a desperate effort, clutching the pipe with his knees so hard that cramp took him. But he got up, and through the window.

He felt like being sick.

He wasn't going to be, though. It wouldn't come.

"Morlais," she called through the door.

He turned from bending over the pan and quickly shot the

bolt back.

Easier to open it straight away than go on hiding.

But he didn't expect the flush of power that came into him as he faced her. Liquid heat.

"Well?" he said loudly, "what d'you want to say?"

She looked bewildered, very pale and gentle and uncertain.

"I thought I saw you outside the front window," she said. She frowned, putting her hand over the bridge of her nose. "I must be seeing you everywhere. Must try and think about you less."

"You did see me," he said.

"Did I? I thought I did." She sounded half-there, lost.

"What are you going to say?" he asked, forcing the issue while he could stand it.

"Say? Say?," she said slowly. Then, seeing his hands, "Oh dear, your knuckles are dripping blood. Oh Morlais." She shuddered. "Come to the bathroom, let's iodine them and get the dirt out."

She turned the hot water tap on and poured some iodine into the water,

"Now," she said, taking his hand and he letting her, simply.

She bathed it carefully, taking the grit out with a swab of cotton wool.

"Is it hurting?" she asked gently.

"No," he answered, watching the white nape of her neck.

There were starlings outside, bowing and scraping like street fiddlers. Long ago, when he came here first, the starlings had been there. On summer nights he could hear the hungry youngsters th-th-th-ing for food. In years past. He felt terribly lonely, old, tired, dead tired.

"Is that better?"

"Yes," he answered, seeing the crows-feet at the corner of her eye.

"Remember," she said, looking up; her face was raw and haggard, "all the black coal dust in David's wounds when he was killed."

She was still holding his hand. And his gaze. He didn't move.

"I watched the old woman washing him, I thought it must be hurting him still. Terribly. As if you'd skinned a plum and dropped it in the dirt."

She smiled. He couldn't bear the smile, and turned away, seeing nothing.

"That night I was afraid to go to bed. I stayed in the sitting room, doing nothing." Her voice was slow and measured. "When the pain left me – it was like having a child, coming in long pangs and leaving me sweating – I thought I'd never believe in anything again. And Denis – oh my God, he said – he said "We can have another son, dear." He never liked David, really. I knew that then, for certain. I was engaged to a man called David. He jilted me. Denis hated the name. Oh God, I'm a mess."

She put her shaking head softly against his shoulder, just resting her forehead against the rough tweed. Her whole body was quivering.

"Oh, Mums," Morlais said, two or three times. "Please, Mums."

She shook her head, jerking upright, tautening with an effort of will.

"I'm sorry," she said, unnaturally steady, "I wanted to say something else. This came out. Yes, that's what I intended to say – it's about you. The day David had his coffin, the first day, Margaret brought me some lemon juice before going to bed. She told me they were searching the mountain for you, that you'd run away from your scholarship exam. I made Denis help in the search. I remember the lights, like stars in black velvet on the mountain. They might have been looking for me up there in the darkness, for when Denis said you'd been found I laughed with joy. It was astonishing. Pure joy. Redemption. You don't know the world of shadows through and through, do you? Lovers know it. It's the price they pay. I thought having a child would dispel it. And then again having you. Bless you always, – Morlais Jenkins."

There are moments when we see into a person, when words have a supernal lucidity and power to explain and when the soul and all the lifetime's desires and defeats take to themselves the lineaments of the face. It is impossible to describe the first meeting of man with God, a stooping apeman with hanging forepaws, low forehead, lidless red eyes, standing on a mountain glacier among eternal snows, very old and hairy and trembling before God, the power that turned the icefields to grass and runnels of water before those bewildered red eyes that could not close or blink. Impossible to describe what Morlais saw, looking at the map of her face, the valleys running down to the sea, the black reefs, the impasses of granite, the devastated meadows.

"Stop looking at me," she said, shuddering. Her eyes grew warm and glazed. She looked at him searchingly, embracing him with that look, then dropped his hand and took up a roll of bandage to bind his clean knuckles.

"Thank you," he said when she had finished.

"And now I think I'll have a bath," she said. "I'm filthy after that long journey. It seems years ago, doesn't it?"

"Yes," he said automatically, turning from her.

"Morlais."

He stopped in the doorway,

"Yes?"

"You won't stay out late, will you?"

"No, Mums."

He smiled to her and closed the door softly behind him. He went into his room, closing the door, and stood by the window for a long time, just looking out. Then he went to his desk and began writing a letter. To Nora. He tore up three sheets of paper, pushed the pad away, and sat till it was dusk, his head buried in his hands. He heard the bath water gurgle down the drain pipe. Long after that he got up and opened the door softly. The landing was empty, dim; the stairs went down to a well of dusk. He tiptoed downstairs and slipped out into the garden. The moon was up, behind the mist, a soft effulgence like the bloom of lilies. The garden was silent and among the vague bushes he was safe. Alone. Precious, this interlude of stillness, of neither asking nor being asked, lonely on a sailing boat between the islands, the tiller lifeless under the dreaming hands. Then he went into the house, summoned by the shaft of green light falling across the lawn from the uncurtained French windows.

They had a pass-round supper and a pass-round talk, casually. Then they all three went to bed. Morlais fell asleep listening to the rain, which had come on again, and to the stillness....

He woke under her touch. Not her physical touch. But he knew she was in the room, in the pitch dark. He felt her presence, tingling in him. But he didn't move. His eyes opened, that was all.

She sat on his bedside, softly, carefully. Her hand touched him, his hair, his ear. He closed his eyes. Her fingers touched his eyelids.

He could hear her breathing. She moved and he felt her breath warm on his forehead. Her lips glanced over his cheek and forehead.

In a whisper she spoke.

I loved you, Atthis, once, long long ago;
You seemed to me a small ungainly child.

The words were familiar, under a drift of memories, in the warmth and the slumber stirring some association.

She left his bedside, and he heard the soft rustle of her silk dressing gown in the darkness, going away from him, like a moth....

Waking was like being tied down to the muddy bed of a pond and struggling up. Filmy unidentifiable dreams loomed monstrously about him.

"Nora," he gasped, pushing the overheated clothes off his prone body.

There was something insistent deep in the morass of apprehensions that must be released, dredged for by memory. That must be done first.

He couldn't remember anything at all.

He got out of bed quickly, in a panic, and went to the bathroom for a cold bath. He passed the boxroom. The door was open.

On the makeshift bed inside the boxroom Mums was sleeping. Her hair was down and she wore her dressing gown.

He scurried back to his room. His watch on the dressing table said six thirty. Nobody was awake yet.

He leaned out of the window, gulping at the raw air. He remembered her coming now. Therefore he sucked at the cold and neutral day. He could hear the sound of men calling in the coal sidings, and working boots in the lane. And then the hooter sounded from the pithead. Icy cold, he went back to bed and pulled the clothes over his head.

The opposing armies slept, the past and the future, yesterday and today; a brief uneasy truce while the sun delayed.

For the next hour he slept sweetly like a nut ripening in its shell, alive for the sounds of movement in the house, listening subconsciously and yet untroubled. The sound of Maggie's key in the back door woke him, an electrical contact. He listened to her movements half-awake, and drowsily they came to him, lulling him with their familiarity. The sound of a poker raking the ashes out of the grate, of carpets beaten against the back wall, of a cheap love song, of banter with the milkman and the clink of can and gill. And then that feeling of yesterday came back, deep deep sadness. Each well-known sound rang through and through him with a poignancy that wounded him and yet brought such delight that he didn't know whether he was weeping silently for sorrow or for joy.

Then a hurried step on the landing, coming from the front bedroom.

"Edith," Morlais heard him say, "Oh my darling."

Morlais put his fingers against his ear drums to shut out the anguish of that voice. He was always so strong, so quiet, and so much hidden, like the winding machine in the pit engine house before the mechanic set the great steel wheels whirring. And now it was as if his heart was being retched up.

When he woke again the sun had made the mirror a sheet of bright water, long indented reaches of light dazzling his uncovered eyes. He threw the clothes off, hot and dark and repulsive now like another animal's lair. He was thinking of the fox he had seen, long long ago, in the back lane, cooped in a barrel covered with wire netting.... The day he came here to tea with.... him.... and.....

He washed and dressed and ran downstairs, hungry.

The table was laid for himself only, starched white cloth and twinkling knives with the sun caught in the thin column of the grapefruit cup, a clean serviette in his ring of white bone, and a bowl of newly cut rhododendrons, purple brimming over and spilt across the light. Mums must have had breakfast.

"Hallo," he said loudly. "Maggie?"

Mums came out of the scullery.

"She's gone to town for some fish," she said. "Will I do instead?"

"Oh yes," he said, laughing back at her. "You'll do nicely."

She had his coffee ready for him, and a plate of fried bread and bacon, garnished with mushrooms. He ate with a primitive relish. His fingers even partook of food, breaking the fine white bread and feeling its goodness like ears of corn, rough, starchy.

"Are you going to go to school today?" she asked, putting

the newspaper down.

"Need I?" he said, feeling somehow on holiday.

She laughed and shrugged her shoulders.

"As you like it," she said. "Stay and dig the garden and if it's a nice afternoon we can take the chairs onto the lawn and read."

He could see she wanted him to stay.

"Yes, alright," he said gladly. And then he remembered and frowned.

"It's the last day of term, Mums."

"Mm." She considered. "You'd like to go back?"

"It'll be my last day there."

"Alright," she said. "Off you go. You've only got a few minutes."

Heavens, yes. Twenty-five past eight. Three minutes before the bus left the station.

He jumped up from the table, letting his serviette fall onto the floor, the desire to see school again, for the last time, flooding through him. To say goodbye to old Bony, and Hughes the new master who took them on rambles and bird watching, and the sixth form room and the library and the lavatories where they smoked surreptitiously. And lots of things besides. The little kid in form two he'd saved from a beating and Mrs Tomkins the cook who gave him second helpings of pudding because she thought he was spoiling his looks through overwork.... He rammed his books into his satchel, snatched his cap from the hall stand and ran into the kitchen to say goodbye.

"Mums, I'm off," he shouted. She wasn't there.

She came in from the scullery.

"Alright," she said, standing in the door. Something checked him. She had an envelope in her hand and she wasn't looking straight at him. Her shoulders were lifted unnaturally high. She was trying to say something.

"Goodbye, then," he said.

"Goodbye."

He turned slowly,

"You'd better take this," she said, holding the envelope out to him.

"It came this morning." She held her eyes averted.

He took it from her. A blue envelope, slit open neatly with a knife.

Addressed to Mr Morlais Jenkins. An Aberystwyth postmark. In Nora's quick sensitive hand.

"Hurry up. You'll miss your bus," she said, catching at her breath.

She stood there like a stone column.

He turned and hurried down the passage way, pushing the letter into his pocket. The front door was open to the fresh morning. He ran out into it, leaping over the worn steps and racing across the wet grass.

His head was singing like a kettle, his blood drumming.

Nora.

And – Mums.

She'd opened it, read it.

He ran down the lane and just caught the bus. There was a junior in his seat.

"Come on, Hicks," he said, falling into school habits unthinkingly, "get out of there."

"What's wrong?" little Hicks said cockily. "You been away, mun."

"Come on, you little pimple," Morlais said roughly. "Get out."

He took Hicks by the collar and tugged him out.

"Alright, alright," Hicks shouted. "Leggo then."

Morlais took his proper place, where he could see the road and the people on the pavements.

He was daft, imagining things. She'd naturally open it. Of course. It would be to her as much as to him. She'd left her cigarette case behind; she said so in the train.

He took the letter out of his pocket and pulled the creamy notepaper out of the envelope with fingers suddenly clumsy and unsteady.

For the next five minutes he was dissolved into her words, utterly.

Dear Morlais, she wrote, *The sudden departure of you and Auntie has affected me oddly. I'm not very great at entertaining people or wanting to be with people for long at a time, and I didn't think I'd miss you. Perhaps I mean something more negative than that. You see, ever since your beastly train went out and I turned back to the wet streets and the impersonal world of dripping raincoats and umbrellas I've been feeling – I suppose the word is* alone. *It's drizzled all day and I've just come into digs at midnight from a subhuman world where I found nothing recognisable at all – only rain and wind and great banks of shingle tormented by the sea and all the lamps extinguished. They're all in bed. In the house and the street, and the silence has got into my bones. I ought to go to bed, but want to warm myself first by writing to someone I know.*

Really I've got a hangover from that talk we had along Nannigoat's Walk, and what you said about Auntie. I've been thinking of it subconsciously ever since, and it exudes a grey 'influence' that decolours all my thoughts and makes the people I see and meet in the road as unreal as dummies. I've been thinking – I'm wondering whether you're afraid of Auntie, and avoid her in your mind, because she's unhappy. *You seemed ashamed of unhappiness, I thought, of being called a misery, wet blanket, pessimist, kill-joy – choose your own word. Well, I think unhappiness is proof of a capacity for pure joy. Only shallow people are perpetually in a pleasant mood. And Auntie is fighting some inner conflict to release her happiness. So you should be happy to see her strife. We live by strife, and deep things are always dark. A tall tree thrusts its roots down into the black subsoil. There it sucks up the essential water. I think I almost envy her. She isn't neutral and shut in, and she isn't just a dry ditch bearing no water except when the sky bursts or spring rains. I waste so much – it's only when something touches me, Beethoven or Blake or that afternoon on the bridge when the tramp passed us, that I realise what a frightful amount of my life I don't live.*

This is pure self-indulgence. What do I matter now? By tomorrow I'll be like brass, ashamed of my self-pity. But really, all I wanted to say was Be Yourself. *Let Auntie settle her own fate. It's not yours. You are alive – at least when I talked to you I felt alive myself, you quicken everything you touch – and so you'll know what to do, know it instinctively. Go and do it. Don't let other people dissuade you. Pity only misleads. We're alone, really, each one of us. God, yes, we're alone. My fingers are white at the tips and this pen makes a terrible scratchy noise, like a devilish rat. Please pardon this moralising and morbid letter and forget it as I'll have forgotten it in a week's time. Goodbye, Morlais,*

> *Nora.*

He read, and reread it, listening to all the thoughts that moved silently under the inadequate words. When the bus stopped outside school he folded the letter up and put it in his pocket. The mountains towered about the town, and in the blue haze of the expanding day a flock of white gulls circled about, like crumpled sheets of white paper tossed from gust to gust. They made no sound, silently stirring the transparent liquid in the bowl of the morning. Like the words of her letter.

A boy running out of the school gates with a shout, chasing another boy who had stolen his cap, crashed into Morlais, winding him.

"Look where you're going," Morlais shouted, angry with shock. The boy stopped,

"Oh, it's you, Morly, is it? Thought you'd left. Or got the sack like your old man. Watch where you're going yourself, mun."

Morlais dropped his satchel and caught the boy by the lapels of his coat. He was big and flabby, with red hair and fat cheeks. His face dropped, the cheekiness leaving it, Morlais shook him.

"Say that again, Billy Bunter," he said.

His eyes were burning with anger.

"Alright, alright, keep your hair on. I didn't mean nothing."

Morlais let him go and went into school.

The day passed. A rush of commissions, carrying piles of books to the store-room for the seven weeks' holiday; making out terminal lists; rushing round the corridors and classrooms saying goodbye to the corner seats he had occupied years ago, dreaming through the droning weeks of winter and spring; Arith, Algy, English, Bony, Sloper, Foxy with their gowns and mannerisms and sarcastic fits of spleen; locking the cricket pads and bats in the sports pavilion, the cold and draughty shack where the excitement of the game warmed their gawky bodies while they changed into rugger togs.

But it was all over, and he was glad; he wouldn't go through it again. There was something else, deeper, more urgent. The fire that Billy Bunter's jibe had set alight was burning him up. There must be a burning of more things than discarded school exercise books.

The boys assembled in the main hall before dismissal and the Head swept in in mortar board and gown. The chatter of the crowded room became a disciplined silence, and the Head made a speech. He thanked all those who had helped to make another school year, the prefects, the actors in the Christmas play, the football and cricket teams; he hoped all those who were leaving would think of their school days with pleasure (he smiled a little, permitting the boys to laugh, too) and that those who were going out into the world, to business or to the University, would work hard and deal honestly and prosper in their callings. He would like to mention two or three names in particular – Dafydd Rees for winning an open scholarship to Cambridge, John James for playing in the Welsh Secondary Schools' team, and Morlais Jenkins. And, finally, he hoped that no boy would desecrate the countryside by littering it with peels and paper bags. If Mr Morgan would take his seat at the organ they would conclude the term by singing the usual hymn, Lord Dismiss Us With Thy Blessing.

Morlais couldn't sing because his throat was burning and constricted and cold waves were shaking his body. He rubbed his eyes roughly. He fought his way out of school through the shouting press of boys. Struggling in the crush of bodies gave him control of his emotions. Silly, bloody soft. The boss was glad to see the last of them, and they of him.

He let the bus go and walked home over the mountain, fortifying himself. There was nothing to be had from the mountain. The trees might as well be lampposts, the grass path that was a lighter green than the fields of whin and heather merely an arterial road, the larks and the blue sky a roof in need of repair, the slates fallen from the rotting beams through age and poverty. There was no happiness there.

Then he came to the crest above Tredwr and stood watching the great wave of rock roll on into the valley in a downward sweep of green. The paths diverged, one to the right leading to The Elms, the other forking down the valley past the Blackmore's farm and Mountain Row to the cluster of grey streets where the colliers lived and bought food and worshipped and drank and set their children to school. Tredwr. Home.

He didn't know which path he must take.

He struggled to resolve his mood, to decide. Which path to renounce? His indecision tormented him, and still he stayed there. He threw his satchel down and sprawled on the grass, gasping for breath although he hadn't run at all. Then his eyes caught sight of someone coming up the path from Tredwr. A boy in a dark suit with a greyhound on the leash. He concentrated his attention on the boy, thankful for any diversion. After watching for ten minutes he was certain that it was his brother. The same indecision, transferred to the new problem

– whether to stand up and wave and hail Dilwyn or run down the path away from him – towards The Elms. He felt shaky and loathsome again, with that whiff of black oozing slime in his nostrils and throat again. He knew frantically that he must do something, decide, decide. His will must snatch mastery out of this turmoil. Oh, he wanted only to lie down on the grass and all his body twitch, his pores break into weeping.

All the time Dilwyn was coming slowly nearer. At first a black insect making no progress, a mile and a half of falling bracken away; then the minute likeness of a man, too small to have power or humanity, a little effigy of matchsticks now striding across the crest with the dog straining on the leash and the wind making him bend forward to prevent it snatching the breath out of his mouth. He was singing. Morlais neither got up nor made any sign.

Dilwyn came straight to him. Morlais made an immense effort to control his limbs and the nervous muscles of his face, his twitching eyes.

When still twenty yards off Dilwyn shouted, "Got a match, chum?"

Morlais pushed himself onto his hands.

"Dilwyn," he said.

Dilwyn stopped. The dog reared ups forelegs, suddenly constrained by the taut leash.

"Well, I be damned," he said, pushing his cap back from his forehead, "if it isn't Morlais, eh?"

"Yes, it's me," Morlais laughed.

The laugh came from deep in him, like a released spring, cleansing and restoring. Just to be known, and welcomed – there was welcome in Dilwyn's grinning surprise; he felt it warm him, like the taste of brandy – and by his own brother, somebody from his childhood, a voice and a face from that inner complex of tangled voices and faces which he had been striving to recall into his orbit as a conscious sun might strive to attract a remote planet, how it gave him strength, and laughter, and a new urgency in his blood. He felt the power in his fingers to tear down the fibres of his bleeding brain and break through the thicket of thorns that imprisoned the silent castle and its beloved inmates.

"When did I see you last?" Dilwyn said. "Not this ages. Going for a walk?"

Morlais stood up.

"No. Home from school. You've grown a lot, Dil."

Dilwyn stretched up proudly.

"No' bad," he conceded. "Plenty of muscle, too. Been boxing down the Y.M.C.A. C'n you box?"

Morlais laughed.

"Not much," he said.

"C'm on, 'en. Put your mitts up; let's try you out."

Dilwyn dropped the leash.

"You keep your right bent like this, see? For guard. Then lead with your left –"

His face had all the looseness and eagerness of adolescence. His mouth was like a slash, his top lip full and overhanging; his teeth already bad and yellow with lack of cleaning; his cheeks hollow and his skin blotchy. But his eyes gave his features a dare-devil unity. He was all out for life, for the thrills of life, boxing, greyhounds, anything like that.

"The dog's running away," Morlais warned.

It was loping off over the high field dragging its leash.

"'Ere, Gyp, 'ere boy," Dilwyn shouted, forgetting the sparring lesson at once. He blew a long piercing whistle, sticking his two forefingers into his mouth and pulling his lips out like an elastic garter.

The white greyhound stopped and gracefully turned its lithe neck, crooking one of its forepaws and delicately considering its next movement, poised in a perfect equilibrium of speed and check.

"Isn't she a blem?" Dilwyn said, like a lover.

"Is it yours?" Morlais asked.

"No, she's Ben James's," he replied. "Only I took a fancy to her as a pup and Ben said I could train her. She 'aven't 'ad a race yet. You wait till I get 'er on the track, boy."

He whistled again.

The dog came easily back. Dilwyn kneeled down and she ran her slender muzzle into his lap. He laughed with pleasure, kissing her fine skull.

Morlais watched him.

"We're shifting houses," Dilwyn said suddenly, looking up. "I been carrying furniture all day."

"Where to? Why?" Morlais asked, instantly alive.

"Why?" Dilwyn looked surprised. "Because Dad's lost 'is job and the rent's too high in the old 'ouse. You knew 'e'd lost 'is job didn't you?"

"Yes," Morlais said slowly. "Why did he lose it?"

Dilwyn's face became bitter. Automatically. He was saying what he'd heard, unconsciously imitating the reaction of the grown ups to this question.

"Because 'e asked for the minimum wage, that's why," he almost snarled

"And Reames gave 'im the minimum and then sacked 'im." His face lightened again. "Oh boy, there was riots for you. Don't talk." He became more excited, his eyes fired. "You know Bobby Linton? Well, 'im and three others – Bolshies they were – they took a slam at the cops. They're coming on in the court next week. I climbed into an empty railway truck. I seen it all, boy."

"Dil," Morlais laid his hand on his brother's frayed sleeve. "Can I come down with you to the house? Have they left it yet?. Are you going back home now?"

"I was going for a stretch with old Gyppy 'ere," he replied. "She've been kennelled all day. You wouldn't believe the exercise a good dog needs to keep in trim. I c'n take 'er down the road instead, though. Come on, 'en. Mam's still in the 'ouse, I expect. Blackmore the milk is bringing 'is 'orse and cart round to carry the beds up."

He picked up the leash and both boys took the path to the left, away from the Elms.

Dilwyn was talking about Gyp all the way down. Morlais kept silent. When they got to Blackmore's farm they caught sight of Nan, in a summer frock, hitting a tennis ball against the wall of the cowshed.

"'Owbe, Nan," Dilwyn shouted cheerily. "Know 'er?" he said, turning to Morlais. "She's a tidy bit of stuff, i'n't she?"

Morlais shuddered.

"Hallo," Nan waved her racket; and then, seeing Morlais, dropped racket and ball and came running across the yard.

"Come on," said Morlais, hurrying past the yard gate. "Hallo, Nan," he waved. "Alright?"

They were past before she reached the gate. Seeing that they weren't going to stop Nan faltered, halted, and with no one to see her stamped her foot on the rough stone and lowered her head to hide the trembling of her mouth.

"Why didn't you stop?" Dilwyn asked. "'Fraid of girls you are, or what?"

"Come on, mun," Morlais said, with the gruffness of an elder brother "and don't talk so daft."

Dilwyn laughed, his old taunting laugh, with the old power to infuriate.

He and Morlais were brothers again.

When they reached the village Dilwyn stopped.

"I can't come to the 'ouse with Gyp," he said, "Dad would put 'is boot be'ind me. 'E's as bad as a minister, our Dad is. Always on to me about the greyhound. Nothing doing, though, is there, Gyppy?"

He fondled the dog's head roughly.

"I'll take 'er down to Ben James's," he said.

He left Dilwyn and walked slowly along the back lane, slouching, hands in trouser pockets. As if his nerves were curling back like fern fronds he dawdled, stopping to read children's chalk marks on the wall, looking over the crumbling walls at the blousy back gardens with patched and frayed underclothing flapping on the lines. The lane was closing round him, its familiarity recovering him. He was breathing it through his nostrils, his eyes were re-awakening old images in his brain. He, Morlais Jenkins, hadn't been here for years – not since he went to buy corned beef in James the Grocer's for Monday dinner. It was not a pleasant feeling – but only trivial experiences, like eating sweets, are definitely pleasureable. He was full of wildness and unrest; but not now of indecision.

He turned out of the lane past the little cobbler's shop in the ramshackle shed at the bottom of the corner garden. He found it derelict; the discovery brought with it a flat desolate feeling, a tiny lapse. The grizzled cobbler with a mouth full of nails and a hammer that never hit his fingers when he was banging the sprigs in – was gone. And he couldn't remember his name.

There was a horse and milk cart outside the side door – Blackmore's old cart with a step on which Luther used to let him ride down hill and high wheel guards and Dunlop tyres on the wheels. A pile of dung was steaming under the mare's tail; she tossed her old head at the flies.

He patted her and put his cheek against her neck for a moment. He'd always wanted to do that in the days when he used to watch her slow journey down the street with melting patience. He hadn't been tall enough then.

He pushed the door open and went into the back.

It was just the same, even to the old rag mat over the rabbits' hutch.

The kitchen door was open, the room empty. No furniture or anything.

How empty it was. The life had gone out of it.

He tapped at the door, nervously, like a poor relation.

No answer. He could hear voices upstairs. He knocked

Alun Lewis

louder.

He heard his mother's shuffling step in the passage and there was a great leap inside him, wrenching him. He could have run away. Only that feeling would have been plucking at his face and clothes like a gale of wind, wherever he went.

He caught a glimpse of her in that storm of feeling – a sight of her gasping face and red hands and the sack tied round her skinny hips. But the gasp coming out of her smothered him and he stepped into the kitchen trembling. She stood goggling at him.

"Hallo, Mam," he said in a small voice.

"Morlais," she said, and smiled.

Her eyes were red; she'd been crying. The smile was like great light on her.

"Come to see the 'ouse before we go from it?" she said.

He nodded.

"'Ad any food?" she asked, "I'm doing a bit of bacon for Dad 'gainst 'e comes 'ome."

"No thanks, Mam. I – I only wanted to see you."

He went hot with shame; still afraid to step into the house? The weakness went down to his knees, through a gulf in him.

"Blackmore've lent 'is cart for the beds," she said. She didn't know what to say, "'Tisn't like our 'ouse no more, is it?"

"No," he said, looking round.

There were white patches on the grimy wall paper where the Sunday School certificates had been, and a white patch where the wooden settle had been placed against the wall. In the corner by the fire the floorboards had rotted away; there was water underneath. The armchair Dad used to sleep in after work always covered that. All the hidden things were coming out now, like slugs and black beetles. A poor house quickly throws off humanity.

"Come upstairs?" she asked. "I'm folding the mattresses."

"Righto."

He followed her up the bare stairs. He glimpsed the

parlour as he passed. Well, there'd never been any fun in there.

The bedrooms were empty, curtainless and drab, no longer small and intimate with sleep. The mattresses were stacked in the corners.

She turned round and looked at him. She seemed to be wilted, standing in her old clothes, in her stockinged feet out of habit – they always had to leave their shoes at the foot of the stairs not to dirty the loft; the inherited custom from generations of farm servants kicking off their muddy clogs before climbing to the straw. Her hat and coat were on the sill, her old varnished straw hat and shiny black coat. She let her hands drop, looking round at the desolation of dismantled beds.

"Shall I carry the mattresses down, Mam?"

"A'right. Only be careful. That one's split. Watch the stuffing don't come out."

He carried one mattress down and stacked it in the cart. On the way back he took his jacket off and hung it on the foot of the stairs.

"Proper navvy now," she laughed.

He picked the second one up.

"Where's Dad?" he asked, half stifled under the bulging mattress.

"Up in Mountain Row, weeding the garden a bit."

"Mountain Row? What's he doing up there?"

"Well, that's where we're going to live now, mun."

She couldn't see his face, the horror on it.

"The empty 'ouse on the end," she went on. "Blackmore's renting it for three shilling a week."

"Does he own them, then?" he asked casually.

"Aye," she said slowly. "That's where we're going."

He put the mattress down, stood up, and faced her.

"Will you have room for me to live with you, Mam?"

She took a sharp breath and her eyes dilated. Her face was

pinched and sharp.

"What?" she said.

"Can I come and live with you?"

"But you wouldn't –" she said, her face trembling.

"Yes," he said, looking intensely at her. "Yes. If you're willing'."

"Morlais," she breathed. And then, pulling herself up, she said hurriedly, "But there's no room – no bath, bach, nor somewhere quiet for you to go with your books – only three rooms it is. And the roof leaking."

"Can I tell Dad you're willing?" he said insistently.

She turned away. "Go and talk to 'im," she said, her voice cracked with withheld tears.

"I'll be back now," he said.

He ran downstairs, pulled his jacket on as he ran through the passage, and leaped across the yard into the lane. Soon he was through the mountain gate and hurrying up the stony path, running and walking and out of breath.

He reached Mountain Row panting and hysterically calm. It was all swimming round him. Like a dream, he was going back, back, back, down a tunnel narrowing in perspective so that he sweated with the fear of being stuck and smothered in that down, down, down dropping; faster, sliding down the smooth incline. Until he was through, out of that tunnel and in the wild sunlight among trees and banks of wild flowers, the laughter of angels on the threshold of the cold cell and joy shattered like glass all about. Only to go on, and clinch it with a promise.

He found his father in his old clothes, loosening the weedy garden with a fork. A pile of weeds and tins and rags and ashes against the tumbledown wall at the top of the garden.

"Dad," Morlais said feverishly.

His father slowly looked up and as slowly wiped his streaming forehead.

"'Owbe, son," he said. "Come on; nip over that wall, mun."

Morlais steadied up; there was such calmness in his father's deliberate actions. He'd weeded a good patch, the earth fresh turned and clean.

"You're our first visitor," his father said, wiping his hands and grinning. "'ow's it going?" He began digging again.

"Alright," Morlais said. He didn't want to speak in a hurry now; better to take his father's time, his poise and deliberation, and watch him digging with the rhythm of practice as he used to watch him on Saturday afternoons and summer evenings long ago. He was always ready to chat with somebody over the wall while he was digging. He was chatting to Morlais in the same way now, and Morlais was soothed by his casual companionship.

"Aye, indeed," his father said, turning a sod over with a twist of spade and mouth. "Living up 'ere we are now. Retired from work and taking a country 'ouse on the mountain. Good view from the front, i'n't it?"

Morlais had come expecting turbulence. On the way up the mountain he had realised that his father had been the spear-head and butt of all the trouble; the storm in his own body must be trivial, a little shower, compared with his father's enduring. His had been a war among grown men, for bread and money, and he'd lost his living, his right hand. And he wasn't the sort to be beaten. When he found him, not raving and violent and full of hurt, but quietly digging the choked garden, he felt a sudden flow of assurance spread its level waters through the arid channels of his fever. His own fight now was nearly over.

"Aye," his father said, "digging ourselves in we are for the second round. Give an 'and with these weeds. Put them on the pile there. We'll 'ave a bonfire tonight for an 'ouse-warming."

Morlais bent down and collected the uprooted nettles and dock and dandelions.

"How will you manage with such a small house, Dad?" he

asked.

"Manage?" his father straightened his back, "We got to manage, mun. It's easy then. We'll grow a tidy bit of spuds and cabbage in this garden. Patch that chicken run up and keep a few Rhode Islands. There's good grazing outside; only save up and buy a nice little nanny goat. Goat's milk is richer than cow's." He turned round and looked at the back of the house. The lean-to roof was slanting and sagging, the tiny window pane cracked and filmed with dirt. "As for that," he said, pulling out his clay pipe and tin of Ringers, "well, I'm a tidy carpenter and I'll 'ave plenty of time for it. You wait, boy. Come back in September and see if you know the place."

Morlais never remembered him saying so much, so easily. He took a quick breath and looked up.

"Can I come and live with you, Dad? – I'll get a job. I'll keep myself alright –"

His father looked him over carefully, sizing him up.

"They 'aven't made a Reames of you yet, then?" he said levelly.

Morlais winced, feeling the challenge probing him.

"They've been kind to me, whatever else they've done," he said, returning his father's look.

His father laughed, not unkindly.

"When a fine woman takes a fancy there's trouble flying," he said.

"'Ave you told 'er?"

Morlais looked away, guiltily. He was going behind her back. Yes.

"Go and tell 'er first, then. No running away, see?" He began weeding again, pulling at a deeply rooted tangle of woody nightshade.

"Tell 'er this: I let you go with 'er when you was a kid to see if water was thicker than blood. Damn this weed. Ah. That's got 'im." He shook the earth out of the roots in a dry shower. "See?" He looked at Morlais. "Come back after – if you *want* to live with us."

Morlais hesitated,

"Sleep with Dilwyn you'll 'ave to," his father said, "when you're 'ome from college,"

Morlais turned away, his eyes misty and his throat tight, choking.

"I'm not going to college," he said. "I'm going to work."

He heard his father strike a match and suck at his pipe.

"You go on up that mountain and think what you're deciding," his father said.

Morlais faced him,

"I have decided," he said. "I'm going to tell Mums – Mrs Reames. Solong."

"Solong."

It was as simple as that. Like saying the Lord's Prayer for the first time, after a long and tormented agnosticism. I have decided.

I have decided, I have decided, his feet said to the earth, to the stones of the garden wall, to the springy grass of the mountain. He took long strides, energy hardening his limbs, breaking through the wild orchestration of his nerves and steadying the theme for its final gathering up in the last statement. The music had hold of him; he neither knew nor cared whither it was transporting him. At the end there would be silence, and in that silence, reunion. Music always effected that – if it effected anything.

His path ran along the skirt of the hill, the walls of the allotments buttressing it against the tremendous pressure of the upward soaring mountain. The walls were drystone, built up by the colliers who had hired the allotments from the Blackmores and won the land back from the waste. They were a yard thick, and must have taken ages to build, to carry the stones from the river bed and lay them together so that even the wind was kept out. And there was so little to protect – only a few rows of pickling cabbage stalks, knuckled and run to seed, and bean-stalks rotting with a season's rain. His blood was like a noisy mountain stream, saying to the walls and the allotments and the stones along the path "I'm here, I'm here, I'm here again."

He crossed the stream and the open patch below the station, not noticing the bus or the people in it or the children playing rounders against the pine end of Glannant Street. He was concentrating, all his powers upon this last task and ordeal. He pushed the green gate open and entered the garden of the Elms. He kept to the path, like a stranger. Usually he cut across the lawn.

He walked round to the front door, opened it and went in. He felt he had taken a liberty in not ringing the bell. He stood in the hall and listened, like a trespasser. It was all quiet and spacious and refined, the floor blocks waxed and polished, the brass dinner gong on the dark wallpaper gleaming like the mirror. She was particular about the look of things.

He pushed the front room door open. She was looking through her music, the piano lid unlocked; he was stretched out in a chair.

"Hallo," he said.

She was glad to see him, too glad to say anything. She smiled and let her music drop, turning away from the piano.

"Hallo, dear," she said. "You're late, aren't you? You must be hungry."

"I'm alright," he said.

Mr Reames turned round.

"I nearly ate your dinner myself," he said. "Salmon and Russian salad and a fresh fruit salad. Go and remove the temptation, will you?"

"It's ready laid on the table," she said.

"I don't want to," Morlais said, sickly pale.

"What's the matter, dear?" she asked, quick with concern. "Let's feel your head."

"No," he said, a touch of hysteria in his voice. He stepped

back. "I'm alright. I don't want – that is – I want to – there's something I want to say."

"Well?" she said, her lips opening breathlessly. He looked away from her, struggling with the unmanagable words, seeing nothing with his eyes, nothing.

"What is it?" she asked.

"I'm going to live with my father," he said.

"Oh," she said, less a word than an audible gasp of breath. Mr Reames stood up, the newspaper rustling down from his lap to the carpet.

"This is sudden, Morlais," he said.

"No," she said slowly. "It isn't sudden. I knew it would come."

"What is it?" Mr Reames said. His voice was so strong and level that it dominated the room and disciplined Morlais's spirit. "Is it this strike?"

Morlais didn't reply. "Well, speak, boy. Surely you're not afraid to tell us." His voice had that gritty sound in it, the short shrift of a man who forces complexity to make a simple and essential statement and will not abide evasion. "*Is* it because of the strike?"

Morlais looked straight at him, trying to steel his voice.

"You've been so good to me," he said as steadily as he could. "Please let me go."

Mr Reames shrugged his shoulders and bent down to pick up the paper. That shrug of insouciance cut Morlais to the bone. He turned away, clenching his hands.

She put her hand on his shoulder.

"Alright, Morlais, we *do* understand. Go and eat your dinner first."

He knew he must get out at once. The cord in his brain would snap if she touched it again.

"I don't want any," he said. He turned round on her. "Can I go now?"

She drew back with a convulsive start.

"Yes," she said in a whisper, her hand feeling behind her for something to touch, a chair, the piano.

"What about your clothes, your books?" Mr Reames said.

"I don't want anything," Morlais said. His lungs seemed to be constricting, knotting up like clenched fists.

"Don't be silly," Mr Reames said. "You'd better go and pack."

"No," she said. "Let him go. I'll send his things along tomorrow. Just leave the address."

"Mountain Row," Morlais said.

"What?" she gasped. "Not those little pigsties by the white farm?"

"Yes," Morlais said. He stood up, feeling his self come back, the anguish subside.

Mr Reames held out his hand.

"Goodbye then," he said. "Come and see us when you're home from college."

As Morlais stepped across the thick pile of the carpet to take his hand something went cold in him. He was over the verge of feeling, in the ice belt now. He shook hands.

"Good luck," Mr Reames said.

"Goodbye, Mums," Morlais turned to her.

She took him by the arm and led him from the room. Through the hall and down the two stone steps into the porch.

"Tell me this only," she said, stopping. Then hastily, "I'm not asking for a confession. No scene."

"Yes?" he said.

"I want to know whether this is a victory for yourself, or a defeat."

"What d'you mean?" he asked, frowning.

"All that's happened recently – has it been like a quicksand, dragging you down? *Has* it dragged you down? Why are you going home?"

"Because –" he swallowed; his body was shaking again, "I

don't know, Mums. I – I couldn't – I *had* to –"

"Alright," she said, her voice soothing over, "Never mind. Only remember that the hardest way is the easiest – in the long run. Goodbye."

She was gone, a rustle of silk and the door pushed to, hiding the hall. He stood still for a moment; there was something to say, some unsaid thing, something incomplete. Standing in the empty porch he knew he couldn't go in although the door had swung open again. Nor was there anywhere else. Where else? His body made no response. He began to feel hysteria, a prickling in his skin. There was no shape to it, no way after all. He'd fought to forge his will in the furnace of circumstances. And now there was nothing, only grey; no eminence, only sand. Infinity. The landmarks were gone, even the landmark he knew best, his body. And there was no recognisable thing in all this familiar landscape. Too strange to touch, even; there would be no feel in anything – grass, cloth, tree, gate. He opened the gate. The touch of it, and its opening under his hand surprised him. He was at the gate. The *gate*. Must have walked here across the lawn. He looked back to see if the lawn was behind him. Yes, and the house, its two red gables. His eyes considered them, and saw her standing in the window of the front bedroom, watching him. She looked very small and white, like a doll smeared with flour. He looked back at her, neither of them smiling or lifting a hand, and closing the gate behind him he gravely turned away.

He went back through the village, calling first at the old house in the hope of seeing his mother or Hetty. The house was empty and locked up. He left it quickly, disheartened by the resistance of the back door. The dead shell oppressed him. There was nothing there; the thought frightened him. If he was hollow and locked up, too, and all his childhood scooped out, thrown away?

When Hetty called his name out excitedly and came running down Mountain Row, her thin lanky legs in black school stockings flying about he could have cried with the sharpness of renewed life. Hetty. Hetty. Hetty. Calling him. Brother, big brother; little sister, ink on her fingers, laughing with the pleasure of seeing *him*, and bubbling over with excitement at some tremendous news.

"You're coming to live with us," she shouted, rushing helter-skelter at him.

"I know that, silly noodles," he laughed, sweeping her up by the armpits so that her legs were a foot off the ground. "I knew first."

"You're hurting," she said, laughing and frowning at the same time. "Let me go."

He let her slip down. She took his hand in both of hers, jumping up and down. "Won't we have some fun? Isn't it a teeny house, isn't it?"

"Yes," he said. "We'll all sleep in one bed as they do in Mrs Bruin's, won't we?"

"Yes," she laughed. "Won't we? And d'you know the wind? It's huge up here. I'm going to be Whitie in winter and you can be Brownie and Dilwyn Blackie if he's willing and the wind can be the bad wolf, see?"

"Go on," he said, ruffling her hair. "I thought you were grown up."

"I am, too," she said, shaking herself free and strutting like a cock sparrow. "And I'll ask you to leave my hair alone in future. I spent some little time putting it tidy."

"Garn, you minx. I'll huff and puff you if I catch you," he snarled.

"*If*," she shouted back and ran from him, squeaking with excited and breathless laughter, and he coming after her, stamping his feet and taking care not to catch her.

It was nice to go into the house, too, and see it with Hetty's eyes. There was only one room downstairs; a rickety stairs led to the two attics above.

"I'm going to sleep on the couch," Hetty preened. "So

you'll have to go to bed early, and I'll have the whole room to myself. And a fire, too. Mam's going to put the couch so I can watch the goblins hop out of the fire and put whiting on their tails if they make a row."

"Well, indeed," he said. "And where are they putting all the furniture, then?"

"Dad's sold half of it to Bluestein the Auctioneer for a goat and chickens and wood," she said.

"Did Bluestein have a spare goat in his office, then?"

She pealed with laughter.

"No, silly, it's from Blackmore's the goat is. And I know its mummy, too. She's only got one eye and she tried to butt me only the rope was too short."

"Gosh, what a spinky house. I feel like a giant with feet like boats," he said. "Look. I can touch the ceiling when I stretch."

"I can too," she replied boastingly, "if I get on the chair."

"Where's Mam?" he asked.

"Down Tredwr, buying a bucket and scrubbing brush in the iremongers. Dad's down there, too. Got a meeting. He's got meetings like I get homework. You got to keep quiet if he's thinking about a meeting, but he won't shut up when I got sums to do. Can you do equations?"

"Don't bother about that now," he said, "You've got seven weeks' holiday before your next homework."

"Yes," she said. "You got a pimple where your collar is. I don't want you to *do* them for me. I can do them myself. I only wanted to know if you can do them."

"Well, go and ask the goat," he said, "and leave me alone for half hour. I want to write a letter. Is there any note paper?"

"What a hope," she said. "You won't find *anything* here now. Anyroads nobody ever writes letters much with us."

There wasn't much hope of finding anything, truly. The floor was piled with pots and frying pans and a basket of crockery, blankets and clothes and patched sheets were heaped high on the table. It would be worse when Mam and

Dad and Dilwyn came in. There'd be no privacy at all. Never would be any. The place was upside down.

Hetty was pouring milk into a saucer.

"I'm going down Tredwr for an hour," he said,. "Will you be O.K.?"

"Sure," she replied. "I'm going to tame a wild cat. Nobody belongs to her and she's got a coat of white and treacle and I'm going to watch till she comes for this milk."

"Solong then," he said.

He left the house by the back door, going up the garden and over the wall. Somehow he didn't like using the front door.

When he got to the village he stopped outside the newsagent's, feeling in his pocket for some money. He had three pennies. And a sixpence. He went in and bought a cheap pad of notepaper, a packet of envelopes and a bottle of ink. In the act of paying he had a sudden qualm. It wasn't his money. The girl was waiting for the money, holding her hand out for it. He started, realising he was holding his hand in the air. He gave it to her quickly, flushing.

He had no money.

It was like a great stone falling into a deep narrow well.

Tomorrow he'd begin.

He crossed the square and entered the Workmen's Institute. The old men were sitting on the bench outside. Just the same. Spitting and talking in Welsh about the people who passed them. The same old men. Dai Stop-a-pig, bandy and dwarfish, with a bowler that was too big for him and was supported by his bushy eyebrows and his bent ears; Twm Carmarthen, that used to sell the religious weeklies to the Welsh chapel people when his legs were good enough to walk on. He remembered what his mother had told him about them, bit by bit as he went along the shabby corridor with its bare distempered walls and its notices forbidding smoking and spitting. He pushed the door of the reading room open and passed the newspaper stands to the small table by the window. An old man was reading The Dog Fancier – reading it aloud with his nose so close to the page that it seemed to be reading the words by a sort of Braille. Morlais sat next to him, pushed the litter of journals away and uncorked the bottle of ink.

"Wha's the good of keeping a St Bernard these days, eh?" the old man wheezed. "Can't feed yourself for a start, can you?"

"That's true," Morlais said politely, beginning to write; he had written the address, 2, Mountain Row, Tredwr, when the old man spoke.

"Wha's 'at?" he said. "Do you remember who you're speaking to?"

"I said you were right," Morlais answered.

"Of course I'm right. I know. I've seen life, boyo. Yes indeed. It's no good telling me I –" his voice liquefied into a muddled mutter and his puckered eyes strayed back to the journal.

Dear Nora, Morlais wrote. *I want to answer your letter, but first I've got to tell you that it's happened here. It's been moving all the time like feeling a bit sick and then more and more in different parts of your body and you know you'll have to see the doctor. And now it's happened I don't know when exactly it did take place. Only I'm living with my mother and father now in a little house on the mountain and I'm not living in The Elms any more.*

You can see by the address that we're high up. We're going to live on goat's milk, too. Our own goat. I hope I won't have to milk it, I can't bear touching goats. Can you? I don't think I'll be able to go to college, I haven't got the time or the money and my father has lost his job. He was the one who was sacked. He has been very kind to me today. I was terrified they wouldn't want me with them but they did. My mother and sister are glad, and we're like a family.

You see I'm happy really, and it's marvellous because I thought I was going to die today sometimes. You said to be myself, but I was all torn to pieces. Last night I was rotting like cabbage stalks in a heap in the corner of the garden turning into black liquid. And this afternoon it was as if claws were tearing the fibres of my brain apart, all blood and grey matter. I tried to be brave, but it made it worse, much worse. I was so frightened, because I knew I couldn't go on like that for long. And it didn't seem as if anything could change it. I'm thinking if Mums is like that – but she can't be. I expect it's more an argument in her mind. It wouldn't be the same for grown ups.

I was so very very glad to get your letter this morning. I was thinking about it all day in school, and I wish I could tell you how I felt when I read it. I've never met any one who can turn the world in and out like you, make it move, all its tremendousness. I could see a marvellous future when I was reading it and thinking about it afterwards. As if your words were clouds which parted and in the bright gap I could see leagues and leagues of islands in a sea that dazzled me with its brightness. You know how the birds sing in the morning sometimes when you wake early? It was like that, and I don't know how you do it. I wonder who invented life? Did somebody think it out? It sounds silly, doesn't it. But it's too wonderful to be an accident, I think. My mind seems to expand.

"'Ave you seen my daughter looking for me?" the old man asked, putting his withered brown hand on Morlais's sleeve.

"No," said Morlais. "No, I haven't."

"Th's alright, 'en. I thought she would be worrying where I was. Tha's alright, my son." He turned back to his paper. Morlais watched his nose running; he was as insensitive to it as a baby; his moustache was bedraggled and damp with it; his pores were black and unwashed.

I must finish now and go home," Morlais continued writing. *It's getting dark, I'm tired, too; it's been a day alright. I was talking to my sister when I suddenly realised I hadn't been think-ing about you all the evening. You were more real than ever when I remembered that suddenly. And I felt heaps stronger, more myself. It had seemed – oh, I can't describe it – as if I was just walking from one person to another, asking them something and getting no answer, only being told to ask the next one. When I was with Hetty, and you woke up in my mind, I knew I'd decided my own fate myself. I can't make out exactly when, though, just as you can't see the hands of a clock move, but it goes on until it strikes the hour.*

Please write to me when you have time, will you please? And thank you, thank you. You make me feel a pig.

Goodbye, Morlais.

He put the letter in the envelope, addressed it, and went out into the street. The old men had gone. The fresh air went to his head; he was in a dizzy and exalted state. The evening had a quietness in it, the dusk a privacy permitting him to laugh without having to explain why, even to himself.

When he got to the post office he remembered that he had no money to buy a stamp.

He put the letter back into his breast pocket, resisting the first impulse, which was to rip it up.

"Oh God," he swore. "Oh God."

Then he had an idea. He could pawn his wrist watch tomorrow in town. Perhaps there'd be enough money from that to buy Mums a present.

He wanted to show her, somehow....

Going up the mountain in the dark was like scaling some breathless peak. It wanted him, that darkness; it tingled in him. He hurried, knowing that his mother was waiting for him, the table laid.

The third week he stayed in bed till eleven each morning and only went up to town twice. Each time he drew a blank. When he came home on the second occasion, late on Friday afternoon, he was exhausted; his mind and body were in tatters, his nerves frayed. He entered the house through the front door. There was nobody in the kitchen except Dilwyn, who was stretched out on the settle in a doze. He was in an old pair of dirty grey trousers, cheap cottony flannel, torn and baggy at the knees, an old red shirt with rolled up sleeves, and a pair of his father's thick working socks. His face and arms were black with coal dust. Morlais looked at him distastefully.

The rest of the kitchen was just as bad. The table was covered with greasy plates left there since dinner; the walls were still waiting a papering. Everything was insufferably hot and small. There was no privacy, no space; everything cluttered up, a bag of potato peelings on one chair, Hetty's coat on another, and flies buzzing round the unwashed frying pan and untidy table.

He shrugged his shoulders and went through the back door into the little yard where his mother did her washing. She was beating the rag mat against the wall. When he saw her he changed.

"Hallo, Mam," he called. "Let's beat that mat for you, shall I? I haven't done anything useful all day."

She turned round, glad to see him. There was a tired droop about her, despite her smile.

"I should think you want a rest yourself after walking to town on a day like this," she said.

"I didn't get up till dinner time," he replied.

"Well, you needed a good sleep," she said. "That first fortnight knocked it out of you. You went at it like a bull at a gate, didn't you?"

He took the mat from her and swiped it against the wall.

"Steady on," she said. "You'll knock it to pieces if you don't watch. How'd *you* like to 'ave a leathering like that if you'd given ten years good service?"

"If I was trodden on for ten years I'd drown myself," he said.

She looked at him anxiously.

"Down in the dumps again, son?" she said.

He straightened himself slowly.

"I don't know," he said moodily. "Everything seems to be against me."

"Don't talk such nonsense, boy," she said. "Against you, indeed. D'you know what they're saying down in the village about you?"

"What?" he asked listlessly.

"They're saying you're a son I ought to be proud of," she said.

"Oh, Mam," he said, bitterly hurt. "That's only talk. They don't know. They think Mrs Reames is a snob and they're glad of something to triumph over her about. Anyway, that's all done with. It's *now* that matters, I'm not doing anything except hanging about, living on you and Dad. And I *must* do something. I *must*. Can't you see?"

"Morlais bach," she said. "Don't fret yourself, boy. Wait a bit. Wait a bit. Go and help Dad to make the chicken cwtch, or fetch some coal off the tip with Dilwyn. Or go up the river and 'ave a swim with the boys. It's summer 'olidays for you, by rights."

He turned away with a helpless shrug.

"You're saying I don't understand what you're feeling, aren't you?" she said. "Morlais bach. D'you think I've lived fifty odd years without knowing what it is to feel beat? And the worst of living is that it don't get any better as you gets older. When I think of all the years I been mothering you children – you wouldn't throw all that away for me, Morlais, would you?"

"No," he said, almost in a whisper. "It's because I want to do something for you that I feel so – oh Mam. I hate myself." He turned round, his face contorted.

"Now then, don't call your best friend out of names," she said. "Only a fool quarrels with himself. You 'ave a good rest now. And next week there'll be the result of your exams out. P'r'aps you'll win a scholarship to college, you never know."

"Mam," he said, suddenly very calm. "Listen now. I can

see it now. Listen. I'm not going to college, it's no good me going there. I wanted to, terribly, once. I wanted all the pleasant things then. I don't want that now. I want something else. I don't know what it is, exactly. I don't think you can say it in words. Mrs Reames made me see it. She knows what it is. I can see it now. She'll get it in the end, even if it kills her."

He was breathless with excitement and his eyes seemed to burn in a filmy haze.

His mother watched him. When she saw he wasn't going to say any more she said quietly, "It was God you were talking about then."

He seemed to wake with a jolt, his face took on a definite look, as though he had been shaken from sleep.

"God?" he said, looking at her and puzzling over the word. It was her word, expressing a whole experience that mystified him because he hadn't shared it.

"Yes," she said. "And even when you was a little boy I used to watch you and pray you wouldn't go crucifying yourself when you came a man."

Suddenly he caught her hands, folding them together inside his own, squeezing them with the urgency of his apprehension.

"Tell me what to do, Mam," he said. "Tell me what to do. I don't know what – only I must do something. I go all bad doing nothing."

"I can't tell you that," she said. "Nobody can tell you that. Better for you to forget all this we been saying and be like Dilwyn for a bit. Anyway, don't be too 'ard on yourself. 'Come on, now. Let go my 'ands. The floor 'aven't been scrubbed yet."

She shook herself loose and turned away quickly, making an unnecessary fuss with the bucket and scrubbing brush.

"Look at this good-for-nothing," she jeered, shaking Dilwyn. "Get up, you old sluggard."

"Oh what the 'ell," Dilwyn said, getting up in a temper. "Can't you leave me be? I fetched a barrow of coal for you, didn't I?"

"It's only a sinner can count 'is good deeds," she shouted back. "Out the back with you and put your dirty face under the tap."

Dilwyn came out from the kitchen, sticking his hands inside the top of his trousers like a collier and spitting into the air. His hair was matted with sweat. "Oh Christ," he said, yawning heavily.

"Dilwyn," Morlais called.

"'Allo," he replied sleepily. "You still living with us?"

Morlais flushed.

"Dilwyn," he said. "Listen a minute, I've got something important to say to you,"

"Better let me wash first, then," Dilwyn said with a grin. He spat again, further this time, "Well, let's 'ave it."

"Well, I'd like you to tell me," Morlais shuffled uncomfortably, "if there's anything I've done to you, any wrong. Or – or any way I can help you, or anything."

Dilwyn's loose mouth gaped open.

"What's wrong with you?" he said, "Joined the pentecostals or what?"

"I'm serious," Morlais replied, "I want to help you. Isn't there any way?"

Dilwyn guffawed.

"Better go and ask Nan Blackmore," he roared. "Go and ask her. Oh 'ell." He turned towards the kitchen. "Oi, Mam. Our Morlais wants to know if –"

"Shut up." Morlais hissed.

"– wants to know if 'e can –" Dilwyn shouted, louder still.

That was as far as he got. Morlais hit him in the stomach and he doubled up with a gasp.

"Eh, what's all this?" Mrs Jenkins said, coming to the door. "Fighting again, you two? For shame on you, both."

Dilwyn got to his feet groaning. Morlais stood still, white and shameful.

"There's a fine start, indeed," she said, overwrought herself.

"It was 'e did it," Dilwyn moaned. "I didn't do nothing."

"Serve you right, whatever it's about," she said, cuffing him. "Go and make yourself tidy, for goodness sake."

"Oh alright," Dilwyn said. He fetched a lump of carbolic soap and a towel from the windowsill and turned the tap on in the yard. Mrs Jenkins went back into the kitchen. Dilwyn lifted his wet and soapy face. "I'll 'ave my own back for this," he said sullenly.

Morlais was standing there still, and his eyes were moist.

He looked helplessly at Dilwyn and turned away from his resentful face, climbing the tumble-down steps to the steep little garden. The path was laid with ashes; on each side of it the small strip of stony soil had been weeded and broken up. But nothing had been planted; it had a dry starved look, holding out no promise. Beyond and above it the steep barren mountain rose precipitously to the broken crest of rocks. The grass was parched and scorched, the whole stretch of it rigid and dusty. Summer had gone beyond its pitch of ripeness and had gripped the high valley in a hard drought, as arid as winter.

He retraced his steps and went through the kitchen and up the rickety stairs to his bedroom. He kept his few possessions in an orange box at the foot of the bed. Taking out the notepaper he had bought on the first evening of his homecoming he uncapped his pen and sat on the edge of the bed, the paper tabled on his lifted knee.

Dear Nora, he wrote, *I'm not going to write to you again, because I won't have anything to say for a long time to come. It's all much harder and less definite than I ever thought it could be, and if I wrote to you my letter would be wild and full of questions that nobody could answer. You see, I've really got to start again, from the beginning. And everything that's happened to me so far is just a weight that I must throw off. It was like that with Mums,*

*I think; the past was like a load on her, a millstone round her neck.
It was much better for me to leave her. Perhaps she and Uncle
Denis will settle things somehow now. I was only a drag on them.
And I wanted to be free, too. And thought I was at first. But of
course I'm not. I was silly to expect freedom simply by running out
of one house into another. And I tried to throw away too many
things Mums sent my books and clothes after me and a letter with
a cheque for five pounds in it. I gave them all to my brother, except
the letter, to return to her. I'm sorry I did it now. It must have hurt
her, and it wouldn't have been so difficult for me to keep them.
Only I was so stubborn. I suppose I thought it was manly, being
like that. False pride.*

*But the real reason why I'm not going to write again is because
I want to stop thinking so much. It only muddles and tires me. I
saw in a book once that pigeons dirty their drinking water before
lapping it because a muddy colour suits their pensive minds better.
I watch the pigeons wheeling in the clear air – our Row is so high
up that I can look down on their flight – and I wish I was as
natural as they. But there you are. They go round and round in
emptiness and come back to the same place in the end. So if ever
you come down to visit Mums you'll probably find me flapping
my artificial wings in silly circles. But I mustn't go on like this. I
seem full of bad black blood. If I could only get a job, a decent job
where I'd be doing something useful, I'm sure things would take
shape again. I don't want to read anything – I don't think I could
settle down to any book until my exam results are out and I've
definitely put college behind me. Then I must start. What shall I
read? The Bible? And what shall I do? My hands are trembling –
I know I can do something good – but what? That's what won't
give me any peace. Do you understand? I feel you do, and it's like
cool water refreshing me. And it's all so simple, really. Patience –
just that. Oh well, I'll try not to run away any more. And goodbye
for ages and ages, –*

He paused, poising his pen over the signature; looked up as
if to make sure the room was really empty, then bent his head

to the letter again and concluded it.

I love you, love you, love you, dark little Nora,
                    Morlais.

He put his pen down, went to the window, and read the letter slowly through. Then he put it in an envelope, addressed it and licked the flap down.

"Morlais," his mother called. "Dad's got news for you."

"O.K." he replied. "Just a sec."

He ripped the letter into pieces and stuffed it into his trousers pocket. Then he went downstairs.

His mother was standing waiting for him, her lined face dimpling with delight. She caught his hands and shook them excitedly.

"Guess what?" she said, laughing. "Guess what Dad's got for you?"

"What?" he said, infected by her spirits.

"Go up the back and see," she said. "'E's up the lav."

Mr Jenkins was sitting comfortably on the lavatory seat at the top of the garden – the door was tied back during the hot weather.

"Well, what's the great news?" Morlais asked.

Mr Jenkins pushed his cap onto the back of his head.

"Mam didn't tell you, then?" he grinned. "A wonder she could 'old 'er tongue. Well, I got you the offer of a job," he said.

Morlais caught his breath.

"Wait a minute now," his father cautioned. "Don't go jumping over the wall yet. It's only seventeen bob a week, mind."

"What is it?" Morlais asked excitedly.

"Library assistant in the Workmen's Institute," his father replied.

"One of the committee asked me if you wanted it, so I said right you are. You're only pining up 'ere doing nothing, I know."

"Of course I want it," Morlais said. "Oh, thank you, Dad."

"There you are, then," his father said. "You've joined the working class proper now, 'aven't you? Fetch me a bit of newspaper from the kitchen, son there's none left 'ere."

"If you hadn't got me a job I'd leave you out here all night," Morlais replied, and went off to obey his father's behest.

"Oh, thank God," he said softly, going down the cinder path. His eyes seemed to open wider, his fingers to stretch further, and when he tilted his head back the good sunlight made him laugh, releasing him.

"Dad wants some paper, Mam," he said, entering the dark kitchen. They both laughed, looking at each other happily.

"Under the cushion by there," she said. "Well, my boy."

And she put her hands up to his face and kissed him.

"I've got a job, Mam," he said, simply for the delight of saying it.

"Yes," she said. "You've got a start. It'll come now, you see." Her face grew serious. "Pity you wouldn't go to college, though."

He laughed.

"I'll read a lot of books down there," he said. "I'll learn more."

"Aye, no doubt," she replied. "But maybe it won't get you so far,"

"You don't understand, Mam," he said. "I've got to go my own way about this thing, see?"

"Oi, Morlais," his father bellowed from up the garden. "Are you *making* that paper?"

"Go on, take it to 'im quick," she said, "'fore they come running out of next door."

Morlais hung about while his father washed and shaved. He stripped his coat and shirt off, propped a broken piece of mirror against the garden steps and squatted down on his heels, his braces hanging on the ground behind him. Morlais sat and watched him wield his cut-throat.

He was getting a bit skinny, despite his thick woollen vest.

"You're working too hard, Dad," he said. "You're as thin as a rake."

"All gristle I am, my boy," Mr Jenkins said. "As for working, it'll be my tongue will do all the work in future, by the look of it. Nobody wants these."

He held out his hands, rough and horny and pocked with blue weals.

"I'm proud of these, boy," he said. "They been good servants to me, these 'ave. But you can't fight the boss classes with your fists – they got the soldiers and the magistrates be'ind them. And they're not too soft-'earted to string you up by the neck, neither. Same as they did with old Dic Penderyn and Lewis the 'untsman when they led the attack on old Crawshay's castle over in Cyfartha."

"We did that in history for Senior," Morlais said. "That was over a century ago, wasn't it?"

"Aye," his father said. "It's an old cause we're fighting for, my lad. An old cause. I don't reckon I'll see the end of the struggle in my lifetime. It's like that old tree on top of the quarry. I didn't see it planted and I won't see it die. But I see it putting out its leaves every year."

Morlais looked at the tree his father's razor was pointing at. It was the old hawthorn on the slanting brow of the hill.

"I remember thinking that tree was like you, Dad," he said.

His father laughed.

"Did you indeed?" he said. "Well, if I go on talking much more I'll 'ave to go to the meeting in my vest and pants."

"What meeting?"

"Committee meeting in the Institute," he replied, relathering his face. "They're asking me to stand for this ward in the Council Elections."

Morlais jumped up and slapped him on the shoulders.

"Councillor Jenkins," he exclaimed.

"Steady on, you daftie. D'you want to cut my throat?" his father said, hiding his pleasure at Morlais's enthusiasm under a show of alarm. "Go and tidy your 'air a bit and I'll take you down with me to see old Dai Garibaldi."

"Mr Thomas the Librarian, you mean?"

"Same feller," his father said, "When 'e come back from the Boer War they chaired 'im and cheered 'im right round the village. But Dai Garibaldi 'e was at the end of it all, and better as a collier too, than shooting the Dutch farmers, poor dabs. 'E'll tell you some tales, boy; 'cording to old Dai there's nothing 'e 'aven't done 'cept kiss Queen Victoria. Before you been there a week 'e'll be giving you lectures with the magic lantern, you watch."

His cheerful talk made Morlais light-hearted. Ever since he'd come home to live his father had treated him in this kindly equal way. And it was all the more heartening because it was unexpected. He had been so unyielding and hard all the time Morlais had lived with the Reameses. Queer.

"Well, don't you listen to me," Mr Jenkins said, "It's Karl Marx and Kier Hardie with me, and John the Baptist and William Williams Pantycelyn with your mother. Better for you to make up your own mind, being as you've got a mind. Not like that Dilwyn of ours that can't see further than a football match or a grey'ound, the bastard."

Ten minutes later they went down the mountain path into the village. The colliers squatting in the shade of the back lane wall smoking Woodbines before their bath all shouted some greeting to Mr Jenkins. He went over to chat with them and Morlais nervously followed him.

"'Ere's my new mate," Mr Jenkins said, pointing to Morlais. "'E's going to see to the grammar side of my speeches, i'n't you, son?"

"'Owbe, Morlais," the men said, with genuine goodwill, looking him over with unconcealed interest.

"A tidy lad, too, Will," a white-haired old collier said. "It don't need nobody to make a man out of 'im, I can see."

Morlais grinned and rubbed his knuckles against the grimy wall. He felt this renewal of contact with intense discomfort, almost anguish.

He hadn't spoken to any of the colliers since he went to live in The Elms and it was hard, bitterly hard, standing in front of them now, not knowing what to say, conscious of a subtle change in their attitudes, a prudent withdrawal of their rough easiness, and a corresponding embarrassment in himself. And it was something deeper than the usual discomfort that the sensitive introvert experiences when meeting people. It was a complex that had matured slowly, in the seclusion of The Elms; that had been fed by the daily evasions of contact with the village, the choice of empty back lanes or lonely mountain paths in going to and from school, by the perpetual feeling of shame at this shrinking from his own people as though he were diseased or hunted. He knew he had gone outside the community, broken their law and forfeited their familiarity. It was the hardest thing of all, this humiliating petition for reinstatement. The pain of it frightened him.

"Oh well, we'll see a good bit of you now, Morlais," another said.

"Rugby you played in the County, isn't it?" one of the younger men said.

"Yes," Morlais answered.

"What about taking up Soccer again. We got a few positions we want filling, with some of the lads left the district," he went on. "Teddy Barnes – 'member 'im? 'e was in school same time as you – 'e's joined the Wolves."

"I don't think I'd be much use," Morlais said. "Thanks all the same."

"You never know till you try, mun," the boy persisted. "Your brother Dilwyn's a tidy little player. Plenty of guts. Turn out in the trial next Thursday, mun?"

"I really wouldn't be any good," Morlais said, desperately.

"Well, 'ow about joining our golf club?" another one butted in.

They all laughed. Morlais felt easier.

"Come on, then son," his father said. "Solong, boys."

"Solong, Will boy," they replied.

"There you are," said Mr Jenkins as they went down the steep hill to the Square. "They're the boys to shout for Wales town in Cardiff Arms Park. Nothing wrong with them."

All the men hailed Mr Jenkins and Morlais was aware that they held him in respect and rough and ready admiration. But he was glad when they entered the little door marked SILENCE at the foot of the Institute stairs and the attention of the street dissolved into the privacy of the library. It was a small room with two grimy windows and narrow strips of green distempered wall showing between the bookshelves. Piles of books, torn and dog-eared, were stacked on the floor and the table on which the periodicals were arranged seemed to be standing knee-deep in the tide in terror of being completely engulfed. And there was old Dai Garibaldi Thomas, snoring in the basket chair which he had brought into the library to make it more home-like.

'No wonder 'e wants an assistant,' Mr Jenkins said. "The old flies must be a proper nuisance, this 'ot weather."

He stood over the sleeping man and, winking to Morlais, bellowed out "Mr Thomas."

The old man leaped up in a tremendous fluster.

"Will, is it?" he said. "I was waitin' for my tea. You put me in a proper stew then, boy." He pushed his fingers under his silver-rimmed spectacles and rubbed his grey wrinkled eyes. Both his eyebrows came to a point in the middle and hung over the rim of his glasses like creeping plants. Although his skin was lined and leathery with age and his hair a faded grey, his features had a placid ease, his eyes a proneness to laughter that showed no signs of the hardening and constriction so common in the appearance of aging colliers.

"I brought a visitor to see you, Dai," Mr Jenkins said. "Your new secretary."

Dai Garibaldi took off his spectacles and peered closer, puckering up his eyes. It was fifteen years since he had left the mine with advanced nystagmus, and although he had recovered his sight, his eyes retained an unnatural staring sharpness, a sort of vacancy, so that when he looked at you his mind seemed to be considering some distant problem.

"Morlais, is it? Your eldest boy, eh?" he said.

Morlais took his proffered hand.

"Well, I 'ope you'll like it 'ere, my boy," he said. "It's a tidy little place – nice and warm in winter – I do like it fine, whatever."

"You can show 'im round a bit, Dai," Mr Jenkins said, "whiles I goes down to the committee meeting."

"Right you are, Will fach. Go you." And with an absent-minded wave of his hand he dismissed William Jenkins from his mind. "Now let me see," he said. "let me see," nibbing his hands and brushing the dandruff and cigarette ash off his worn grey jacket and waistcoat, "What 'ave we got 'ere altogether, eh?"

Mr Jenkins winked at Morlais as he slipped through the door. As the door closed slowly Morlais took a deep breath and considered the stuffy ugly room in which he was to earn his living. And he wanted to tug the door open and run out into the sunlight on the mountain side and crush his panicky heart against the green ferns.

"Well, indeed, there isn't much to show you, coming to think of it," the old man said, putting his spectacles on carefully. "You'll drop into it as you go along, no doubt. There's not much doing, except when the kiddies comes out of school. Then you gives them any of these 'ere books on the floor and enters the number on their cards and in this ledger by 'ere. See?"

"Yes," Morlais said. "What do you do the rest of the day? Is there any cataloguing to be done?"

"No, nothing much," he replied. "We don't 'ave many new books these days. No room for them in any case. Once you've put the papers out in the reading room in the morning you'll 'ave time for a bit of a chat, like, or a read if you want to."

"Oh yes, I like reading," Morlais said, as enthusiastically as he could.

"There you are, then. That's the way to get on, my boy. Read you whatever you can lay your 'ands on. There's near everything 'ere. All that corner by there is 'istory – all about Chartism and the War and a new book just come in about the General Strike. Then all over by there is stories. Good writers, too. Charles Dickens and Scott. You'll enjoy yourself, right enough."

"Yes, I'm sure," Morlais replied.

"Got any 'obbies, son?"

"No, I don't know that I have."

"Pity, too. I thought you might be interested in stamps or bee-keeping per'aps. I been collecting stamps since I was a kid. I brought a tidy few back from the Boer War with me. And bees – I been keeping bees ever since my old woman died, God rest 'er. It's very good, 'aving an 'obby, you know."

Morlais peeped out through the grimy window. There was a yard filled with ash cans, a load of coal, a pile of stones and a few packing cases; round it a cement wall; beyond that an ashtip running down to the gorge of the river; and beyond the river a coal tip and a disused working on the scarred and blackened hill side.

"Nice view you've got," he said, laughing.

"Eh? View? Indeed, I doubt if I know what's there, indeed," Dai Garibaldi said, coming to the window. "This glass could do with a scrubbing, too. I'll 'ave to remember to tell Mrs Jones about it."

He picked up his keys from the table.

"Well, I got to go down the billiard room now," he said. "Them lads 'ave 'ad their 'alf-hour. I expect you'll be starting on Monday morning, isn't it?"

"Right-ho," Morlais said. "Solong till then."

"Solong, my boy. And glad to see you."

Morlais went out of the library, through the grey lobby, and into the blown coal dust of the parched street.

The old men had left the bench in front of the Institute and gone home for tea. Most of the shops were shut for the same reason, blue blinds over the closed doors of the Maypole, the Meadow Dairy, Ben James's Save As You Spend Stores, the Emporium and the ironmonger's. Only the indefatigable Italian's shop was still open. And as Morlais passed it Bob Linton came out. Four illkempt urchins were mobbing him, hanging on to his arms and shouting at him,

"Let's come with you, Bobby boy."

"Goin' 'ome, Bobby?"

"Come an' see the football match with us, Bob."

"Oh, go to 'ell, 'fore I knock your bloody blocks off," Bob shouted, shaking them off. "Leave me be, can't you?"

Then he saw Morlais and his face lit up.

"Well, Morlais," he called. "How's it going, boy?"

"Hallo, Bobby."

They shook hands in the middle of the street. The urchins went into a whispered conference. Morlais heard one of them say, "That's Mrs Reames the Manager's pet. I 'eard my mother sayin' about 'im."

"Come on," Bob said. "Let's get out of 'ere. These kids 'ave been 'anging onto me ever since I came out of jail."

Morlais laughed,

"You've made a name for yourself in Glannant, Bob," he said. "They'll be putting you on the Council before much longer."

Bob laughed, sardonically.

"My mother always said I'll end up on the gallows," he

said. "But it won't be in Tredwr. I been thinking of clearing out of here for good."

"Where to" Morlais asked, eagerly.

"Why? You thinking of escaping, too? "Bob said, surprised at Morlais's quick interest.

Morlais shrugged his shoulders.

"No, not really, I suppose," he said. "I've just been appointed to my first job."

"No?" Bob's gladness was genuine. "Good boy. Where to?"

"Assistant librarian in the Institute," Morlais said morosely.

Bob grimaced.

"Alright if you like it, I suppose," he said, "I've just spent ten days in jail – that was enough for me."

"Well, I can read," Morlais said. "There's that about it. And I want to read a lot, too. I don't know anything, really. I *must* learn before I can do anything."

"Learn what?" Bob said, watching Morlais carefully.

"I can't tell you exactly," Morlais said. "Only I want to know how coal is mined, how the winder works, how wages and hours are fixed, and who's behind it all. I want to read about other countries, too, and about government. And the *reason* for it all," – he was very excited – "why it causes so much suffering, and death. I know there's something badly wrong with it, Bob. Look at the mess it's making of Glannant. There's no *real* happiness in the village, is there?"

Bob was kindled; his eyes alive.

"I wish I was good enough to work with you," he said. "Remember Luther Blackmore being killed in work?"

"Well, come up the library with me next week," Morlais said eagerly. "We'll make a plan of reading, shall we, Bob?"

"I'm no good at studying," Bob said. "I couldn't do it."

"Of course you can," Morlais said, pressing him. "Please, Bob. Have a shot at it. You haven't got a job, yet, have you?"

"No," Bob said moodily. He looked at Morlais, struggling to say something, his face drawn and mobile. "I don't know. I nearly ran away somewhere last night," he said. "I wish I'd gone, in a way."

"What would you have done?"

"Joined the army, or got work somewhere, navvying, or in an hotel – I don't know," he said despondently. "Look here," he said, "you don't mind me saying something to you?" he said.

There was a queer forced calmness about him.

"Go on," Morlais said.

Bob paused in the middle of pushing the mountain gate open.

"Why don't you go near Blackmore's farm?" he asked. "You live right by them. Hetty's always there, playing about the yard."

Morlais flushed, gripping the gate so hard that the blood left his knuckles.

"I don't know," he said, clumsily. "I don't happen to. Why then?"

Bob laughed unsteadily.

"Well, I know Nan would like to see you a bit more," he said.

Morlais, acutely distressed, stared back at Bob's white face. There was a pain, a stab, in Bob's look.

"How d'you know?" Morlais said, struggling for his balance.

"Well, she told me," Bob said. "If you must know."

His voice had become hard and hostile.

Morlais gripped himself.

"Well, I don't want to go with her," he said levelly.

Bob breathed heavily.

"Can I tell her that?" he asked.

"If you want to," Morlais said.

Bob was silent for a moment.

"Is it still on, what you said about making a plan to read books?" he said hesitantly,

Morlais looked up and his face opened, mouth and eyes smiling.

"Of course," he said. "Why not?"

"Shake on it, then," Bob said, trembling slightly with a huge relief. He laughed like a child. "I don't want to run away now," he said.

Morlais heard that laugh again, just as the blue obscurity of the hot evening softly rubbed out the hard lines of the jagged rocks. He was standing at the top of the garden, pensively watching the white chickens strut arrogantly and impatiently among the cabbage stalks of the next door garden, clucking and pecking. What a silly fuss to be making on such a calm evening. Hetty was singing in the kitchen, waiting for the kettle to boil –

Now the day is over,
Night is drawing nigh

– the old dismissal song of the elementary school. She was still entirely a child, for all her fifteen years and her quadratics, flowing along like a little brook. All the better. There was no heart searching in him this evening as to where she was heading, what would come of them all, boxed up in this unhealthily small ramshackle cottage that winter would subject to such a bombardment. It was all simple enough, if you only had peace like this, to watch the kindly dusk come quietly round you and know that you had a job, no matter what sort, and to feel a potency in the calm of physical and mental weariness. And when he heard that laugh and, looking up, saw a dark boyish figure come slithering down the path above the quarry, helping a slight, white-frocked, dark-blazered girl, Morlais smiled to himself, stirred by a feeling that was neither pleasant nor painful, but compounded of such contradictory emotions that it could only be called a distillation of being alive. He took the torn scraps of the letter he had written and ripped up that afternoon and opening the hand in which he held them, blew them out. They fluttered down like confetti emptied from a high window. He turned and went indoors, for bread and cheese and bed.

The next week went more easily than the three previous ones, and his fear of the morrow, that had kept him awake every night while he was looking for a job, dissolved into the first acceptance of the new routine. He got up each morning at eight, went out the back to wash under the tap and, if no one was looking, exercise himself with Dilwyn's skipping rope, then upstairs again to finish dressing, and back down for breakfast. All the time his mother was moving about, shaking the mat, brushing the floor, dusting, emptying the ashes from the grate and setting the fire ready to boil her son's tea and fry his bread and dripping. Hetty lay on the couch under an old rug, watching sleepily, lulled by the movements about her. And Mrs Jenkins was happy to be getting the house ready and making breakfast for the boys who were going out to work again. There was no shape on the house when all the men folk were idle. With Morlais at the Library and Dilwyn working in Ben James's shop – even though Ben and Doris never came near them they had shown that much goodwill – and her husband busy with electioneering, the old rhythm was coming back into the house. With the garden and the poultry and the goats, and a bit of tarred felting and corrugated iron to patch up the roof, they'd shift alright. Dilwyn was the only one who didn't look after his clothes; well, he'd have to manage with patched trousers and shiny elbows and worn soles until winter; and put by a shilling a week out of his five bob wages to buy new things. So she planned her way into the winter, silently and carefully, as she riddled the ashes and filled the kettle and set the table ready for food.

Morlais was aware of his mother's calmness, although neither of them spoke about it. It was evident in his cheery goodbye as he hurried from the kitchen after breakfast – he knew that if he turned round on his way down the mountain he would see her standing at the front door watching him – and in her quiet welcome on his return. She always had his meals ready for him to sit down to. And the refinements of The Elms – coffee and serviettes, cut glass and flowers and standing up when Mums came into the room – became as unreal and fantastic as the music of the mountain to which he listened dreamily from the pastures of sleep.

Bob called in the library at the beginning of the week and they went through the shelves, compiling a list of books they intended reading. Morlais knew the standard works on History and literature and found them conspicuous by their absence. Bob on the other hand was dismayed by the magnitude of the undertaking and the mass effect of shelf upon shelf of books. They were going to start with a copy of the Hammond's Industrial Revolution which Morlais had unearthed. Then Morley's three volume Life of Gladstone and Marx's Capital, Morlais explaining to Bob that they would get both sides of the question in that way. These books they were to study together, in the afternoons and two evenings a week – Bob said with embarrassment that he wouldn't be able to come more than two evenings a week. Dai Garibaldi was inquisitively interested in their scheme. Too old and easy-going to be ambitious or intellectually curious himself, he took a vicarious pleasure in Morlais's evident seriousness, both as a compensation for his own shortcomings and because he attributed it to his own influence. He talked endlessly about the old days when the pits were doing well and the colliers newly come from the rural counties of west Wales.

"Good independent farming stock they was, then," he said, never tiring of repeating himself. "Knew their Bibles and feared God, my boy. Every chapel 'ad it's own minister then, and didn't they fight for Disestablishment and education, eh? No old cinemas and grey'ounds and dole in them days, I can tell you. And Lloyd George working wonders for little Wales and putting the fear of God into the top 'ats across the border. And then the Unions, and the I.L.P. Free fights on the Square very near every week, boy, with the old shoppies. And singing all the better in chapel for it we was, too...."

Morlais liked old Dai; his enthusiasm for vanished causes had something pathetic and dignified about it, like a parlour furnished in the grace of an out-moded period; and his detachment from daily gossip made Morlais at home with him as he would not have been with a man who knew all the talk about the Reameses and Morlais's association with them. Actually, it never occured to him to ask Morlais any personal questions. He was out of touch, not with human beings but with individuals. Morlais was a boy who listened to him and asked him questions and helped him with his work; a very nice boy. Indeed.

Mr Jenkins was glad to see Morlais planning, too. In the evenings he would talk to Morlais intermittently while he was nailing odd pieces of wood and strips of felting onto the broken down chicken run and when he wanted help Morlais would lay aside his book, jump off the garden wall, and hold the felting up while his father drove nails into it. When Bob was up there too, the two boys spent more time in hammering and patching than in study. Bob was a good boy with his hands, having done a stretch of repairing in the pit, and he took a secret delight in showing his skill before Morlais, whom he considered so infinitely cleverer than himself in every other respect. During those late August evenings, with the dry heat of summer touched by the first gentle breath of autumn, Morlais settled down in Mountain Row.

He had a visit from Doris, too, which gave him added warmth of feeling. She called at the library late one afternoon, shortly before closing time. Dai Garibaldi had gone home to his lodgings for the day; Morlais was sitting reading in the empty room; Doris pushed the door open quietly and peeped in.

When he saw her he leaped to his feet and hugged her. They were both delighted. Morlais had worried so much about her, her 'trouble' that he remembered so clearly had taken such a deep root in his deep and far-off memories, that her actual presence was like a light in a nightmare-dark bedroom.

"Oh, Doris," was all he could say, or had need to say.

She was deeply affected too, but held herself in by a show of her old devilment.

"Alright, don't go choking me," she said, pushing him away and laughing with him. "I didn't ask you to be familiar with me, did I? Remember you're quite a stranger."

"No, I'm not," he said. "It's you're the stranger. You never come near us in Mountain Row."

"Oh well," she said. "I never go where I'm not welcome." And before he could rejoin she said quickly, "I've got a stranger outside, too, waiting to see you. Shall I bring 'im in?"

"Who is it?" he said. "Ben James?"

She laughed, almost derisively.

"Can you see dear Benjamin waiting on the door mat to be called in?" she said. "No fear. It's the cause of all the trouble I've got outside for you." She went to the door and called softly. "Come on, Charlie-is-my-darling. Come on in and show yourself to your rich uncle."

"Your son?" Morlais said excitedly.

"Daniel James himself," she said. "Oh, this boy. You want a sheep dog to round 'im up. I've never seen such a shy baby."

She went out into the lobby to fetch him, Morlais held the door open. Doris came back a moment later carrying a dark, curly-headed boy of six in her arms. He was hiding his face against her shoulder.

"Come on, Dan," she said. "For shame on you. This is a nice uncle. No need to be shy of him."

She let the child down. He took a quick glance at Morlais and hid his head in her skirts again.

Morlais's heart thumped at the glimpse of his face; it was a statement of something too secret and innocent to be defined or captured. It wasn't a pretty face; the cheeks were too drawn, the cheekbones and forehead too prominent for prettiness. Besides, the little wax-pale lips were distorted slightly, the doctor having failed to remove every trace of the hare-lip with which he had been born, and the mouth had a look of breathlessness, of readiness to flee, of cunning almost. But the hair and eyes – they were what gripped Morlais; exceptionally dark and glossy, especially the eyes, even which were bigger even and more intense than children's eyes usually are, and sharp with apprehension.

"Come on, my treasure," Doris said. "Don't you know a friend when you see one?"

"He's very nervous, isn't he? Highly strung?" Morlais said.

"Don't talk," she said, ruffling the child's hair. "If you feel cross with him he knows it. You don't need to say anything."

"Won't you speak to me, Dan?" Morlais said gently, bending down and softly taking his small clean hands.

"He doesn't like men," Doris said. "He thinks they all come home drunk and shout at their wives."

Morlais looked up sharply. It was right enough, his first impression. It wasn't the same Doris, the spontaneous lissom sister who had danced through his childhood and awed him with the beauty of her flowering womanhood. There was a hard restraint about her now, a coarseness, a lack of sincerity. Her cheeks were artificially flushed, her face powdered, her hair permed. She had adopted a mode of life, hiding herself in a cage of calculated behaviour complete to the minutest detail – a pair of red ear-rings, for example. Only the shrinking he caught in her dark eyes showed him that the real Doris was still there, hidden and hurt.

"How's he getting on at school?" Morlais asked.

"Not very good," she said. "I don't think he likes it there much. I've got to take him and fetch him. When I've tried sending him by himself the little devil mitches and goes off somewhere by himself."

"Well, you come to the library when you feel like that," Morlais said to Dan. "We'll do writing and drawing together here, shall we?"

Dan looked at him with his great wondering eyes, then nodded assent, and, most marvellous, he smiled.

"He's yours," Doris said, laughing. "I'll know where to find him when he's missing now."

"I hope you're right," Morlais said. "I feel like hugging him."

"Well, come on, Daniel. Back to the lion's den," Doris said, pulling on her gloves. "Got to get tea ready for the master. He's very touchy these days. I don't think the shop is doing much trade."

"No wonder," Morlais said. "People can't pay when the pits are only work half time."

"I suppose so," she said moodily. "Anyway, Ben's making a big gamble of it, I'm afraid. You know he's gone shares in the greyhound track they've just opened in Tredwr, don't you?"

"Yes. Dilwyn was telling me. He's full of it."

Doris laughed.

"It's queer the way Ben and Dilwyn get along together," she said.

"Dilwyn will do anything for him. I don't like seeing them so thick together. I don't suppose Mam and Dad do, either."

Morlais hesitated.

"I don't think Dad likes him spending so much time with the greyhounds," he said. "He's told him that if he ever catches him gambling he won't let him enter the house again."

"Well, I don't like it, anyway," she said with a slight shudder.

"Come on then, Danny. And call to see us, Mor, will you? Number five, Council Houses, we live."

"I think it's you ought to call at Mountain Row," Morlais said earnestly. "Why don't you, Dor?"

She shrugged her shoulders in a weary, jaded gesture.

"I don't know," she said. "P'r'aps I will – when I'm beat."

He didn't say anything.

"Solong then," she said.

"Solong, Dor. Goodbye, Dan."

Little Dan gave him another furtive smile and disappeared through the door with his smart mother.

The library door closed slowly. Morlais watched it shut, then sat down again with his book, but did not turn over a single page during the next half hour.

Afterword

Morlais tells the story of Morlais Jenkins from the day before he sits his scholarship examination to the County School, aged 11, until his last term there. It has two unusual features: first, Morlais is the only fully-drawn character, the others being projections of the forces in himself, and, second, his close identification with the narrator, as Lewis himself suggested when he told Gwyn Jones in October 1939, shortly after completing the novel, that it was an attempt

> to synthesise two lines – that of the industrial novel and of the intellectual-aesthetic novel. It's my own life, I suppose, & that's why I find it so difficult to be honest.

To Jean Gilbert, a librarian friend in France, he wrote:

> I eat it, dream it, sleep with it. It is very thrilling & exacting and sometimes disappointing....

There is no authorial perspective in it to counterpoint Morlais's point of view or place it in a wider context. His life is substantially that of his author, though the portrait is not naively autobiographical. For example, Morlais's parents are unlike Lewis's (as is the case in all his fiction), his father being a collier, his mother a Mam who washes and scrubs.

From the start, the boy is in a state of turmoil, one that is both exciting and terrifying, like a perpetual churning of the stomach or whirring of the brain. The reasons for this are several: he is suffering from anxiety, he is apart from his family and friends and, perhaps most tellingly, he is a poet (something revealed only later – and then glancingly – in the novel), not simply one who wishes to write but one who is compelled to do so, making and unmaking himself in acts of creation that leave him shoring up his fragments against his ruin. Writing is his gift and his fate, related to his isolation and depression, as the existence of novel testifies.

Morlais's anguish is not simply neurotic, however. As a sensitive boy from a south Wales mining valley in the 20s and 30s, he knows the devastating effect of the Depression on Glannant (Lewis's Cwmaman) but he also knows his fate is not theirs. The very exam he is about to sit points in a different direction for him, as does his vocation as a poet.

Dai Smith has said of the collective experience of the valleys that it was the driver of individual (though not necessarily individuated) lives, thereby inverting 'the novel's more traditional concept or relationship between distinctive 'character' and nebulous 'society' by making the outcome of the former the creation of the latter'. While Morlais is the novel's concerted theme, therefore, Glannant is its granted one. Passage after passage is given over to descriptions of it. Of all those who wrote about the mining valleys of south Wales at this time, Lewis, I believe, is the most penetrating thanks to his liminal position, being of the valleys but not wholly in them. Painfully, steadily, seriously, sensuously, he describes Glannant in a way that suggest why Dylan Thomas should have granted him pride of place in his essay on 'Welsh Poets':

> But out of the mining valleys of South Wales, there were poets who were beginning to write in a spirit of passionate anger against the inequality of social conditions. They wrote, not of the truths and beauties of the natural world, but of the lies and ugliness of the unnatural system of society under which they worked – or, more often during the nineteen-twenties and thirties, under which they were not allowed to work. They spoke, in ragged and angry rhythms, of the Wales they knew: the coal-tips, the dole-queues, the stubborn bankrupt villages, the children, scrutting for coal on the slag-heaps, the colliers' shabby allotments, the cheap-jack cinema….
>
> (*Quite Early One Morning*)

A passage that begins with a noble oratorical cadence ('out of the mining valleys...') lapses into a prose paraphrase of Lewis's 'The Mountain over Aberdare'.

> From this high quarried ledge I see
> The place for which the Quakers once
> Collected clothes, my fathers' home,
> Our stubborn bankrupt village sprawled
> In jaded dusk beneath its nameless hills;
> The drab streets strung across the cwm,
> Derelict workings, tips of slag
> The gospellers and gamblers use
> And children scrutting for the coal
> That winter dole cannot purvey;
> Allotments where the collier digs
> While engines hack the coal within his brain;
> Grey Hebron in a rigid cramp,
> White cheap-jack cinema, the church
> Stretched like a sow beside the stream....

In Lewis, Dylan recognised that rare thing, a writer who captures the spirit of the age.

II

Morlais's agony begins early and continues unabated. His alienation was not uncommon among the gifted young in the valleys but its intensity is. It descends on him like darkness, depressing all his natural vitality. Lewis's account of it is like the thing itself, febrile and penetrating.

The boy first appears when 'the hot day [is] burning out his whole being with its ruthless pitiless glare' (35). The pitch of the writing immediately arrests: Morlais is trapped in a hostile universe of 'broken pavements and stony roads and grey rows of houses', a 'transcendent over-reaching world of great metal objects and fists, foreign to him in its cold unyielding power'. Above all, there is 'the pit, the inscrutable skeleton of power whose whirring wheels attracted him as completely as a nightmare' (52). Lewis's teenage years were spent in the shadow of Brown's colliery and the experience left its mark, as the recurrence of the wheel image in 'Ward 'O' 3 (b)' four years later (a year before his death) indicates. It appears again later in the novel when Morlais discusses girls with a friend:

> Morlais felt the cold sweat burst out of his forehead and under his arms and round his loins. His body cramped with sudden nausea and a wheel spun round behind his eyes. (147)

Once more, the neurotic and social run together. Morlais's sexual nausea may be less explicit than the other causes of his suffering but it is just as significant. The shame of puberty leaves him 'soft' (13), 'trembling like a jelly inside himself' (13) and weeping tears that are 'black rivers of pain' (38); his nerves are

> like highly charged wires pulled across each other, pulled to the limit of endurance and ringing terrible alarms in the anarchic wilderness of his mind. (59).

Such Lawrentian anguish renders the boy virtually incapable, unable to express his feelings or experience the need to do so. The novel does that for him.

The central event of Morlais's life comes early when his friend, David Reames, the pit manager's son, is killed in a pit-head accident. That same night, Mrs Reames visits his parents and offers to adopt him. They agree, foreseeing advantages to him in the arrangement, and Morlais promptly goes off with her. Such a magical transformation highlights a division already latent in him, which explains why it is so calmly accepted by everyone. The boy exchanges working class life for a world of leisure and culture, though without losing his 'dissolved fluid terror' (65). The whole episode plays on Lewis's move to Cowbridge Grammar School in 1926, the very year of the General Strike (or lock-out), a move that induced in him a sense of social guilt and a conviction that he had been abandoned by his parents.

Mrs Reames is a mysterious figure, a B.A., cool and aloof. (Morlais's sister, Doris, calls her an 'icebug' (86)). She is the Gravesian Muse and her arrival in the novel signals the moment when Morlais becomes conscious of his poetic destiny, one that blights him even as it lights up the darkness of his mind. This is how it will be for the rest of his life.

III

The cultivated atmosphere at The Elms with 'Mums' and her husband, Denis Reames, leaves Morlais numbly compliant, somewhere between contentment and repression. Everything appears 'neat and familiar and untroubled' (116) but he has effectively been neutralised.

> It is so lonely, I can't explain. It's so quiet the air moves round and round you and it whispers but I can't hear it, only I must listen. (91)

In Mrs Reames, he discovers a kindred spirit who appreciates 'the hard wrenching of gears inside him, steel crowbars hacking at the living coal' (82). She warns him he possesses 'the power of understanding, a terrible power' (131) but he yearns for Glannant:

> It was so narrow and deep; the mountains possessed it, overpowered it. It was theirs, this narrow valley with its straggle of grey streets, its ruck of railways sidings where the timber was stacked and the coal trucks waited, its tips and its colliery whose great wheel seemed so tiny. (118)

A moving passage, affection vying with distaste:

> So he sat down on the sun-ripened rock, quiet in the hope
> of seeing a fox trot past, a streak of autumn through the
> green uncurled ferns, and quietly he saw the grey streets in
> the lower reach of the valley, the sun flashing from the
> cheap ferro-concrete council houses above the park where
> the gramophone blared the Desert Song, the long ruck of
> sidings and stacked pitprops that looked no bigger than
> matchsticks, the turning wheel above the pitshaft bringing
> the men up to the surface, and at the top of Glannant street
> the red gables of the Elms standing haughtily in their
> private greenery... (153)

Out walking one day, he visits Mountain Row, a group of
20 miners' cottages, one room below, two above. Their
wooden walls and felt-covered corrugated iron roofs front a
lane of ashes, their backs up against the mountain. To Mrs
Reames they are 'little pigsties' (221) but they are the
favourite haunt of children and gamblers and where Morlais
would like to live as a collier.

This feeling of his for the pit catches up with him in a
different way when the miners threaten a strike in support of
their claim for a minimum wage, his father being their
committee chair). This crisis, however, is immediately
overshadowed by another when he picks up a volume of Mrs
Reames's Keats and hears 'a frantic deadly earnest voice' – it
is hers – reading two lines from it:

> When I have fears that I may cease to be,
> Before this pen has gleaned my teeming brain.

He climbs up to her room ('The silence tried to thrust him
back as he ran up the stairs' (150)) and discovers her night-
marishly transformed, haggard and sallow and trying to hide
a chamber pot under the bed while spilling a 'thick whitish
liquid' over the counterpane.

> 'Why didn't you leave me alone?' she said tonelessly over
> his head.
> 'I knew,' he said....

'I ought to thank you, I suppose, for fetching me back....
I don't want you to tell Denis ... It would have been better
in the long run for him...'

(150/1)

That this acme of coolness should be revealed 'incomplete,
unfinished, beaten' (186) is shocking.

These two crises – the political and the Keatsian – leave
Morlais uncertain which side in the coming strike to support.
Mrs Reames tells him he owes allegiance to neither:

Your struggle must be first to find yourself. Don't you
understand? You must become yourself first of all. It will
take all your courage and sweat to do that. (153)

There speaks the Muse, having first introduced him to the act
which will allow him to do so. This quest for selfhood was
supremely significant for Lewis, who saw his life as a spiritual
journey 'east and east and east'. The pain of living without his
identity, without knowing who he was, of being at the mercy
of forces outside himself, was daunting and writing his way of
rescuing something from it for himself. Hence his fear
(Keats's fear, Mrs Reames's fear) of ceasing to be before his
pen could glean his brain.

Only when he reached India and fell in love with a second
Muse figure, Freda Aykroyd, did he eventually find himself –
for good and ill.

IV

After Mrs Reames's 'inner failure and bitterness' (163), she
and Morlais go off on a visit to Aberystwyth, where her niece,
Nora, is studying. Only now is it revealed he is a poet, which
implies that everything until now has been a throwing of the
patterns of his mind onto the page. Morlais tells Nora:
'There's something all smashed up inside her [Mrs Reames].

I know.' (172); she and Denis are 'poisoning each other, the three of us. In that big house. I hate it sometimes. Hate it.' (173). He himself feels he is 'strangling' Mrs Reames (174).

Standing on the beach with Nora, he sees the ocean 'coming in naked',

> casting its marriage veils over the bridal beach. Earth and sea, water and stone, eternally in intercourse, the thrust of the inward flow, the caress of the ebb… for the first time he felt his manhood respond to the attraction of Being without at the same time being tormented with shame. (167)

For the first time, he experiences an erection without guilt. Puritan repression and emotional deadlock have created in him a 'blurred indecisive pain' (182) that neutralises any attraction he may feel for women like Nora or Nan Blackmore back home.

On his return to Glannant, Morlais finds that his father has been sacked by Mr Reames for his part in the miners' campaign. The Jenkinses now move to Mountain Row and Morlais calls on them to beg for readmittance:

> he had gone outside the community, broken their law and forfeited their familiarity. It was the hardest thing of all, this humiliating petition for reinstatement. The pain of it frightened him. (240)

Here is the novel's second magical stroke and much less convincing it is. Indeed, it flouts the whole tenor of the novel, a product of Morlais's acute social guilt and his author's belief that the search for selfhood could be found in solidarity with Glannant and a country at war. These two struggles were one – fighting Hitler meant fighting for an improvement in the workers' condition, and that is what happened with the election of a Labour government in 1945. Writing to Jean Gilbert (like most of Lewis's correspondence, this letter is unpublished), he declared that the novel traced Morlais's development 'through poverty and love to disenchantment and wisdom' but there is no development in it, only repetition and variation. Life at The Elms turns out to be a blind alley, but so is that at Mountain Row.

Lewis's belief in social solidarity and historical inevitability was fuelled by two developments at this time: his meeting his wife-to-be, Gweno Ellis, in May 1939 and his securing a teaching post at the Lewis School that autumn. The spirit of the phoney war reached him early, culminating in his enlistment in the Royal Engineers in May 1940, despite his being in a reserved occupation.

Morlais's father is glad to find that water isn't thicker than blood and gets Morlais a job as librarian in the Workmen's Institute.

> His blood was like a noisy mountain stream, saying to the walls and the allotments and the stones along the path 'I'm here, I'm here again.' (219)

But there is no 'here' for Morlais: he is neither 'Morlais Jenkins' nor 'Morlais Reames', only 'Morlais', a possibility rather than a definition:

> He'd fought to forge his will in the furnace of circumstances. And now there was nothing, only grey; no eminence, only sand. Infinity. The landmarks were gone, even the landmark he knew best, his body. (222)

And into that wilderness he vanishes. Earlier, he feared he was 'rotting like cabbage stalks...turning into black liquid'; now, it is 'as if claws were tearing the fibres of my brain apart, all blood and grey matter' (227). A novel which opens with a butterfly's hysterical attempt to survive the elements takes this struggle of life and death as its major theme. It is the work of a young man who, through Mrs Reames, discovers what his fate will be. 'She'll get it in the end,' he remarks, 'even if it kills her' (231).

V

In December 1943-January 1944, two months before his death, Lewis wrote 'The Jungle', his last poem, in which there appears the following retrospect of Morlais's world:

> The weekly bribe we paid the man in black,
> The day shaft sinking from the sun,
> The blinding arc of rivets blown through steel,
> The patient queues, headlines and slogans flung
> Across a frightened continent, the town
> Sullen and out of work, the little home
> Semi-detached, suburban, transient
> As fever or the anger of the old,
> The best ones on some specious pretext gone.

Lewis then begs forgiveness from his loved ones for deserting them – this time, for good.

VI

Morlais appears here for the first time. It is impossible to say why it was not published in his lifetime. In 1937, he wrote another fictional autobiography based on an Aberystwyth student called Adam who, like Lewis, has recently returned from a period of research in London. *Morlais* may have been intended as a development (or conclusion) of this, reaching back to Adam's childhood and clarifying what had previously lain untested, a voyage into uncharted waters as much as a finished product. Lewis's turn to prose narrative occurred when his poetry wasn't coming right but, having finished the novel, he may have decided it was unlikely a London publisher would want to print it once war had been declared. At the same time, he prepared a short story based on the same characters as the novel and set at the same time, which was also unpublished. It appears in his *Collected Stories* (ed.

Cary Archard, 1990, pp. 329-347) under the title 'It was very warm and welcome'.

It is less easy to understand why it did not appear after his death. His publisher, Philip Unwin, pressed his wife more than once about a novel he felt sure had been left behind. First, implied that it did not exist, then expressed doubts about publishing anything from an earlier, less finished stage of his writing. Perhaps she had grown wary about the rumours that had begun to circulate about his experiences in India. She knew how prone to depression he was but may not have wished to emphasise it, tainting her happier memories of him.

Whatever, here it is, 70 years after his death, a remarkable addition to the work of a writer who burned more brightly than most.

John Pikoulis
2015

Also available by

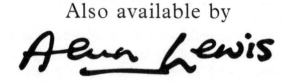

To celebrate the centenary of Alun Lewis, Seren brings you the uniform paperback reprints of his Collected Poems, Stories and Letters.

www.serenbooks.com